THE ADVENTURES

OF A

SPECIAL CORRESPONDENT

D1663503

THE ADVENTURES
OF A
SPECIAL CORRESPONDENT

AMONG THE VARIOUS RACES AND COUNTRIES OF CENTRAL ASIA

Being the Exploits and Experiences of
Claudius Bombarnac of "The Twentieth Century"

JULES VERNE

TARK CLASSIC FICTION
AN IMPRINT OF

MANOR
Rockville, MARYLAND
2008

ISBN: 978-1-60450-228-2

Published by TARK Classic Fiction
An Imprint of Arc Manor
P. O. Box 10339
Rockville, MD 20849-0339
www.ArcManor.com

Printed in the United States of America/United Kingdom

Biography and Bibliography

Jules Verne, French author, was born at Nantes, France, in 1828, and died in 1905. In 1850 he wrote a comedy in verse, but he eventually confined himself to the writing of scientific and geographical romances, achieving a great reputation. He visited the United States in 1867, sailing for New York on the *Great Eastern*, and his book, *A Floating City*, was the result of this voyage. His best-known books are: *A Captain at Fifteen, A Two Years' Vacation, A Voyage to the Center of the Earth* (1864), *From the Earth to the Moon* (1865), *20,000 Leagues Under the Sea* (1870), *A Tour of the World in Eighty Days* (1873), *Michael Strogoff* (1876), *Mrs. Branica* (1891), *Clovis Dordentor* (1896), *The Brothers Kip* (1902). Most of his works have been translated into English.

Claudius Bombarnac

Chapter I

Claudius Bombarnac,
Special Correspondent,
"Twentieth Century."
Tiflis, Transcaucasia.

Such is the address of the telegram I found on the 13th of May when
I arrived at Tiflis.

This is what the telegram said:

"As the matters in hand will terminate on the 15th instant Claudius
Bombarnac will repair to Uzun Ada, a port on the east coast of the
Caspian. There he will take the train by the direct Grand Transasiatic
between the European frontier and the capital of the Celestial Empire.
He will transmit his impressions in the way of news, interviewing re-
markable people on the road, and report the most trivial incidents by
letter or telegram as necessity dictates. The Twentieth Century trusts
to the zeal, intelligence, activity and tact of its correspondent, who can
draw on its bankers to any extent he may deem necessary."

It was the very morning I had arrived at Tiflis with the intention of
spending three weeks there in a visit to the Georgian provinces for the
benefit of my newspaper, and also, I hoped, for that of its readers.

Here was the unexpected, indeed; the uncertainty of a special correspondent's life.

At this time the Russian railways had been connected with the line
between Poti, Tiflis and Baku. After a long and increasing run through
the Southern Russian provinces I had crossed the Caucasus, and imagined I was to have a little rest in the capital of Transcaucasia. And here
was the imperious administration of the *Twentieth Century* giving me

7

only half a day's halt in this town! I had hardly arrived before I was obliged to be off again without unstrapping my portmanteau! But what would you have? We must bow to the exigencies of special correspondence and the modern interview!

But all the same I had been carefully studying this Transcaucasian district, and was well provided with geographic and ethnologic memoranda. Perhaps it may be as well for you to know that the fur cap, in the shape of a turban, which forms the headgear of the mountaineers and cossacks is called a "papakha," that the overcoat gathered in at the waist, over which the cartridge belt is hung, is called a "tcherkeska" by some and "bechmet" by others! Be prepared to assert that the Georgians and Armenians wear a sugar-loaf hat, that the merchants wear a "touloupa," a sort of sheepskin cape, that the Kurd and Parsee still wear the "bourka," a cloak in a material something like plush which is always waterproofed.

And of the headgear of the Georgian ladies, the "tassakravi," composed of a light ribbon, a woolen veil, or piece of muslin round such lovely faces; and their gowns of startling colors, with the wide open sleeves, their under skirts fitted to the figure, their winter cloak of velvet, trimmed with fur and silver gimp, their summer mantle of white cotton, the "tchadre," which they tie tight on the neck—all those fashions in fact so carefully entered in my notebook, what shall I say of them?

Learn, then, that their national orchestras are composed of "zournas," which are shrill flutes; "salamouris," which are squeaky clarinets; mandolines, with copper strings, twanged with a feather; "tchianouris," violins, which are played upright; "dimplipitos," a kind of cymbals which rattle like hail on a window pane.

Know that the "schaska" is a sword hung from a bandolier trimmed with studs and silver embroidery, that the "kindjall" or "kandijar" is a dagger worn in the belt, that the armament of the soldiers of the Caucasus is completed by a long Damascus gun ornamented with bands of chiseled metal.

Know that the "tarantass" is a sort of berline hung on five pieces of rather elastic wood between wheels placed rather wide apart and of moderate height; that this carriage is driven by a "yemtchik," on the front seat, who has three horses, to whom is added a postilion, the "faletre," when it is necessary to hire a fourth horse from the "smatritel," who is the postmaster on the Caucasian roads.

Know, then, that the verst is two-thirds of a mile, that the different nomadic people of the governments of Transcaucasia are composed of

8

Kalmucks, descendants of the Eleuthes, fifteen thousand, Kirghizes of Mussulman origin eight thousand, Koundrof Tartars eleven hundred, Sartof Tartars a hundred and twelve, Nogais eight thousand five hundred, Turkomans nearly four thousand.

And thus, after having so minutely absorbed my Georgia, here was this ukase obliging me to abandon it! And I should not even have time to visit Mount Ararat or publish my impressions of a journey in Transcaucasia, losing a thousand lines of copy at the least, and for which I had at my disposal the 32,000 words of my language actually recognized by the French Academy.

It was hard, but there was no way out of it. And to begin with, at what o'clock did the train for Tiflis start from the Caspian?

The station at Tiflis is the junction of three lines of railway: the western line ending at Poti on the Black Sea, where the passengers land coming from Europe, the eastern line which ends at Baku, where the passengers embark to cross the Caspian, and the line which the Russians have just made for a length of about a hundred miles between Ciscaucasia and Transcaucasia, from Vladikarkaz to Tiflis, crossing the Arkhot range at a height of four thousand five hundred feet, and which connects the Georgian capital with the railways of Southern Russia.

I went to the railway station at a run, and rushed into the departure office.

"When is there a train for Baku?" I asked.

"You are going to Baku?" answered the clerk.

And from his trap-door he gave me one of those looks more military than civil, which are invariably found under the peak of a Muscovite cap.

"I think so," said I, perhaps a little sharply, "that is, if it is not forbidden to go to Baku."

"No," he replied, dryly, "that is, if you are provided with a proper passport."

"I will have a proper passport," I replied to this ferocious functionary, who, like all the others in Holy Russia, seemed to me an intensified gendarme.

Then I again asked what time the train left for Baku.

"Six o'clock to-night."

"And when does it get there?"

"Seven o'clock in the morning."

"Is that in time to catch the boat for Uzun Ada?"

"In time."

9

And the man at the trap-door replied to my salute by a salute of mechanical precision.

The question of passport did not trouble me. The French consul would know how to give me all the references required by the Russian administration.

Six o'clock to-night, and it is already nine o'clock in the morning! Bah! When certain guide books tell you how to explore Paris in two days, Rome in three days, and London in four days, it would be rather curious if I could not do Tiflis in a half day. Either one is a correspondent or one is not!

It goes without saying that my newspaper would not have sent me to Russia, if I could not speak fluently in Russian, English and German. To require a newspaper man to know the few thousand languages which are used to express thought in the five parts of the world would be too much; but with the three languages above named, and French added, one can go far across the two continents. It is true, there is Turkish of which I had picked up a few phrases, and there is Chinese of which I did not understand a single word. But I had no fear of remaining dumb in Turkestan and the Celestial Empire. There would be interpreters on the road, and I did not expect to lose a detail of my run on the Grand Transasiatic. I knew how to see, and see I would. Why should I hide it from myself? I am one of those who think that everything here below can serve as copy for a newspaper man; that the earth, the moon, the sky, the universe were only made as fitting subjects for newspaper articles, and that my pen was in no fear of a holiday on the road.

Before starting off round Tiflis let us have done with this passport business. Fortunately I had no need for a "poderojnaia," which was formerly indispensable to whoever traveled in Russia. That was in the time of the couriers, of the post horses, and thanks to its powers that official exeat cleared away all difficulties, assured the most rapid relays, the most amiable civilities from the postilions, the greatest rapidity of transport, and that to such a pitch that a well-recommended traveler could traverse in eight days five hours the two thousand seven hundred versts which separate Tiflis from Petersburg. But what difficulties there were in procuring that passport!

A mere permission to move about would do for to-day, a certificate attesting in a certain way that you are not a murderer or even a political criminal, that you are what is called an honest man, in a civilized country. Thanks to the assistance I received from our consul at Tiflis, I was soon all in due order with the Muscovite authorities.

It was an affair of two hours and two roubles. I then devoted myself entirely, eyes, ears, legs, to the exploration of the Georgian capital, without taking a guide, for guides are a horror to me. It is true that I should have been capable of guiding no matter what stranger, through the mazes of this capital which I had so carefully studied beforehand. That is a natural gift.

Here is what I recognized as I wandered about haphazard: first, there was the "douma," which is the town hall, where the "golova," or mayor, resides; if you had done me the honor to accompany me, I would have taken you to the promenade of Krasnoia-Gora on the left bank of the Koura, the Champs Elysees of the place, something like the Tivoli of Copenhagen, or the fair of the Belleville boulevard with its "Katchelis," delightful seesaws, the artfully managed undulations of which will make you seasick. And everywhere amid the confusion of market booths, the women in holiday costume, moving about with faces uncovered, both Georgians and Armenians, thereby showing that they are Christians.

As to the men, they are Apollos of the Belvedere, not so simply clothed, having the air of princes, and I should like to know if they are not so. Are they not descended from them? But I will genealogize later on. Let us continue our exploration at full stride. A minute lost is ten lines of correspondence, and ten lines of correspondence is—that depends on the generosity of the newspaper and its managers.

Quick to the grand caravanserai. There you will find the caravans from all points of the Asiatic continent. Here is one just coming in, composed of Armenian merchants. There is one going out, formed of traders in Persia and Russian Turkestan. I should like to arrive with one and depart with the other. That is not possible, and I am sorry for it. Since the establishment of the Transasiatic railways, it is not often that you can meet with those interminable and picturesque lines of horsemen, pedestrians, horses, camels, asses, carts. Bah! I have no fear that my journey across Central Asia will fail for want of interest. A special correspondent of the *Twentieth Century* will know how to make it interesting.

Here now are the bazaars with the thousand products of Persia, China, Turkey, Siberia, Mongolia. There is a profusion of the fabrics of Teheran, Shiraz, Kandahar, Kabul, carpets marvelous in weaving and colors, silks, which are not worth as much as those of Lyons.

Will I buy any? No; to embarrass oneself with packages on a trip from the Caspian to the Celestial Empire, never! The little portmanteau I can carry in my hand, the bag slung across my shoulders, and a traveling suit will be enough for me. Linen? I will get it on the road, in English fashion.

Let us stop in front of the famous baths of Tiflis, the thermal waters of which attain a temperature of 60 degrees centigrade. There you will find in use the highest development of massage, the suppling of the spine, the cracking of the joints. I remember what was said by our great Dumas whose peregrinations were never devoid of incidents; he invented them when he wanted them, that genial precursor of high-pressure correspondence! But I have no time to be shampooed, or to be cracked or suppled.

Stop! The Hotel de France. Where is there not a Hotel de France? I enter, I order breakfast—a Georgian breakfast watered with a certain Kachelie wine, which is said to never make you drunk, that is, if you do not sniff up as much as you drink in using the large-necked bottles into which you dip your nose before your lips. At least that is the proceeding dear to the natives of Transcaucasia. As to the Russians, who are generally sober, the infusion of tea is enough for them, not without a certain addition of vodka, which is the Muscovite brandy.

I, a Frenchman, and even a Gascon, am content to drink my bottle of Kachelie, as we drank our Chateau Laffite, in those regretted days, when the sun still distilled it on the hillsides of Pauillac. In truth this Caucasian wine, although rather sour, accompanied by the boiled fowl, known as pilau—has rather a pleasant taste about it.

It is over and paid for. Let us mingle with the sixteen thousand inhabitants of the Georgian capital. Let us lose ourselves in the labyrinth of its streets, among its cosmopolitan population. Many Jews who button their coats from left to right, as they write—the contrary way to the other Aryan peoples. Perhaps the sons of Israel are not masters in this country, as in so many others? That is so, undoubtedly; a local proverb says it takes six Jews to outwit an Armenian, and Armenians are plentiful in these Transcaucasian provinces.

I reach a sandy square, where camels, with their heads out straight, and their feet bent under in front, are sitting in hundreds. They used to be here in thousands, but since the opening of the Transcaspian railway some years ago now, the number of these humped beasts of burden has sensibly diminished. Just compare one of these beasts with a goods truck or a luggage van!

Following the slope of the streets, I come out on the quays by the Koura, the bed of which divides the town into two unequal parts. On each side rise the houses, one above the other, each one looking over the roof of its neighbors. In the neighborhood of the river there is a good deal of trade. There you will find much moving about of vendors of wine, with their goatskins bellying out like balloons, and vendors of water with their buffalo skins, fitted with pipes looking like elephants' trunks.

Here am I wandering at a venture; but to wander is human, says the collegians of Bordeaux, as they muse on the quays of the Gironde.

"Sir," says a good little Jew to me, showing me a certain habitation which seems a very ordinary one, "you are a stranger?"

"Quite."

"Then do not pass this house without stopping a moment to admire it."

"And why?"

"There lived the famous tenor Satar, who sang the *contre-fa* from his chest. And they paid him for it!"

I told the worthy patriarch that I hoped he would be able to sing a *contre-sol* even better paid for; and I went up the hill to the right of the Koura, so as to have a view of the whole town.

At the top of the hill, on a little open space where a reciter is declaiming with vigorous gestures the verses of Saadi, the adorable Persian poet, I abandon myself to the contemplation of the Transcaucasian capital. What I am doing here, I propose to do again in a fortnight at Pekin. But the pagodas and yamens of the Celestial Empire can wait awhile, here is Tiflis before my eyes; walls of the citadels, belfries of the temples belonging to the different religions, a metropolitan church with its double cross, houses of Russian, Persian, or Armenian construction; a few roofs, but many terraces; a few ornamental frontages, but many balconies and verandas; then two well-marked zones, the lower zone remaining Georgian, the higher zone, more modern, traversed by a long boulevard planted with fine trees, among which is seen the palace of Prince Bariatinsky, a capricious, unexpected marvel of irregularity, which the horizon borders with its grand frontier of mountains.

It is now five o'clock. I have no time to deliver myself in a remunerative torrent of descriptive phrases. Let us hurry off to the railway station.

There is a crowd of Armenians, Georgians, Mingrelians, Tartars, Kurds, Israelites, Russians, from the shores of the Caspian, some taking their tickets—Oh! the Oriental color—direct for Baku, some for intermediate stations.

This time I was completely in order. Neither the clerk with the gendarme's face, nor the gendarmes themselves could hinder my departure.

I take a ticket for Baku, first class. I go down on the platform to the carriages. According to my custom, I install myself in a comfortable corner. A few travelers follow me while the cosmopolitan populace invade the second and third-class carriages. The doors are shut after the visit of the ticket inspector. A last scream of the whistle announces that the train is about to start.

Suddenly there is a shout—a shout in which anger is mingled with despair, and I catch these words in German:

"Stop! Stop!"

I put down the window and look out.

A fat man, bag in hand, traveling cap on head, his legs embarrassed in the skirts of a huge overcoat, short and breathless. He is late.

The porters try to stop him. Try to stop a bomb in the middle of its trajectory! Once again has right to give place to might.

The Teuton bomb describes a well-calculated curve, and has just fallen into the compartment next to ours, through the door a traveler had obligingly left open.

The train begins to move at the same instant, the engine wheels begin to slip on the rails, then the speed increases.

We are off.

CHAPTER II

We were three minutes late in starting; it is well to be precise. A special correspondent who is not precise is a geometer who neglects to run out his calculations to the tenth decimal. This delay of three minutes made the German our traveling companion. I have an idea that this good man will furnish me with some copy, but it is only a presentiment.

It is still daylight at six o'clock in the evening in this latitude. I have bought a time-table and I consult it. The map which accompanies it shows me station by station the course of the line between Tiflis and Baku. Not to know the direction taken by the engine, to be ignorant if the train is going northeast or southeast, would be insupportable to me, all the more as when night comes, I shall see nothing, for I cannot see in the dark as if I were an owl or a cat.

My time-table shows me that the railway skirts for a little distance the carriage road between Tiflis and the Caspian, running through

Saganlong, Poily, Elisabethpol, Karascal, Aliat, to Baku, along the valley of the Koura. We cannot tolerate a railway which winds about; it must keep to a straight line as much as possible. And that is what the Transgeorgian does.

Among the stations there is one I would have gladly stopped at if I had had time, Elisabethpol. Before I received the telegram from the *Twentieth Century*, I had intended to stay there a week. I had read such attractive descriptions of it, and I had but a five minutes' stop there, and that between two and three o'clock in the morning! Instead of a town resplendent in the rays of the sun, I could only obtain a view of a vague mass confusedly discoverable in the pale beams of the moon!

Having ended my careful examination of the time-table, I began to examine my traveling companions. There were four of us, and I need scarcely say that we occupied the four corners of the compartment. I had taken the farthest corner facing the engine. At the two opposite angles two travelers were seated facing each other. As soon as they got in they had pulled their caps down on their eyes and wrapped themselves up in their cloaks—evidently they were Georgians as far as I could see. But they belonged to that special and privileged race who sleep on the railway, and they did not wake up until we reached Baku. There was nothing to be got out of those people; the carriage is not a carriage for them, it is a bed.

In front of me was quite a different type with nothing of the Oriental about it; thirty-two to thirty-five years old, face with a reddish beard, very much alive in look, nose like that of a dog standing at point, mouth only too glad to talk, hands free and easy, ready for a shake with anybody; a tall, vigorous, broad-shouldered, powerful man. By the way in which he settled himself and put down his bag, and unrolled his traveling rug of bright-hued tartan, I had recognized the Anglo-Saxon traveler, more accustomed to long journeys by land and sea than to the comforts of his home, if he had a home. He looked like a commercial traveler. I noticed that his jewelry was in profusion; rings on his fingers, pin in his scarf, studs on his cuffs, with photographic views in them, showy trinkets hanging from the watch-chain across his waistcoat. Although he had no earrings and did not wear a ring at his nose I should not have been surprised if he turned out to be an American—probably a Yankee.

That is my business. To find out who are my traveling companions, whence they come, where they go, is that not the duty of a special correspondent in search of interviews? I will begin with my neighbor in front of me. That will not be difficult, I imagine. He is not dreaming or sleeping, or looking out on the landscape lighted by the last rays of the sun. If I am not mistaken he will be just as glad to speak to me as I am to speak to him—and reciprocally.

I will see. But a fear restrains me. Suppose this American—and I am sure he is one—should also be a special, perhaps for the *World* or the *New York Herald*, and suppose he has also been ordered off to do this Grand Asiatic. That would be most annoying! He would be a rival!

My hesitation is prolonged. Shall I speak, shall I not speak? Already night has begun to fall. At last I was about to open my mouth when my companion prevented me.

"You are a Frenchman?" he said in my native tongue.

"Yes, sir," I replied in his.

Evidently we could understand each other.

The ice was broken, and then question followed on question rather rapidly between us. You know the Oriental proverb:

"A fool asks more questions in an hour than a wise man in a year."

But as neither my companion nor myself had any pretensions to wisdom we asked away merrily.

"*Wait a bit,*" said my American.

I italicize this phrase because it will recur frequently, like the pull of the rope which gives the impetus to the swing.

"*Wait a bit!* I'll lay ten to one that you are a reporter!"

"And you would win! Yes. I am a reporter sent by the *Twentieth Century* to do this journey."

"Going all the way to Pekin?"

"To Pekin."

"So am I," replied the Yankee.

And that was what I was afraid of.

"Same trade?" said I indifferently.

"No. You need not excite yourself. We don't sell the same stuff, sir."

"Claudius Bombarnac, of Bordeaux, is delighted to be on the same road as—"

"Fulk Ephrinell, of the firm of Strong, Bulbul & Co., of New York City, New York, U.S.A."

And he really added U.S.A.

We were mutually introduced. I a traveler in news, and he a traveler in—In what? That I had to find out.

The conversation continues. Ephrinell, as may be supposed, has been everywhere—and even farther, as he observes. He knows both Americas and almost all Europe. But this is the first time he has set foot in Asia. He talks and talks, and always jerks in *Wait a bit*, with inexhaustible loquacity. Has the Hunson the same properties as the Garonne?

I listen to him for two hours. I have hardly heard the names of the stations yelled out at each stop, Saganlong, Poily, and the others. And I really should have liked to examine the landscape in the soft light of the moon, and made a few notes on the road.

Fortunately my fellow traveler had already crossed these eastern parts of Georgia. He pointed out the spots of interest, the villages, the watercourses, the mountains on the horizon. But I hardly saw them. Confound these railways! You start, you arrive, and you have seen nothing on the road!

"No!" I exclaim, "there is none of the charm about it as there is in traveling by post, in troika, tarantass, with the surprises of the road, the originality of the inns, the confusion when you change horses, the glass of vodka of the yemtchiks—and occasionally the meeting with those honest brigands whose race is nearly extinct."

"Mr. Bombarnac," said Ephrinell to me, "are you serious in regretting all those fine things?"

"Quite serious," I reply. "With the advantages of the straight line of railway we lose the picturesqueness of the curved line, or the broken line of the highways of the past. And, Monsieur Ephrinell, when you read of traveling in Transcaucasia forty years ago, do you not regret it? Shall I see one of those villages inhabited by Cossacks who are soldiers and farmers at one and the same time? Shall I be present at one of those merry-makings which charm the tourist? those djiquitovkas with the men upright on their horses, throwing their swords, discharging their pistols, and escorting you if you are in the company of some high functionary, or a colonel of the Staniza."

"Undoubtedly we have lost all those fine things," replies my Yankee. "But, thanks to these iron ribbons which will eventually encircle our globe like a hogshead of cider or a bale of cotton, we can go in thirteen days from Tiflis to Pekin. That is why, if you expect any incidents, to enliven you—"

"Certainly, Monsieur Ephrinell."

"Illusions, Mr. Bombarnac! Nothing will happen either to you or me. Wait a bit, I promise you a journey, the most prosaic, the most homely, the flattest—flat as the steppes of Kara Koum, which the Grand Trans-asiatic traverses in Turkestan, and the plains of the desert of Gobi it crosses in China—"

"Well, we shall see, for I travel for the pleasure of my readers."

"And I travel merely for my own business."

And at this reply the idea recurred to me that Ephrinell would not be quite the traveling companion I had dreamed of. He had goods to sell, I had none to buy. I foresaw that our meeting would not lead to a sufficient intimacy during our long journey. He was one of those Yan-kees who, as they say, hold a dollar between their teeth, which it is impossible to get away from them, and I should get nothing out of him that was worth having.

And although I knew that he traveled for Strong, Bulbul & Co., of New York, I had never heard of the firm. To listen to their representa-tive, it would appear that Strong, Bulbul & Co. ought to be known throughout the world.

But then, how was it that they were unknown to me, a pupil of Chincholle, our master in everything! I was quite at a loss because I had never heard of the firm of Strong, Bulbul & Co.

I was about to interrogate Ephrinell on this point, when he said to me:

"Have you ever been in the United States, Mr. Bombarnac?"

"No, Monsieur Ephrinell."

"You will come to our country some day?"

"Perhaps."

"Then you will not forget to explore the establishment of Strong, Bulbul & Co.?"

"Explore it?"

"That is the proper word."

"Good! I shall not fail to do so."

"You will see one of the most remarkable industrial establishments of the New Continent."

"I have no doubt of it; but how am I to know it?"

"Wait a bit, Mr. Bombarnac. Imagine a colossal workshop, immense buildings for the mounting and adjusting of the pieces, a steam en-gine of fifteen hundred horse-power, ventilators making six hundred revolutions a minute, boilers consuming a hundred tons of coals a day, a chimney stack four hundred and fifty feet high, vast outhouses for the storage of our goods, which we send to the five parts of the world, a general manager, two sub-managers, four secretaries, eight under-secretaries, a staff of five hundred clerks and nine hundred workmen, a whole regiment of travelers like your servant, working in Europe, Asia, Africa, America, Australasia, in short, a turnover exceeding annually one hundred million dollars! And all that, Mr. Bombarnac, for making millions of—yes, I said millions—"

At this moment the train commenced to slow under the action of its automatic brakes, and he stopped.

"Elisabethpol! Elisabethpol!" shout the guard and the porters on the station.

Our conversation is interrupted. I lower the window on my side, and open the door, being desirous of stretching my legs.

Ephrinell did not get out.

Here was I striding along the platform of a very poorly lighted station. A dozen travelers had already left the train. Five or six Georgians were crowding on the steps of the compartments. Ten minutes at Elisabethpol; the time-table allowed us no more.

As soon as the bell begins to ring I return to our carriage, and when I have shut the door I notice that my place is taken. Yes! Facing the American, a lady has installed herself with that Anglo-Saxon coolness which is as unlimited as the infinite. Is she young? Is she old? Is she pretty? Is she plain? The obscurity does not allow me to judge. In any case, my French gallantry prevents me from claiming my corner, and I sit down beside this person who makes no attempt at apology.

Ephrinell seems to be asleep, and that stops my knowing what it is that Strong, Bulbul & Co., of New York, manufacture by the million.

The train has started. We have left Elisabethpol behind. What have I seen of this charming town of twenty thousand inhabitants, built on the Gandja-tchai, a tributary of the Koura, which I had specially worked up before my arrival? Nothing of its brick houses hidden under verdure, nothing of its curious ruins, nothing of its superb mosque built at the beginning of the eighteenth century. Of its admirable plane trees, so sought after by crows and blackbirds, and which maintain a supportable temperature during the excessive heats of summer, I had scarcely seen the higher branches with the moon shining on them. And on the banks of the stream which bears its silvery murmuring waters along the principal street, I had only seen a few houses in little gardens, like small crenelated fortresses. All that remained in my memory would be an indecisive outline, seized in flight from between the steam puffs of our engine. And why are these houses always in a state of defence? Because Elisabethpol is a fortified town exposed to the frequent attacks of the

Lesghians of Chirvan, and these mountaineers, according to the best-informed historians, are directly descended from Attila's hordes.

It was nearly midnight. Weariness invited me to sleep, and yet, like a good reporter, I must sleep with one eye and one ear open.

I fall into that sort of slumber provoked by the regular trepidations of a train on the road, mingled with ear-splitting whistles and the grind of the brakes as the speed is slowed, and tumultuous roars as passing trains are met with, besides the names of the stations shouted out during the short stoppages, and the banging of the doors which are opened or shut with metallic sonority.

In this way I heard the shouts of Geran, Varvara, Oudjarry, Kiourdamir, Klourdane, then Karasoul, Navagi. I sat up, but as I no longer occupied the corner from which I had been so cavalierly evicted, it was impossible for me to look through the window.

And then I began to ask what is hidden beneath this mass of veils and wraps and petticoats, which has usurped my place. Is this lady going to be my companion all the way to the terminus of the Grand Transasiatic? Shall I exchange a sympathetic salute with her in the streets of Pekin? And from her my thoughts wander to my companion who is snoring in the corner in a way that would make all the ventilators of Strong, Bulbul & Co. quite jealous. And what is it these big people make? Is it iron bridges, or locomotives, or armor plates, or steam boilers, or mining pumps? From what my American told me, I might find a rival to Creusot or Cokerill or Essen in this formidable establishment in the United States of America. At least unless he has been taking a rise out of me, for he does not seem to be "green," as they say in his country, which means to say that he does not look very much like an idiot, this Ephrinell!

And yet it seems that I must gradually have fallen sound asleep. Withdrawn from exterior influences, I did not even hear the stentorian respiration of the Yankee. The train arrived at Aliat, and stayed there ten minutes without my being aware of it. I am sorry for it, for Aliat is a little seaport, and I should like to have had a first glimpse of the Caspian, and of the countries ravaged by Peter the Great. Two columns of the historico-fantastic might have been made out of that, with the aid of Bouillet and Larousse.

"Baku! Baku!"

The word repeated as the train stopped awoke me.

It was seven o'clock in the morning.

CHAPTER III

The boat did not start until three o'clock in the afternoon. Those of my companions who intended to cross the Caspian hurried off to the harbor; it being necessary to engage a cabin, or to mark one's place in the steamer's saloon.

Ephrinell precipitately left me with these words:

"I have not an instant to lose. I must see about the transport of my baggage."

"Have you much?"

"Forty-two cases."

"Forty-two cases!" I exclaimed.

"And I am sorry I have not double as many. Allow me—"

If he had had a voyage of eight days, instead of one of twenty-four hours, and had to cross the Atlantic instead of the Caspian, he could not have been in a greater hurry.

As you may imagine, the Yankee did not for a moment think of offering his hand to assist our companion in descending from the carriage. I took his place. The lady leaned on my arm and jumped—no, gently put her foot on the ground. My reward was a *thank you, sir,* uttered in a hard, dry, unmistakably British voice.

Thackeray has said somewhere that a well-brought-up Englishwoman is the completest of the works of God on this earth. My only wish is to verify this gallant affirmation in the case of my companion. She has put back her veil. Is she a young woman or an old girl? With these Englishwomen one never knows! Twenty-five years is apparently about her age, she has an Albionesque complexion, a jerky walk, a high dress like an equinoctial tide, no spectacles, although she has eyes of the intense blue which are generally short-sighted. While I bend my back as I bow, she honors me with a nod, which only brings into play the vertebrae of her long neck, and she walks off straight toward the way out.

Probably I shall meet this person again on the steamboat. For my part, I shall not go down to the harbor until it is time to start. I am at Baku: I have half a day to see Baku, and I shall not lose an hour, now that the chances of my wanderings have brought me to Baku.

It is possible that the name may in no way excite the reader's curiosity. But perhaps it may inflame his imagination if I tell him that Baku is the town of the Guebres, the city of the Parsees, the metropolis of the fire-worshippers.

21

Encircled by a triple girdle of black battlemented walls, the town is built near Cape Apcheron, on the extreme spur of the Caucasian range. But am I in Persia or in Russia? In Russia undoubtedly, for Georgia is a Russian province; but we can still believe we are in Persia, for Baku has retained its Persian physiognomy. I visit a palace of the khans, a pure product of the architecture of the time of Schahriar and Scheherazade, "daughter of the moon," his gifted romancer, a palace in which the delicate sculpture is as fresh as it came from the chisel. Further on rise some slender minarets, and not the bulbous roofs of Moscow the Holy, at the angles of an old mosque, into which one can enter without taking off one's boots. True, the muezzin no longer declaims from it some sonorous verse of the Koran at the hour of prayer. And yet Baku has portions of it which are real Russian in manners and aspect, with their wooden houses without a trace of Oriental color, a railway station of imposing aspect, worthy of a great city in Europe or America, and at the end of one of the roads, a modern harbor, the atmosphere of which is foul with the coal smoke vomited from the steamer funnels.

And, in truth, one asks what they are doing with coal in this town of naphtha. What is the good of coal when the bare and arid soil of Apcheron, which grows only the Pontic absinthium, is so rich in mineral oil? At eighty francs the hundred kilos, it yields naphtha, black or white, which the exigencies of supply will not exhaust for centuries.

A marvelous phenomenon indeed! Do you want a light or a fire? Nothing can be simpler; make a hole in the ground, the gas escapes, and you apply a match. That is a natural gasometer within the reach of all purses.

I should have liked to visit the famous sanctuary of Atesh Gah; but it is twenty-two versts from the town, and time failed me. There burns the eternal fire, kept up for centuries by the Parsee priests from India, who never touch animal food.

This reminds me that I have not yet breakfasted, and as eleven o'clock strikes, I make my way to the restaurant at the railway, where I have no intention of conforming myself to the alimentary code of the Parsees of Atesh Gah.

As I am entering, Ephrinell rushes out.

"Breakfast?" say I.

"I have had it," he replies.

"And your cases?"

"I have still twenty-nine to get down to the steamer. But, pardon, I have not a moment to lose. When a man represents the firm of Strong, Bulbul & Co., who send out every week five thousand cases of their goods—"

"Go, go, Monsieur Ephrinell, we will meet on board. By the by, you have not met our traveling companion?"

"What traveling companion?"

"The young lady who took my place in the carriage."

"Was there a young lady with us?"

"Of course."

"Well you are the first to tell me so, Mr. Bombarnac. You are the first to tell me so."

And thereupon the American goes out of the door and disappears. It is to be hoped I shall know before we get to Pekin what it is that Strong, Bulbul & Co. send out in such quantities. Five thousand cases a week—what an output, and what a turnover!

I had soon finished my breakfast and was off again. During my walk I was able to admire a few magnificent Lesghians; these wore the grayish tcherkesse, with the cartridge belts on the chest, the bechmet of bright red silk, the gaiters embroidered with silver, the boots flat, without a heel, the white papak on the head, the long gun on the shoulders, the schaska and kandijar at the belt—in short men of the arsenal as there are men of the orchestra, but of superb aspect and who ought to have a marvelous effect in the processions of the Russian emperor.

It is already two o'clock, and I think I had better get down to the boat. I must call at the railway station, where I have left my light luggage at the cloakroom.

Soon I am off again, bag in one hand, stick in the other, hastening down one of the roads leading to the harbor.

At the break in the wall where access is obtained to the quay, my attention is, I do not know why, attracted by two people walking along together. The man is from thirty to thirty-five years old, the woman from twenty-five to thirty, the man already a grayish brown, with mobile face, lively look, easy walk with a certain swinging of the hips. The woman still a pretty blonde, blue eyes, a rather fresh complexion, her hair frizzed under a cap, a traveling costume which is in good taste neither in its unfashionable cut nor in its glaring color. Evidently a married couple come in the train from Tiflis, and unless I am mistaken they are French.

But although I look at them with curiosity, they take no notice of me. They are too much occupied to see me. In their hands, on their shoulders, they have bags and cushions and wraps and sticks and sunshades and umbrellas. They are carrying every kind of little package you can think of which they do not care to put with the luggage on the steamer.

I have a good mind to go and help them. Is it not a happy chance—and a rare one—to meet with French people away from France?

Just as I am walking up to them, Ephrinell appears, drags me away, and I leave the couple behind. It is only a postponement. I will meet them again on the steamboat and make their acquaintance on the voyage.

"Well," said I to the Yankee, "how are you getting on with your cargo?"

"At this moment, sir, the thirty-seventh case is on the road."

"And no accident up to now?"

"No accident."

"And what may be in those cases, if you please?"

"In those cases? Ah! There is the thirty-seventh!" he exclaimed, and he ran out to meet a truck which had just come onto the quay.

There was a good deal of bustle about, and all the animation of departures and arrivals. Baku is the most frequented and the safest port on the Caspian. Derbent, situated more to the north, cannot keep up with it, and it absorbs almost the entire maritime traffic of this sea, or rather this great lake which has no communication with the neighboring seas. The establishment of Uzun Ada on the opposite coast has doubled the trade which used to pass through Baku. The Transcaspian now open for passengers and goods is the chief commercial route between Europe and Turkestan.

In the near future there will perhaps be a second route along the Persian frontier connecting the South Russian railways with those of British India, and that will save travelers the navigation of the Caspian. And when this vast basin has dried up through evaporation, why should not a railroad be run across its sandy bed, so that trains can run through without transhipment at Baku and Uzun Ada?

While we are waiting for the realization of this desideratum, it is necessary to take the steamboat, and that I am preparing to do in company with many others.

Our steamer is called the *Astara*, of the Caucasus and Mercury Company. She is a big paddle steamer, making three trips a week from coast to coast. She is a very roomy boat, designed to carry a large cargo, and the builders have thought considerably more of the cargo than of the passengers. After all, there is not much to make a fuss about in a day's voyage.

There is a noisy crowd on the quay of people who are going off, and people who have come to see them off, recruited from the cosmopolitan population of Baku. I notice that the travelers are mostly Turkomans, with about a score of Europeans of different nationalities, a few Persians, and two representatives of the Celestial Empire. Evidently their destination is China. .

The *Astara* is loaded up. The hold is not big enough, and a good deal of the cargo has overflowed onto the deck. The stern is reserved for passengers, but from the bridge forward to the topgallant forecastle, there is a heap of cases covered with tarpaulins to protect them from the sea.

There Ephrinell's cases have been put. He has lent a hand with Yankee energy, determined not to lose sight of his valuable property, which is in cubical cases, about two feet on the side, covered with patent leather, carefully strapped, and on which can be read the stenciled words, "Strong, Bulbul & Co., Now York."

"Are all your goods on board?" I asked the American.

"There is the forty-second case just coming," he replied.

And there was the said case on the back of a porter already coming along the gangway.

It seemed to me that the porter was rather tottery, owing perhaps to a lengthy absorption of vodka.

"Wait a bit!" shouted Ephrinell. Then in good Russian, so as to be better understood, he shouted:

"Look out! Look out!"

It is good advice, but it is too late. The porter has just made a false step. The case slips from his shoulders, falls—luckily over the rail of the *Astara*—breaks in two, and a quantity of little packets of paper scatter their contents on the deck.

What a shout of indignation did Ephrinell raise! What a whack with his fist did he administer to the unfortunate porter as he repeated in a voice of despair: "My teeth, my poor teeth!"

And he went down on his knees to gather up his little bits of artificial ivory that were scattered all about, while I could hardly keep from laughing.

Yes! It was teeth which Strong, Bulbul & Co., of New York made! It was for manufacturing five thousand cases a week for the five parts of the world that this huge concern existed! It was for supplying the dentists of the old and new worlds; it was for sending teeth as far as China, that their factory required fifteen hundred horse power, and burned a hundred tons of coal a day! That is quite American!

After all, the population of the globe is fourteen hundred million, and as there are thirty-two teeth per inhabitant, that makes forty-five thousand millions; so that if it ever became necessary to replace all the true teeth by false ones, the firm of Strong, Bulbul & Co. would not be able to supply them.

But we must leave Ephrinell gathering up the odontological treasures of the forty-second case. The bell is ringing for the last time. All the passengers are aboard. The *Astara* is casting off her warps.

Suddenly there are shouts from the quay. I recognize them as being in German, the same as I had heard at Tiflis when the train was starting for Baku.

It is the same man. He is panting, he runs, he cannot run much farther. The gangway has been drawn ashore, and the steamer is already moving off. How will this late comer get on board?

Luckily there is a rope out astern which still keeps the *Astara* near the quay. The German appears just as two sailors are manoeuvring with the fender. They each give him a hand and help him on board.

Evidently this fat man is an old hand at this sort of thing, and I should not be surprised if he did not arrive at his destination.

However, the *Astara* is under way, her powerful paddles are at work, and we are soon out of the harbor.

About a quarter of a mile out there is a sort of boiling, agitating the surface of the sea, and showing some deep trouble in the waters. I was then near the rail on the starboard quarter, and, smoking my cigar, was looking at the harbor disappearing behind the point round Cape Apcheron, while the range of the Caucasus ran up into the western horizon.

Of my cigar there remained only the end between my lips, and taking a last whiff, I threw it overboard.

In an instant a sheet of flame burst out all round the steamer The boiling came from a submarine spring of naphtha, and the cigar end had set it alight.

Screams arise. The *Astara* rolls amid sheaves of flame; but a movement of the helm steers us away from the flaming spring, and we are out of danger.

The captain comes aft and says to me in a frigid tone:

"That was a foolish thing to do."

And I reply, as I usually reply under such circumstances:

"Really, captain, I did not know—"

"You ought always to know, sir!"

These words are uttered in a dry, cantankerous tone a few feet away from me.

I turn to see who it is.

It is the Englishwoman who has read me this little lesson.

❦

CHAPTER IV

I am always suspicious of a traveler's "impressions." These impressions are subjective—a word I use because it is the fashion, although I am not quite sure what it means. A cheerful man looks at things cheerfully, a sorrowful man looks at them sorrowfully. Democritus would have found something enchanting about the banks of the Jordan and the shores of the Dead Sea. Heraclitus would have found something disagreeable about the Bay of Naples and the beach of the Bosphorus. I am of a happy nature—you must really pardon me if I am rather egotistic in this history, for it is so seldom that an author's personality is so mixed up with what he is writing about—like Hugo, Dumas, Lamartine, and so many others. Shakespeare is an exception, and I am not Shakespeare—and, as far as that goes, I am not Lamartine, nor Dumas, nor Hugo.

However, opposed as I am to the doctrines of Schopenhauer and Leopardi, I will admit that the shores of the Caspian did seem rather gloomy and dispiriting. There seemed to be nothing alive on the coast; no vegetation, no birds. There was nothing to make you think you were on a great sea. True, the Caspian is only a lake about eighty feet below the level of the Mediterranean, but this lake is often troubled by violent storms. A ship cannot "get away," as sailors say: it is only about a hundred leagues wide. The coast is quickly reached eastward or westward, and harbors of refuge are not numerous on either the Asiatic or the European side.

There are a hundred passengers on board the *Astara*—a large number of them Caucasians trading with Turkestan, and who will be with us all the way to the eastern provinces of the Celestial Empire.

For some years now the Transcaspian has been running between Uzun Ada and the Chinese frontier. Even between this part and Samarkand it has no less than sixty-three stations; and it is in this section of the line that most of the passengers will alight. I need not worry about them, and I will lose no time in studying them. Suppose one of them proves interesting, I may pump him and peg away at him, and just at the critical moment he will get out.

No! All my attention I must devote to those who are going through with me. I have already secured Ephrinell, and perhaps that charming Englishwoman, who seems to me to be going to Pekin.

I shall meet with other traveling companions at Uzun Ada. With regard to the French couple, there is nothing more at present, but the passage of the Caspian will not be accomplished before I know something about them. There are also these two Chinamen who are evidently going to China. If I only knew a hundred words of the "Kouan-hoa," which is the language spoken in the Celestial Empire, I might perhaps make something out of these curious guys. What I really want is some personage with a story, some mysterious hero traveling *incognito*, a lord or a bandit. I must not forget my trade as a reporter of occurrences and an interviewer of mankind—at so much a line and well selected. He who makes a good choice has a good chance.

I go down the stairs to the saloon aft. There is not a place vacant. The cabins are already occupied by the passengers who are afraid of the pitching and rolling. They went to bed as soon as they came on board, and they will not get up until the boat is alongside the wharf at Uzun Ada. The cabins being full, other travelers have installed themselves on the couches, amid a lot of little packages, and they will not move from there.

As I am going to pass the night on deck, I return up the cabin stairs. The American is there, just finishing the repacking of his case.

"Would you believe it!" he exclaims, "that that drunken moujik actually asked me for something to drink?"

"I hope you have lost nothing, Monsieur Ephrinell?" I reply.

"No; fortunately."

"May I ask how many teeth you are importing into China in those cases?"

"Eighteen hundred thousand, without counting the wisdom teeth!"

And Ephrinell began to laugh at this little joke, which he fired off on several other occasions during the voyage. I left him and went onto the bridge between the paddle boxes.

It is a beautiful night, with the northerly wind beginning to freshen. In the offing, long, greenish streaks are sweeping over the surface of the sea. It is possible that the night may be rougher than we expect. In the forepart of the steamer are many passengers, Turkomans in rags, Kirghizes wrapped up to the eyes, moujiks in emigrant costume—poor fellows, in fact, stretched on the spare spars, against the sides, and along the tarpaulins. They are almost all smoking or nibbling at the provisions they have brought for the voyage. The others are trying to sleep and forget their fatigue, and perhaps their hunger.

It occurs to me to take a stroll among these groups. I am like a hunter beating the brushwood before getting into the hiding place. And I go among this heap of packages, looking them over as if I were a custom house officer.

A rather large deal case, covered with a tarpaulin, attracts my attention. It measures about a yard and a half in height, and a yard in width and depth. It has been placed here with the care required by these words in Russian, written on the side, "Glass—Fragile—Keep from damp," and then directions, "Top—Bottom," which have been respected. And then there is the address,

"Mademoiselle Zinca Klork, Avenue Cha-Coua, Pekin, Petchili, China."

This Zinca Klork—her name showed it—ought to be a Roumanian, and she was taking advantage of this through train on the Grand Transasiatic to get her glass forwarded. Was this an article in request at the shops of the Middle Kingdom? How otherwise could the fair Celestials admire their almond eyes and their elaborate hair?

The bell rang and announced the six-o'clock dinner. The dining-room is forward. I went down to it, and found it already occupied by some forty people.

Ephrinell had installed himself nearly in the middle. There was a vacant seat near him; he beckoned to me to occupy it, and I hastened to take possession.

Was it by chance? I know not; but the Englishwoman was seated on Ephrinell's left and talking to him. He introduced me.

"Miss Horatia Bluett," he said.

Opposite I saw the French couple conscientiously studying the bill of fare.

At the other end of the table, close to where the food came from—and where the people got served first—was the German passenger, a man strongly built and with a ruddy face, fair hair, reddish beard, clumsy hands, and a very long nose which reminded one of the proboscidean feature of the plantigrades. He had that peculiar look of the officers of the Landsturm threatened with premature obesity.

"He is not late this time," said I to Ephrinell.

"The dinner hour is never forgotten in the German Empire!" replied the American.

"Do you know that German's name?"

"Baron Weissschnitzerdoerfer."

"And with that name is he going to Pekin?"

"To Pekin, like that Russian major who is sitting near the captain of the *Astara.*"

I looked at the man indicated. He was about fifty years of age, of true Muscovite type, beard and hair turning gray, face prepossessing. I knew Russian: he ought to know French. Perhaps he was the fellow traveler of whom I had dreamed.

"You said he was a major, Mr. Ephrinell?"

"Yes, a doctor in the Russian army, and they call him Major Noltitz."

Evidently the American was some distance ahead of me, and yet he was not a reporter by profession.

As the rolling was not yet very great, we could dine in comfort. Ephrinell chatted with Miss Horatia Bluett, and I understood that there was an understanding between these two perfectly Anglo-Saxon natures.

In fact, one was a traveler in teeth and the other was a traveler in hair. Miss Horatia Bluett represented an important firm in London, Messrs. Holmes-Holme, to whom the Celestial Empire annually exports two millions of female heads of hair. She was going to Pekin on account of the said firm, to open an office as a center for the collection of the Chinese hair crop. It seemed a promising enterprise, as the secret society of the Blue Lotus was agitating for the abolition of the pigtail, which is the emblem of the servitude of the Chinese to the Manchu Tartars. "Come," thought I, "if China sends her hair to England, America sends her teeth: that is a capital exchange, and everything is for the best."

We had been at the table for a quarter of an hour, and nothing had happened. The traveler with the smooth complexion and his blonde companion seemed to listen to us when we spoke in French. It evidently pleased them, and they were already showing an inclination to join in our talk. I was not mistaken, then; they are compatriots, but of what class?

At this moment the *Astara* gave a lurch. The plates rattled on the table; the covers slipped; the glasses upset some of their contents; the hanging lamps swung out of the vertical—or rather our seats and the table moved in accordance with the roll of the ship. It is a curious effect, when one is sailor enough to bear it without alarm.

"Eh!" said the American; "here is the good old Caspian shaking her skin."

"Are you subject to seasickness?" I asked.

"No more than a porpoise," said he. "Are you ever seasick?" he continued to his neighbor.

"Never," said Miss Horatia Bluett.

On the other side of the table there was an interchange of a few words in French.

"You are not unwell, Madame Caterna?"

"No, Adolphe, not yet; but if this continues, I am afraid—"

"Well, Caroline, we had better go on deck. The wind has hauled a point to the eastward, and the *Astara* will soon be sticking her nose in the feathers."

His way of expressing himself shows that "Monsieur Caterna"—if that was his name—was a sailor, or ought to have been one. That explains the way he rolls his hips as he walks.

The pitching now becomes very violent. The majority of the company cannot stand it. About thirty of the passengers have left the table for the deck. I hope the fresh air will do them good. We are now only a dozen in the dining room, including the captain, with whom Major Noltitz is quietly conversing. Ephrinell and Miss Bluett seem to be thoroughly accustomed to these inevitable incidents of navigation. The German baron drinks and eats as if he had taken up his quarters in some bier-halle at Munich, or Frankfort, holding his knife in his right hand, his fork in his left, and making up little heaps of meat, which he salts and peppers and covers with sauce, and then inserts under his hairy lip on the point of his knife. Fie! What behavior! And yet he gets on splendidly, and neither rolling nor pitching makes him lose a mouthful of food or drink.

A little way off are the two Celestials, whom I watch with curiosity.

One is a young man of distinguished bearing, about twenty-five years old, of pleasant physiognomy, in spite of his yellow skin and his narrow eyes. A few years spent in Europe have evidently Europeanized his manners and even his dress. His mustache is silky, his eye is intelligent his hair is much more French than Chinese. He seems to me a nice fellow, of a cheerful temperament, who would not ascend the "Tower of Regret," as the Chinese have it, oftener than he could help.

His companion, on the contrary, whom he always appears to be making fun of, is of the type of the true porcelain doll, with the moving head; he is from fifty to fifty-five years old, like a monkey in the face, the top of his head half shaven, the pigtail down his back, the traditional costume, frock, vest, belt, baggy trousers, many-colored slippers; a China vase of the Green family. He, however, could hold out no longer, and after a tremendous pitch, accompanied by a long rattle of the crockery, he got up and hurried on deck. And as he did so, the younger Chinaman shouted after him, "Cornaro! Cornaro!" at the same time holding out a little volume he had left on the table.

What was the meaning of this Italian word in an Oriental mouth? Did the Chinaman speak the language of Boccaccio? The *Twentieth Century* ought to know, and it would know.

Madame Caterna arose, very pale, and Monsieur Caterna, a model husband, followed her on deck.

The dinner over, leaving Ephrinell and Miss Bluett to talk of brokerages and prices current, I went for a stroll on the poop of the *Astara*. Night had nearly closed in. The hurrying clouds, driven from the eastward, draped in deep folds the higher zones of the sky, with here and there a few stars peeping through. The wind was rising. The white light of the steamer clicked as it swung on the foremast. The red and green lights rolled with the ship, and projected their long colored rays onto the troubled waters.

I met Ephrinell, Miss Horatia Bluett having retired to her cabin; he was going down into the saloon to find a comfortable corner on one of the couches. I wished him good night, and he left me after gratifying me with a similar wish.

As for me, I will wrap myself in my rug and lie down in a corner of the deck, and sleep like a sailor during his watch below.

At nine o'clock the night is very dark. I try to make out some steamer's lights in the distance, but in vain, for the Caspian has not many ships on it. I can hear only the cry of the sea birds, gulls and scoters, who are abandoning themselves to the caprices of the wind.

During my promenade, one thought besets me: is the voyage to end without my getting anything out of it as copy for my journal? My instructions made me responsible for producing something, and surely not without reason. What? Not an adventure from Tiflis to Pekin? Evidently that could only be my fault! And I resolved to do everything to avoid such a misfortune.

It is half-past ten when I sit down on one of the seats in the stern of the *Astara*. But with this increasing wind it is impossible for me to remain there. I rise, therefore, and make my way forward. Under the bridge, between the paddle boxes, the wind is so strong that I seek shelter among the packages covered by the tarpaulin. Stretched on one of the boxes, wrapped in my rug, with my head resting against the tarpaulin, I shall soon be asleep.

After some time, I do not exactly know how much, I am awakened by a curious noise. Whence comes this noise? I listen more attentively. It seems as though some one is snoring close to my ear.

"That is some steerage passenger," I think. "He has got under the tarpaulin between the cases, and he will not do so badly in his improvised cabin."

By the light which filters down from the lower part of the binnacle, I see nothing.

I listen again. The noise has ceased.

I look about. There is no one on this part of the deck, for the second-class passengers are all forward.

Then I must have been dreaming, and I resume my position and try again to sleep.

This time there is no mistake. The snoring has begun again, and I am sure it is coming from the case against which I am leaning my head.

"Goodness!" I say. "There must be an animal in here!"

An animal? What? A dog? A cat? Why have they hidden a domestic animal in this case? Is it a wild animal? A panther, a tiger, a lion?

Now I am off on the trail! It must be a wild animal on its way from some menagerie to some sultan of Central Asia. This case is a cage, and if the cage opens, if the animal springs out onto the deck—here is an incident, here is something worth chronicling; and here I am with my professional enthusiasm running mad. I must know at all costs to whom this wild beast is being sent; is it going to Uzon Ada, or is it going to China? The address ought to be on the case.

I light a wax vesta, and as I am sheltered from the wind, the flame keeps upright.

By its light what do I read?

The case containing the wild beast is the very one with the address:

"Mademoiselle Zinca Klork, Avenue Cha-Coua, Pekin, China."

Fragile, my wild beast! *Keep from damp*, my lion! Quite so! But for what does Miss Zinca Klork, this pretty—for the Roumanian ought to be pretty, and she is certainly a Roumanian—for what does she want a wild beast sent in this way?

Let us think about it and be reasonable. This animal, whatever it may be, must eat and drink. From the time it starts from Uzon Ada it will take eleven days to cross Asia, and reach the capital of the Celestial Empire. Well, what do they give it to drink, what do they give it to eat, if he is not going to get out of his cage, if he is going to be shut up during

33

the whole of the journey? The officials of the Grand Transasiatic will be no more careful in their attentions to the said wild beast than if he were a glass, for he is described as such; and he will die of inanition!

All these things sent my brain whirling. My thoughts bewildered me. "Is it a lovely dream that dazes me, or am I awake?" as Margaret says in Faust, more lyrically than dramatically. To resist is impossible. I have a two-pound weight on each eyelid. I lay down along by the tarpaulin; my rug wraps me more closely, and I fall into a deep sleep.

How long have I slept? Perhaps for three or four hours. One thing is certain, and that is that it is not yet daylight when I awake.

I rub my eyes, I rise, I go and lean against the rail.

The *Astara* is not so lively, for the wind has shifted to the northeast.

The night is cold. I warm myself by walking about briskly for half an hour. I think no more of my wild beast. Suddenly remembrance returns to me. Should I not call the attention of the stationmaster to this disquieting case? But that is no business of mine. We shall see before we start.

I look at my watch. It is only three o'clock in the morning. I will go back to my place. And I do so with my head against the side of the case. I shut my eyes.

Suddenly there is a new sound. This time I am not mistaken. A half-stifled sneeze shakes the side of the case. Never did an animal sneeze like that!

Is it possible? A human being is hidden in this case and is being fraudulently carried by the Grand Transasiatic to the pretty Roumanian! But is it a man or a woman? It seems as though the sneeze had a masculine sound about it.

It is impossible to sleep now. How long the day is coming! How eager I am to examine this box! I wanted incidents—well! and here is one, and if I do not get five lines out of this—

The eastern horizon grows brighter. The clouds in the zenith are the first to color. The sun appears at last all watery with the mists of the sea.

I look; it is indeed the case addressed to Pekin. I notice that certain holes are pierced here and there, by which the air inside can be renewed. Perhaps two eyes are looking through these holes, watching what is going on outside? Do not be indiscreet!

At breakfast gather all the passengers whom the sea has not affected: the young Chinaman, Major Noltitz, Ephrinell, Miss Bluett, Monsieur Caterna, the Baron Weissschnitzerdoerfer, and seven or eight other passengers. I am careful not to let the American into the secret of

34

the case. He would be guilty of some indiscretion, and then good-by to my news par!

About noon the land is reported to the eastward, a low, yellowish land, with no rocky margin, but a few sandhills in the neighborhood of Krasnovodsk.

In an hour we are in sight of Uzun Ada, and twenty-seven minutes afterward we set foot in Asia.

CHAPTER V

Travelers used to land at Mikhailov, a little port at the end of the Transcaspian line; but ships of moderate tonnage hardly had water enough there to come alongside. On this account, General Annenkof, the creator of the new railway, the eminent engineer whose name will frequently recur in my narrative, was led to found Uzun Ada, and thereby considerably shorten the crossing of the Caspian. The station was built in three months, and it was opened on the 8th of May, 1886.

Fortunately I had read the account given by Boulangier, the engineer, relating to the prodigious work of General Annenkof, so that I shall not be so very much abroad during the railway journey between Uzun Ada and Samarkand, and, besides, I trust to Major Noltitz, who knows all about the matter. I have a presentiment that we shall become good friends, and in spite of the proverb which says, "Though your friend be of honey do not lick him!" I intend to "lick" my companion often enough for the benefit of my readers.

We often hear of the extraordinary rapidity with which the Americans have thrown their railroads across the plains of the Far West. But the Russians are in no whit behind them, if even they have not surpassed them in rapidity as well as in industrial audacity.

People are fully acquainted with the adventurous campaign of General Skobeleff against the Turkomans, a campaign of which the building of the railway assured the definite success. Since then the political state of Central Asia has been entirely changed, and Turkestan is merely a province of Asiatic Russia, extending to the frontiers of the Chinese Empire. And already Chinese Turkestan is very visibly submitting to the Muscovite influence which the vertiginous heights of the Pamir plateau have not been able to check in its civilizing march.

I was about to cross the countries which were formerly ravaged by Tamerlane and Genghis Khan, those fabulous countries of which the Russians in 1886 possessed six hundred and fifteen thousand square kilometres, with thirteen hundred thousand inhabitants. The southern part of this region now forms the Transcaspian province, divided into six districts, Fort Alexandrovski, Krasnovodsk, Askhabad, Karibent, Merv, Pendjeh, governed by Muscovite colonels or lieutenant-colonels.

As may be imagined, it hardly takes an hour to see Uzun Ada, the name of which means Long Island. It is almost a town, but a modern town, traced with a square, drawn with a line or a large carpet of yellow sand. No monuments, no memories, bridges of planks, houses of wood, to which comfort is beginning to add a few mansions in stone. One can see what this, first station of the Transcaspian will be like in fifty years; a great city after having been a great railway station.

Do not think that there are no hotels. Among others there is the Hotel du Czar, which has a good table, good rooms and good beds. But the question of beds has no interest for me. As the train starts at four o'clock this afternoon, to begin with, I must telegraph to the *Twentieth Century*, by the Caspian cable, that I am at my post at the Uzun Ada station. That done, I can see if I can pick up anything worth reporting.

Nothing is more simple. It consists in opening an account with those of my companions with whom I may have to do during the journey. That is my custom, I always find it answers, and while waiting for the unknown, I write down the known in my pocketbook, with a number to distinguish each:

1. Fulk Ephrinell, American.
2. Miss Horatia Bluett, English.
3. Major Noltitz, Russian.
4. Monsieur Caterna, French.
5. Madame Caterna, French.
6. Baron Weissschnitzerdoerfer, German.

As to the Chinese, they will have a number later on, when I have made up my mind about them. As to the individual in the box, I intend to enter into communication with him, or her, and to be of assistance in that quarter if I can do so without betraying the secret.

The train is already marshaled in the station. It is composed of first and second-class cars, a restaurant car and two baggage vans. These cars are painted of a light color, an excellent precaution against the heat and against the cold. For in the Central Asian provinces the temperature ranges between fifty degrees centigrade above zero and twenty below, and in a range of seventy degrees it is only prudent to minimize the effects.

These cars are in a convenient manner joined together by gangways, on the American plan. Instead of being shut up in a compartment, the traveler strolls about along the whole length of the train. There is room to pass between the stuffed seats, and in the front and rear of each car are the platforms united by the gangways. This facility of communication assures the security of the train.

Our engine has a bogie on four small wheels, and is thus able to negotiate the sharpest curves; a tender with water and fuel; then come a front van, three first-class cars with twenty-four places each, a restaurant car with pantry and kitchen, four second-class cars and a rear van; in all twelve vehicles, counting in the locomotive and tender. The first class cars are provided with dressing rooms, and their seats, by very simple mechanism, are convertible into beds, which, in fact, are indispensable for long journeys. The second-class travelers are not so comfortably treated, and besides, they have to bring their victuals with them, unless they prefer to take their meals at the stations. There are not many, however, who travel the complete journey between the Caspian and the eastern provinces of China—that is to say about six thousand kilometres. Most of them go to the principal towns and villages of Russian Turkestan, which have been reached by the Transcaspian Railway for some years, and which up to the Chinese frontier has a length of over 1,360 miles.

This Grand Transasiatic has only been open six weeks and the company is as yet only running two trains a week. All has gone well up to the present; but I ought to add the significant detail that the railway men carry a supply of revolvers to arm the passengers with if necessary. This is a wise precaution in crossing the Chinese deserts, where an attack on the train is not improbable.

I believe the company are doing their best to ensure the punctuality of their trains; but the Chinese section is managed by Celestials, and who knows what has been the past life of those people? Will they not be more intent on the security of their dividends than of their passengers?

37

As I wait for the departure I stroll about on the platform, looking through the windows of the cars, which have no doors along the sides, the entrances being at the ends.

Everything is new; the engine is as bright as it can be, the carriages are brilliant in their new paint, their springs have not begun to give with wear, and their wheels run true on the rails. Then there is the rolling stock with which we are going to cross a continent. There is no railway as long as this—not even in America. The Canadian line measures five thousand kilometres, the Central Union, five thousand two hundred and sixty, the Santa Fe line, four thousand eight hundred and seventy-five, the Atlantic Pacific, five thousand six hundred and thirty, the Northern Pacific, six thousand two hundred and fifty. There is only one line which will be longer when it is finished, and that is the Grand Transsiberian, from the Urals to Vladivostock, which will measure six thousand five hundred kilometres.

Between Tiflis and Pekin our journey will not last more than thirteen days, from Uzun Ada it will only last eleven. The train will only stop at the smaller stations to take in fuel and water. At the chief towns like Merv, Bokhara, Samarkand, Tashkend, Kachgar, Kokhand, Sou Tcheou, Lan Tcheou, Tai Youan, it will stop a few hours—and that will enable me to do these towns in reporter style.

Of course, the same driver and stoker will not take us through. They will be relieved every six hours. Russians will take us up to the frontier of Turkestan, and Chinese will take us on through China.

But there is one representative of the company who will not leave his post, and that is Popof, our head guard, a true Russian of soldierly bearing, hairy and bearded, with a folded overcoat and a Muscovite cap. I intend to talk a good deal with this gallant fellow, although he is not very talkative. If he does not despise a glass of vodka, opportunity offered, he may have a good deal to say to me; for ten years he has been on the Transcaspian between Uzun Ada and the Pamirs, and during the last month he has been all along the line to Pekin.

I call him No. 7 in my notebook, and I hope he will give me information enough. I only want a few incidents of the journey, just a few little incidents worthy of the *Twentieth Century*.

Among the passengers I see on the platform are a few Jews, recognizable more by their faces than their attire. Formerly, in Central Asia, they could only wear the "toppe," a sort of round cap, and a plain rope belt, without any silk ornamentation—under pain of death. And I am told that they could ride on asses in certain towns and walk on foot in others. Now they wear the oriental turban and roll in their carriages if their purse allows of it. Who would hinder them now they are subjects of the White Czar, Russian citizens, rejoicing in civil and political rights equal to those of their Turkoman compatriots?

There are a few Tadjiks of Persian origin, the handsomest men you can imagine. They have booked for Merv, or Bokhara, or Samarkand, or Tachkend, or Kokhand, and will not pass the Russo-Chinese frontier. As a rule they are second-class passengers. Among the first-class passengers I noticed a few Usbegs of the ordinary type, with retreating foreheads and prominent cheek bones, and brown complexions, who were the lords of the country, and from whose families come the emirs and khans of Central Asia.

But are there not any Europeans in this Grand Transasiatic train? It must be confessed that I can only count five or six. There are a few commercial travelers from South Russia, and one of those inevitable gentlemen from the United Kingdom, who are inevitably to be found on the railways and steamboats. It is still necessary to obtain permission to travel on the Transcaspian, permission which the Russian administration does not willingly accord to an Englishman; but this man has apparently been able to get one.

And he seems to me to be worth notice. He is tall and thin, and looks quite the fifty years that his gray hairs proclaim him to be. His characteristic expression is one of haughtiness, or rather disdain, composed in equal parts of love of all things English and contempt for all things that are not. This type is occasionally so insupportable, even to his compatriots, that Dickens, Thackeray and others have often made fun of it. How he turned up his nose at the station at Uzun Ada, at the train, at the men, at the car in which he had secured a seat by placing in it his traveling bag! Let us call him No. 8 in my pocketbook.

There seem to be no personages of importance. That is a pity. If only the Emperor of Russia, on one side, or the Son of Heaven, on the other, were to enter the train to meet officially on the frontier of the two empires, what festivities there would be, what grandeur, what descriptions, what copy for letters and telegrams!

It occurs to me to have a look at the mysterious box. Has it not a right to be so called? Yes, certainly. I must really find out where it has been put and how to get at it easily.

The front van is already full of Ephrinell's baggage. It does not open at the side, but in front and behind, like the cars. It is also furnished with a platform and a gangway. An interior passage allows the guard to go through it to reach the tender and locomotive if necessary. Popof's little cabin is on the platform of the first car, in the left-hand corner. At night it will be easy for me to visit the van, for it is only shut in by the doors at the ends of the passage arranged between the packages. If this van is reserved for luggage registered through to China, the luggage for the Turkestan stations ought to be in the van at the rear.

When I arrived the famous box was still on the platform.

In looking at it closely I observe that airholes have been bored on each of its sides, and that on one side it has two panels, one of which can be made to slide on the other from the inside. And I am led to think that the prisoner has had it made so in order that he can, if necessary, leave his prison—probably during the night.

Just now the porters are beginning to lift the box. I have the satisfaction of seeing that they attend to the directions inscribed on it. It is placed, with great care, near the entrance to the van, on the left, the side with the panels outward, as if it were the door of a cupboard. And is not the box a cupboard? A cupboard I propose to open?

It remains to be seen if the guard in charge of the luggage is to remain in this van. No. I find that his post is just outside it.

"There it is, all right!" said one of the porters, looking to see that the case was as it should be, top where top should be, and so on.

"There is no fear of its moving," said another porter; "the glass will reach Pekin all right, unless the train runs off the metals."

"Or it does not run into anything," said the other; "and that remains to be seen."

They were right—these good fellows—it remained to be seen—and it would be seen.

The American came up to me and took a last look at his stock of incisors, molars and canines, with a repetition of his invariable "Wait a bit."

"You know, Monsieur Bombarnac," he said to me, "that the passengers are going to dine at the Hotel du Czar before the departure of the train. It is time now. Will you come with me?"

"I follow you."

And we entered the dining room. All my numbers are there: 1, Ephrinell, taking his place as usual by the side of 2, Miss Horatia Bluett. The French couple, 4 and 5, are also side by side. Number 3, that is Major Noltitz, is seated in front of numbers 9 and 10, the two Chinese to whom I have just given numbers in my notebook. As to the fat German, number 6, he has already got his long nose into his soup plate. I see also that the Guard Popol, number 7, has his place at the foot of the table. The other passengers, Europeans and Asiatics, are installed, *passim* with the evident intention of doing justice to the repast.

Ah! I forgot my number 8, the disdainful gentleman whose name I don't yet know, and who seems determined to find the Russian cookery inferior to the English.

I also notice with what attention Monsieur Caterna looks after his wife, and encourages her to make up for the time lost when she was unwell on board the *Astara*. He keeps her glass filled, he chooses the best pieces for her, etc.

"What a good thing it is," I hear him say, "that we are not to leeward of the Teuton, for there would be nothing left for us!"

He is to windward of him—that is to say, the dishes reach him before they get to the baron, which, however, does not prevent his clearing them without shame.

The observation, in sea language, made me smile, and Caterna, noticing it, gave me a wink with a slight movement of the shoulder toward the baron.

It is evident that these French people are not of high distinction, they do not belong to the upper circles; but they are good people, I will answer for it, and when we have to rub shoulders with compatriots, we must not be too particular in Turkestan.

The dinner ends ten minutes before the time fixed for our departure. The bell rings and we all make a move for the train, the engine of which is blowing off steam.

Mentally, I offer a last prayer to the God of reporters and ask him not to spare me adventures. Then, after satisfying myself that all my numbers are in the first-class cars, so that I can keep an eye on them, I take my place.

The Baron Weissschnitzerdoerfer—what an interminable name—is not behindhand this time. On the contrary, it is the train this time which is five minutes late in starting; and the German has begun to complain, to chafe and to swear, and threatens to sue the company for damages. Ten thousand roubles—not a penny less!—if it causes him to fail. Fail in what, considering that he is going to Pekin?

At length the last shriek of the whistle cleaves the air, the cars begin to move, and a loud cheer salutes the departure of the Grand Transasiatic express.

❦

Chapter VI

The ideas of a man on horseback are different to those which occur to him when he is on foot. The difference is even more noticeable when he is on the railway. The association of his thoughts, the character of his reflections are all affected by the speed of the train. They "roll" in his head, as he rolls in his car. And so it comes about that I am in a particularly lively mood, desirous of observing, greedy of instruction, and that at a speed of thirty-one miles an hour. That is the rate at which we are to travel through Turkestan, and when we reach the Celestial Empire we shall have to be content with eighteen.

That is what I have just ascertained by consulting my time-table, which I bought at the station. It is accompanied by a long slip map, folded and refolded on itself, which shows the whole length of the line between the Caspian and the eastern coast of China. I study, then, my Transasiatic, on leaving Uzun Ada, just as I studied my Transgeorgian when I left Tiflis.

The gauge of the line is about sixty-three inches—as is usual on the Russian lines, which are thus about four inches wider than those of other European countries. It is said, with regard to this, that the Germans have made a great number of axles of this length, in case they have to invade Russia. I should like to think that the Russians have taken the same precautions in the no less probable event of their having to invade Germany.

On either side of the line are long sandhills, between which the train runs out from Uzun Ada; when it reaches the arm of the sea which separates Long Island from the continent, it crosses an embankment about 1,200 yards long, edged with masses of rock to protect it against the violence of the waves.

We have already passed several stations without stopping, among others Mikhailov, a league from Uzun Ada. Now they are from ten to eleven miles apart. Those I have seen, as yet, look like villas, with balustrades and Italian roofs, which has a curious effect in Turkestan and the neighborhood of Persia. The desert extends up to the neighborhood of Uzun Ada, and the railway stations form so many little oases, made by the hand of man. It is man, in fact, who has planted these slender, sea-green poplars, which give so little shade; it is man who, at great expense, has brought here the water whose refreshing jets fall back into an elegant vase. Without these hydraulic works there would not be a tree, not a corner of green in these oases. They are the nurses of the line, and dry-nurses are of no use to locomotives.

The truth is that I have never seen such a bare, arid country, so clear of vegetation; and it extends for one hundred and fifty miles from Uzun Ada. When General Annenkof commenced his works at Mikhailov, he was obliged to distil the water from the Caspian Sea, as if he were on board ship. But if water is necessary to produce steam, coal is necessary to vaporize the water. The readers of the *Twentieth Century* will ask how are the furnaces fed in a country in which there is neither coal nor wood? Are there stores of these things at the principal stations of the Transcaspian? Not at all. They have simply put in practice an idea which occurred to our great chemist, Sainte-Claire Deville, when first petroleum was used in France. The furnaces are fed, by the aid of a pulverizing apparatus, with the residue produced from the distillation of the naphtha, which Baku and Derbent produce in such inexhaustible quantities. At certain stations on the line there are vast reservoirs of this combustible mineral, from which the tenders are filled, and it is burned in specially adapted fireboxes. In a similar way naphtha is used on the steamboats on the Volga and the other affluents of the Caspian.

I repeat, the country is not particularly varied. The ground is nearly flat in the sandy districts, and quite flat in the alluvial plains, where the brackish water stagnates in pools. Nothing could be better for a line of railway. There are no cuttings, no embankments, no viaducts, no works of art—to use a term dear to engineers, very "dear," I should say. Here and there are a few wooden bridges from two hundred to three hundred feet long. Under such circumstances the cost per kilometre of the Transcaspian did not exceed seventy-five thousand francs.

The monotony of the journey would only be broken on the vast oases of Merv, Bokhara and Samarkand.

But let us busy ourselves with the passengers, as we can do all the more easily from our being able to walk from one end to the other of the train. With a little imagination we can make ourselves believe we are in a sort of traveling village, and I am just going to take a run down main street.

Remember that the engine and tender are followed by the van at the angle of which is placed the mysterious case, and that Popof's compartment is in the left-hand corner of the platform of the first car.

Inside this car I notice a few Sarthes of tall figure and haughty face, draped in their long robes of bright colors, from beneath which appear the braided leather boots. They have splendid eyes, a superb beard, arched nose, and you would take them for real lords, provided we ignore the word Sarthe, which means a pedlar, and these were going evidently to Tachkend, where these pedlars swarm.

In this car the two Chinese have taken their places, opposite each other. The young Celestial looks out of window. The old one—Ta-lao-ye, that is to say, a person well advanced in years—is incessantly turning over the pages of his book. This volume, a small 32mo, looks like our *Annuaire du Bureau des Longitudes,* and is covered in plush, like a breviary, and when it is shut its covers are kept in place by an elastic band. What astonishes me is that the proprietor of this little book does not seem to read it from right to left. Is it not written in Chinese characters? We must see into this!

On two adjoining seats are Ephrinell and Miss Horatia Bluett. Their talk is of nothing but figures. I don't know if the practical American murmurs at the ear of the practical Englishwoman the adorable verse which made the heart of Lydia palpitate:

"Nee tecum possum vivere sine te,"

but I do know that Ephrinell can very well live without me. I have been quite right in not reckoning on his company to charm away the tedium of the journey. The Yankee has completely "left" me—that is the word— for this angular daughter of Albion.

I reach the platform. I cross the gangway and I am at the door of the second car.

In the right-hand corner is Baron Weissschnitzerdoerfer. His long nose—this Teuton is as short-sighted as a mole—rubs the lines of the book he reads. The book is the time-table. The impatient traveler is ascertaining if the train passes the stations at the stated time. Whenever it is behind there are new recriminations and menaces against the Grand Transasiatic Company.

In this car there are also the Caternas, who have made themselves quite comfortable. In his cheery way, the husband is talking with a good deal of gesticulation, sometimes touching his wife's hands, sometimes putting his arms round her waist; and then he turns his head toward the platform and says something aside. Madame Caterna leans toward him, makes little confused grimaces, and then leans back into the corner and seems to reply to her husband, who in turn replies to her. And as I leave I hear the chorus of an operetta in the deep voice of Monsieur Caterna.

In the third car, occupied by many Turkomans and three or four Russians, I perceive Major Noltitz. He is talking with one of his countrymen. I will willingly join in their conversation if they make me any advances, but I had better maintain a certain reserve; the journey has only begun.

I then visit the dining car. It is a third longer than the other cars, a regular dining room, with one long table. At the back is a pantry on one side, a kitchen on the other, where the cook and steward are at work, both of them Russians. This dining car appears to me capitally arranged. Passing through it, I reach the second part of the train, where the second-class passengers are installed. Kirghizes who do not look very intelligent with their depressed heads, their prognathous jaws stuck well out in front, their little beards, flat Cossack noses and very brown skins. These wretched fellows are Mahometans and belong either to the Grand Horde wandering on the frontier between China and Siberia, or to the Little Horde between the Ural Mountains and the Aral Sea. A second-class car, or even a third-class car, is a palace for these people, accustomed to the encampments on the Steppes, to the miserable "iourts" of villages. Neither their beds nor their seats are as good as the stuffed benches on which they have seated themselves with true Asiatic gravity.

With them are two or three Nogais going to Eastern Turkestan. Of a higher race than the Kirghizes, being Tartars, it is from them that come the learned men and professors who have made illustrious the opulent cities of Bokhara and Samarkand. But science and its teaching do not yield much of a livelihood, even when reduced to the mere necessaries of life, in these provinces of Central Asia. And so these Nogais take employment as interpreters. Unfortunately, since the diffusion of the Russian language, their trade is not very remunerative.

Now I know the places of my numbers, and I know where to find them when I want them. As to those going through to Pekin, I have no doubt of Ephrinell and Miss Horatia Bluett nor the German baron, nor the two Chinese, nor Major Noltitz, nor the Caternas, nor even for the haughty gentleman whose bony outline I perceive in the corner of the second car.

As to these travelers who are not going across the frontier, they are of most perfect insignificance in my eyes. But among my companions I have not yet found the hero of my chronicle! let us hope he will declare himself as we proceed.

My intention is to take notes hour by hour—what did I say? To "minute" my journey. Before the night closes in I go out on the platform of the car to have a last look at the surrounding country. An hour with my cigar will take me to Kizil Arvat, where the train has to stop for some time. In going from the second to the first car I meet Major Noltitz. I step aside to let him pass. He salutes me with that grace which distinguishes well-bred Russians. I return his salute. Our meeting is restricted to this exchange of politeness, but the first step is taken.

Popof is not just now in his seat. The door of the luggage van being open, I conclude that the guard has gone to talk with the driver. On the left of the van the mysterious box is in its place. It is only half-past six as yet, and there is too much daylight for me to risk the gratification of my curiosity.

The train advances through the open desert. This is the Kara Koum, the Black Desert. It extends from Khiva over all Turkestan comprised between the Persian frontier and the course of the Amou Daria. In reality the sands of the Kara Koum are no more black than the waters of the Black Sea or than those of the White Sea are white, those of the Red Sea red, or those of the Yellow River yellow. But I like these colored distinctions, however erroneous they may be. In landscapes the eye is caught by colors. And is there not a good deal of landscape about geography?

It appears that this desert was formerly occupied by a huge central basin. It has dried up, as the Caspian will dry up, and this evaporation is explained by the powerful concentration of the solar rays on the surface of the territories between the Sea of Aral and the Plateau of the Pamir.

The Kara Koum is formed of low sandy hills which the high winds are constantly shifting and forming. These "barkans," as the Russians call them, vary in height from thirty to ninety feet. They expose a wide surface to the northern hurricanes which drive them gradually southward. And on this account there is a well-justified fear for the safety of the Transcaspian. It had to be protected in some efficacious way, and General Annenkof would have been much embarrassed if provident Nature had not, at the same time as she gave the land favorable for the railway to be laid along, given the means of stopping the shifting of the barkanes.

Behind these sand hills grow a number of spring shrubs, clumps of tamarisk, star thistles, and that *Haloxylon ammodendron* which Russians call, not so scientifically, "saksaoul." Its deep, strong roots are as well adapted for binding together the ground as those of *Hippophae rhamnoides*, an arbutus of the Eleagnaceous family, which is used for binding together the sands in southern Europe.

46

To these plantations of saksaouls the engineers of the line have added in different places a series of slopes of worked clay, and in the most dangerous places a line of palisades.

These precautions are doubtless of use; but if the road is protected, the passengers are hardly so, when the sand flies like a bullet hail, and the wind sweeps up from the plain the whitish efflorescences of salt. It is a good thing for us that we are not in the height of the hot season; and it is not in June or July or August that I would advise you to take a trip on the Grand Transasiatic.

I am sorry that Major Noltitz does not think of coming out on the gangway to breathe the fresh air of the Kara Koum. I would offer him one of those choice regalias with which my case is well provided. He would tell me if these stations I see on my time-table, Balla-Ischem, Aidine, Pereval, Kansandjik, Ouchak, are of any interest—which they do not seem to be. But it would not do for me to disturb his siesta. And yet his conversation ought to be interesting, for as a surgeon in the Russian army he took part in the campaigns of Generals Skobeleff and Annenkof. When our train ran through the little stations that it honors only with a whistle, he could tell me if this one or that one had been the scene of any incident of the war. As a Frenchman I am justified in questioning him about the Russian expedition across Turkestan, and I have no doubt that my fellow passenger will be pleased to gratify me. He is the only one I can really trust besides Popof.

But why is Popof not in his seat? He also is not insensible to the charms of a cigar. It would seem that his conversation with the engineer has not finished yet.

Ah! Here he is coming from the front of the luggage van. He comes out of it and shuts the door; he remains for a moment and is about to take a seat. A hand which holds a cigar, is stretched out toward him. Popof smiles and soon his perfumed puffs are mingling voluptuously with mine.

For fifteen years I think I said our guard had been in the Transcaspian service. He knows the country up to the Chinese frontier, and five or six times already he has been over the whole line known as the Grand Transasiatic.

Popof was on duty on the section between Mikhailov and Kizil Arvat when the line opened—a section which was begun in the December of 1880 and finished in ten months, in November, 1881. Five years later the locomotive entered Merv, on the 14th July, 1886, and eighteen months later it was welcomed at Samarkand. Now the road through

Turkestan joins the road through the Celestial Empire, and the ribbon of iron extends without interruption from the Caspian Sea to Pekin.

When Popof had given me this information, I asked if he knew anything of our fellow travelers, I meant those who were going through to China. And in the first place of Major Noltitz?

"The major," said Popof, "has lived a long time in the Turkestan provinces, and he is going to Pekin to organize the staff of a hospital for our compatriots, with the permission of the Czar, of course."

"I like this Major Noltitz," I said, "and I hope to make his acquaintance very soon."

"He would be equally pleased to make yours," replied Popof.

"And these two Chinese, do you know them?"

"Not in the least, Monsieur Bombarnac; all I know is the name on the luggage."

"What is that?"

"The younger man's name is Pan-Chao, the elder's is Tio-King. Probably they have been traveling in Europe for some years. As to saying where they come from, I cannot. I imagine that Pan-Chao belongs to some rich family, for he is accompanied by his doctor."

"This Tio-King?"

"Yes, Doctor Tio-King."

"And do they only speak Chinese?"

"Probably; I have not heard them speak any other language together."

On this information from Popof, I will keep to the number nine I have given to young Pan-Chao, and to the ten with which I have labelled Doctor Tio-King.

"The American," began Popof.

"Ephrinell?" I exclaimed, "and Miss Horatia Bluett, the Englishwoman? Oh! You can tell me nothing about them I don't know."

"Shall I tell you what I think about that couple, Monsieur Bombarnac?"

"What do you think?"

"That as soon as they reach Pekin, Miss Bluett will become Mrs. Ephrinell."

"And may Heaven bless their union, Popof, for they are really made for each other."

I saw that on this subject Popof and I held similar ideas.

"And the two French people, that couple so affectionate." I asked, "who are they?"

"Have they not told you?"

"No, Popof."

48

"You need not be anxious, Monsieur Bombarnac. Besides, if you wish to know their profession, it is written at full length on all their luggage.

"And that is?"

"Stage people who are going to a theater in China."

Stage people! If that explains the attitudes, and mobile physiognomy, and demonstrative gestures of Caterna, it does not explain his maritime allusions.

"And do you know what line these players are in?"

"The husband is comic lead."

"And the wife?"

"She is leading lady."

"And where are these lyrical people going?"

"To Shanghai, where they have an engagement at the French theater."

That is capital. I will talk about the theater, and behind the scenes, and such matters, and, as Popof said, I shall soon make the acquaintance of the cheery comedian and his charming wife. But it is not in their company that I shall discover the hero of romance who is the object of my desire.

As to the scornful gentleman, our guide knew nothing beyond that his luggage bore the address in full: Sir Francis Trevellyan, Trevellyan Hall, Trevellyanshire.

"A gentleman who does not answer when he is spoken to!" added Popof.

Well, my number eight will have to be dumb man, and that will do very well.

"Now we get to the German," said I.

"Baron Weissschnitzerdoerfer?"

"He is going to Pekin, I think."

"To Pekin and beyond."

"Beyond?"

"Yes; he is on a trip round the world."

"A trip round the world?"

"In thirty-nine days."

And so after Mrs. Bisland who did the famous tour in seventy-three days, and Train who did it in seventy, this German was attempting to do it in thirty-nine?

True, the means of communication are more rapid the line is more direct, and by using the Grand Transasiatic which puts Pekin within a fortnight of the Prussian capital, the baron might halve the old time by Suez and Singapore—but—

"He will never do it!" I exclaimed.

"Why not?" asked Popof.

"Because he is always late. He nearly missed the train at Tiflis, he nearly missed the boat at Baku—"

"But he did not miss the start from Uzun Ada."

"It doesn't matter, Popof. I shall be much surprised if this German beats an American at globe trotting."

Chapter VII

The train arrived at Kizil Arvat, two hundred and forty-two versts from the Caspian, at thirteen minutes past seven in the evening instead of seven o'clock. This slight delay provoked thirteen objurgations from the baron, one for each minute.

We have two hours to wait at Kizil Arvat. Although the day is closing in, I could not employ my time better than in visiting this little town, which contains more than two thousand inhabitants, Russians, Persians and Turkomans. There is not much to see, however, either within it or around it; there are no trees—not even a palm tree—only pasturages and fields of cereals, watered by a narrow stream. My good fortune furnished me with a companion, or I should rather say a guide, in Major Noltitz.

Our acquaintance was made very simply. The major came up to me, and I went up to him as soon as we set foot on the platform of the railway station.

"Sir," said I, "I am a Frenchman, Claudius Bombarnac, special correspondent of the *Twentieth Century,* and you are Major Noltitz of the Russian army. You are going to Pekin, so am I. I can speak your language, and it is very likely that you can speak mine."

The major made a sign of assent.

"Well, Major Noltitz, instead of remaining strangers to each other during the long transit of Central Asia, would it please you for us to become more than mere traveling companions? You know all about this country that I do not know, and it would be a pleasure for me to learn from you."

"Monsieur Bombarnac," replied the major in French, without a trace of accent, "I quite agree with you."

Then he added with a smile:

"As to learning from me, one of your most eminent critics, if I remember rightly, has said that the French only like to learn what they know."

"I see that you have read Sainte Beuve, Major Noltitz; perhaps this sceptical academician was right in a general way. But for my part, I am an exception to the rule, and I wish to learn what I do not know. And in all that concerns Russian Turkestan, I am in a state of ignorance."

"I am entirely at your disposal," said the major, "and I will be happy to tell you all about General Annenkof, for I was all through the work with him."

"I thank you, Major Noltitz. I expected no less than the courtesy of a Russian towards a Frenchman."

"And," said the major, "if you will allow me to quote that celebrated sentence in the *Danicheffs*, 'It will be always thus so long as there are Frenchmen and Russians.'"

"The younger Dumas after Sainte Beuve?" I exclaimed. "I see, major, that I am talking to a Parisian—"

"Of Petersburg, Monsieur Bombarnac."

And we cordially shook hands. A minute afterwards, we were on our way through the town, and this is what Major Noltitz told me:

It was towards the end of 1885 that General Annenkof finished, at Kizil Arvat, the first portion of this railway measuring about 140 miles, of which 90 were through a desert which did not yield a single drop of water. But before telling me how this extraordinary work was accomplished, Major Noltitz reminded me of the facts which had gradually prepared the conquest of Turkestan and its definite incorporation with the Russian Empire.

As far back as 1854 the Russians had imposed a treaty of alliance on the Khan of Khiva. Some years afterwards, eager to pursue their march towards the east, the campaigns of 1860 and 1864 had given them the Khanats of Kokhand and Bokhara. Two years later, Samarkand passed under their dominion after the battles of Irdjar and Zera-Buleh.

There remained to be conquered the southern portion of Turkestan, and chiefly the oasis of Akhal Tekke, which is contiguous to Persia. Generals Sourakine and Lazareff attempted this in their expeditions of 1878 and 1879. Their plans failed, and it was to the celebrated Skobeleff, the hero of Plevna, that the czar confided the task of subduing the valiant Turkoman tribes.

Skobeleff landed at the port of Mikhailov—the port of Uzun Ada was not then in existence—and it was in view of facilitating his march across the desert that his second in command, Annenkof, constructed the strategic railway which in ten months reached Kizil Arvat.

This is how the Russians built the line with a rapidity superior, as I have said, to that of the Americans in the far west, a line that was to be of use for commerce and for war.

To begin with, the general got together a construction train consisting of thirty-four wagons. Four of these were two-decked for the officers, twenty more had two decks and were used by the workmen and soldiers; one wagon served as a dining room, four as kitchens, one as an ambulance, one as a telegraph office, one as a forge, one as a provision store, and one was held in reserve. These were his traveling workshops and also his barracks in which fifteen hundred workmen, soldiers and otherwise, found their board and lodging. The train advanced as the rails were laid. The workmen were divided into two brigades; they each worked six hours a day, with the assistance of the country people who lived in tents and numbered about fifteen thousand. A telegraph wire united the works with Mikhailov, and from there a little Decauville engine worked the trains which brought along the rails and sleepers.

In this way, helped by the horizontality of the ground, a day's work yielded nearly five miles of track, whereas in the plains of the United States only about half that rate was accomplished. Labor cost little; forty-five francs a month for the men from the oasis, fifty centimes a day for those who came from Bokhara.

It was in this way that Skobeleff's soldiers were taken to Kizil Arvat, and then eighty-four miles beyond to Gheok Tepe. This town did not surrender until after the destruction of its ramparts and the massacre of twelve thousand of its defenders; but the oasis of Akhal Tekke was in the power of the Russians. The inhabitants of the Atek oasis were only too ready to submit, and that all the more willingly as they had implored the help of the czar in their struggle with Kouli Khan, the chief of the Mervians. These latter to the number of two hundred and fifty thousand, followed their example, and the first locomotive entered Merv station in July, 1886.

"And the English?" I asked Major Noltitz. "In what way have they looked upon the progress of the Russians through Central Asia?"

"Jealously, of course. Think for a moment what it means when the Russian railways are united with the Chinese, instead of the Indian. The Transcaspian in connection with the line between Herat and Delhi! And consider that the English have not been as fortunate in Afghanistan as we have been in Turkestan. You have noticed the gentleman in our train?"

"I have. He is Sir Francis Trevellyan of Trevellyan Hall, Trevellyanshire."

"Well, Sir Francis Trevellyan has nothing but looks of contempt and shrugs of the shoulder for all we have done. His nation's jealousy is incarnate in him, and England will never be content that our railways should go from Europe to the Pacific Ocean, while the British railways end at the Indian Ocean."

This interesting conversation had lasted for the hour and a half during which we walked about the streets of Kizil Arvat. It was time to return to the station, and we did so.

Of course, matters did not end here. It was agreed that the major should leave his seat in the third car and occupy that next to mine in the first. We had already been two inhabitants of the same town; well, we would become two neighbors in the house, or, rather, two friends in the same room.

At nine o'clock the signal to start was given. The train leaving Kizil Arvat went off in a southwesterly direction towards Askhabad, along the Persian frontier.

For another half hour the major and I continued to talk of one thing or another. He told me that if the sun had not set, I should have been able to see the summits of the Great and Little Balkans of Asia which rise above the bay of Krasnovodsk.

Already most of our companions had taken up their quarters for the night on their seats, which by an ingenious mechanism could be transformed into beds, on which you could stretch yourself at full length, lay your head on a pillow, wrap yourself in rugs, and if you didn't sleep well it would be on account of a troubled conscience.

Major Noltitz had nothing to reproach himself with apparently, for a few minutes after he had said good night he was deep in the sleep of the just.

As for me, if I remained awake it was because I was troubled in my mind. I was thinking of my famous packing case, of the man it contained, and this very night I had resolved to enter into communication with him. I thought of the people who had done this sort of thing before. In 1889, 1891, and 1892, an Austrian tailor, Hermann Zeitung, had come from Vienna to Paris, from Amsterdam to Brussels, from Antwerp to Christiania in a box, and two sweethearts of Barcelona, Erres and Flora Anglora, had shared a box between them from Spain into France.

But I must wait until Popof had retired to rest. The train would not stop until it reached Gheok Tepe at one o'clock in the morning. During the run from Kizil Arvat to Gheok Tepe I reckoned that Popof would have a good sleep, and then, or never, I would put my plan into execution.

Hold! an idea! Suppose it is Zeitung who makes a trade of this sort of thing and manages to make a little money out of public generosity? It ought to be Zeitung, it must be! Confound it! he is not at all interesting! And here was I reckoning on this fellow. Well, we shall see. I shall know him by his photographs, and perhaps I may make use of him.

Half an hour went by, and the noise of a door shutting on the platform of the car told me that our guard had just entered his little box. In spite of my desire to visit the baggage car I waited patiently, for it was possible that Popof was not yet sound asleep.

Within, all is quiet under the veiled light of the lamps.

Without, the night is very dark, and the rattle of the train mingles with the whistling of the rather high wind.

I rise. I draw aside the curtain of one of the lamps. I look at my watch.

It is a few minutes past eleven. Still two hours to Gheok Tepe.

The moment has come. I glide between the seats to the door of the car. I open it gently and shut it after me without being heard by my companions, without waking any one.

Here I am on the platform, which shakes as the train travels. Amid the unfathomable darkness which envelops the Kara Koum, I experience the feeling of a night at sea when on shipboard.

A feeble light filters through the blind of the guard's box. Shall I wait till it is extinct, or, as is very probable, will it not last till the morning?

Anyhow, Popof is not asleep, as I discover by the noise he makes in turning over. I keep quiet, leaning against the balustrade of the platform.

Leaning forward my looks are attracted by the luminous ray thrown forward by the headlight of the engine. It seems as though we are running on a road of fire. Above me the clouds are racing across with great rapidity, and a few constellations glitter through their rifts, Cassiopeia, the Little Bear, in the north, and in the zenith Vega of Lyra.

At length absolute silence reigns on the platforms. Popof, who is in charge of the train, has his eyes closed in sleep. Assured of safety I cross the gangway and am in front of the baggage van.

The door is only fastened with a bar which is hung between two staples.

I open it and shut it behind me.

I do this without noise, for if I do not want to attract Popof's attention, I do not want as yet to attract the attention of the man in the packing case.

Although the darkness is deep in the van, although there is no side window, I know my position. I know where the case is placed; it is in the left corner as I enter. The thing is not to knock against any other case—not against one of those belonging to Ephrinell, for what a row there would be if I set all those artificial teeth chattering!

Carefully feeling with feet and hands, I reach the case. No cat could have been more gentle or more silent as I felt its edges.

I leaned over and placed my ear timidly against the outer panel.

There was no sound of breathing.

The products of the house of Strong, Bulbul & Co., of New York, could not be more noiseless in their boxes.

A fear seizes upon me—the fear of seeing all my reporter's hopes vanish. Was I deceived on board the *Astara?* That respiration, that sneeze; had I dreamed it all? Was there no one in the case, not even Zeitung? Were these really glass goods exported to Miss Zinca Klork, Avenue Cha-Coua, Pekin, China?

No! Feeble as it is, I detect a movement inside the case! It becomes more distinct, and I ask if the panel is going to slide, if the prisoner is coming out of his prison to breathe the fresh air?

What I had better do to see and not to be seen is to hide between two cases. Thanks to the darkness there is nothing to fear.

Suddenly a slight cracking greets my ear. I am not the sport of an illusion; it is the crack of a match being lighted.

Almost immediately a few feeble rays pierce the ventilation holes of the case.

If I had had any doubts as to the position held by the prisoner in the scale of being, I have none now. At the least it must be an ape who knows the use of fire, and also the handling of matches. Travelers tell us that such animals exist, but we have to take the statement on trust.

Why should I not confess it? A certain emotion came over me and I had to take care I did not run away.

A minute elapsed. Nothing shows that the panel has been moved, nothing gives me reason to suppose that the unknown is coming out.

Cautiously I wait. Then I have an idea to make something out of this light. The case is lighted within; if I were to peep through those holes?

I creep toward the case. A single apprehension chills my brain. If the light were suddenly extinguished!

I am against the panel, which I take care not to touch, and I put my eyes close to one of the holes.

There is a man in the box, and it is not the Austrian tailor, Zeitung! Thank Heaven! I will soon make him my No. 11.

The man's features I can make out clearly. He is from twenty-five to twenty-six years of age. He does not shave, and his beard is brown.

He is of the true Roumanian type, and that confirms me in my notion regarding his Roumanian correspondent. He is good-looking, although his face denotes great energy of character, and he must be energetic to have shut himself up in a box like this for such a long journey. But if he has nothing of the malefactor about him, I must confess that he does not look like the hero I am in search of as the chief personage in my story.

After all, they were not heroes, that Austrian and that Spaniard who traveled in their packing cases. They were young men, very simple, very ordinary, and yet they yielded columns of copy. And so this brave No. 11, with amplifications, antonyms, diaphoreses, epitases, tropes, metaphors, and other figures of that sort, I will beat out, I will enlarge, I will develop—as they develop a photographic negative.

Besides to travel in a box from Tiflis to Pekin is quite another affair than traveling from Vienna or Barcelona to Paris, as was done by Zeitung, Erres and Flora Anglora.

I add that I will not betray my Roumanian; I will report him to no one. He may rely on my discretion; he may reckon on my good offices if I can be of use to him when he is found out.

But what is he doing now? Well, he is seated on the bottom of his case and placidly eating his supper by the light of a little lamp. A box of preserves is on his knee, biscuit is not wanting, and in a little cupboard I notice some full bottles, besides a rug and overcoat hooked up on the wall.

Evidently No. 11 is quite at home. He is there in his cell like a snail in his shell. His house goes with him; and he saves the thousand francs it would have cost him to journey from Tiflis to Pekin, second-class. I know he is committing a fraud, and that the law punishes such fraud. He can come out of his box when he likes and take a walk in the van, or even at night venture on the platform. No! I do not blame him, and when I think of his being sent to the pretty Roumanian, I would willingly take his place.

An idea occurs to me which may not perhaps be as good as it seems. That is to rap lightly on the box so as to enter into communication with my new companion, and learn who he is, and whence he comes, for I know whither he goes. An ardent curiosity devours me, I must gratify it. There are moments when a special correspondent is metamorphosed into a daughter of Eve.

But how will the poor fellow take it? Very well, I am sure. I will tell him that I am a Frenchman, and a Roumanian knows he can always trust a Frenchman. I will offer him my services. I will propose to soften the rigors of his imprisonment by my interviews, and to make up the scarcity of his meals by little odds and ends. He will have nothing to fear from my imprudences.

I rap the panel.

The light suddenly goes out.

The prisoner has suspended his respiration.

I must reassure him.

"Open!" I say to him gently in Russian.

"Open—"

I cannot finish the sentence; for the train gives a sudden jump and slackens speed.

But we cannot yet have reached Gheok Tepe?

There is a noise outside.

I rush out of the van and shut the door behind me.

It was time.

I have scarcely reached the platform before Popofs door opens, and without seeing me he hurries through the van on to the engine.

Almost immediately the train resumes its normal speed and Popof reappears a minute afterwards.

"What is the matter, Popof?"

"What is often the matter, Monsieur Bombarnac. We have smashed a dromedary."

"Poor brute!"

"Poor brute? He might have thrown us off the line!"

"Stupid brute, then!"

Chapter VIII

Before the train reaches Gheok Tepe I am back in the car. Confound this dromedary! If he had not managed to get smashed so clumsily No. 11 would no longer be unknown to me. He would have opened his panel, we would have talked in a friendly way, and separated with a friendly shake of the hand. Now he will be full of anxiety, he knows his fraud is discovered, that there is some one who has reason to suspect his intentions, some one who may not hesitate to betray his secret. And then, after being taken out of his case, he will be put under guard at the next station, and it will be useless for Mademoiselle Zinca Klork to expect him in the capital of the Chinese Empire!

Yes! It would be better for me to relieve his anxiety this very night. That is impossible, for the train will soon stop at Gheok Tepe, and then at Askhabad which it will leave in the first hour of daylight. I can no longer trust to Popof's going to sleep.

I am absorbed in these reflections, when the locomotive stops in Gheok Tepe station at one o'clock in the morning. None of my companions have left their beds.

I get out on to the platform and prowl around the van. It would be too risky to try and get inside. I should have been glad to visit the town, but the darkness prevents me from seeing anything. According to what Major Noltitz says it still retains the traces of Skobeleffs terrible assault in 1880—dismantled walls, bastions in ruins. I must content myself with having seen all that with the major's eyes.

The train starts at two o'clock in the morning, after having been joined by a few passengers who Popof tells me are Turkomans. I will have a look at them when daylight comes.

For ten minutes I remained on the car platform and watched the heights of the Persian frontier on the extreme limit of the horizon. Beyond the stretch of verdant oasis watered by a number of creeks, we crossed wide cultivated plains through which the line made frequent diversions.

Having discovered that Popof did not intend to go to sleep again, I went back to my corner.

At three o'clock there was another stop. The name of Askhabad was shouted along the platform. As I could not remain still I got out, leaving my companions sound asleep, and I ventured into the town.

Askhabad is the headquarters of the Transcaspian, and I opportunely remembered what Boulangier, the engineer, had said about it in the course of that interesting journey he had made to Merv. All that I saw on the left as I went out of the station, was the gloomy outline of the Turkoman Fort, dominating the new town, the population of which has doubled since 1887. It forms a confused mass behind a thick curtain of trees.

When I returned at half-past three, Popof was going through the luggage van, I know not why. What must be the Roumanian's anxiety during this movement to and fro in front of his box!

As soon as Popof reappeared I said to him: "Anything fresh?"

"Nothing, except the morning breeze!" said he.

"Very fresh!" said I. "Is there a refreshment bar in the station?"

"There is one for the convenience of the passengers."

"And for the convenience of the guards, I suppose? Come along, Popof."

And Popof did not want asking twice.

The bar was open, but there did not seem to be much to choose from. The only liquor was "Koumiss," which is fermented mare's milk, and is the color of faded ink, very nourishing, although very liquid. You must be a Tartar to appreciate this koumiss. At least that is the effect it produced on me. But Popof thought it excellent, and that was the important point.

Most of the Sarthes and Kirghizes who got out at Askhabad, have been replaced by other second-class passengers, Afghan merchants and smugglers, the latter particularly clever in their line of business. All the green tea consumed in Central Asia is brought by them from China through India, and although the transport is much longer, they sell it at a much lower price than the Russian tea. I need not say that their luggage was examined with Muscovite minuteness.

The train started again at four o'clock. Our car was still a sleeper. I envied the sleep of my companions, and as that was all I could do, I returned to the platform.

The dawn was appearing in the east. Here and there were the ruins of the ancient city, a citadel girdled with high ramparts and a succession of long porticos extending over fifteen hundred yards. Running over a few embankments, necessitated by the inequalities of the sandy ground, the train reaches the horizontal steppe.

We are running at a speed of thirty miles an hour in a southwesterly direction, along the Persian frontier. It is only beyond Douchak that the line begins to leave it. During this three hours' run the two stations at which the train stops are Gheours, the junction for the road to Mesched, whence the heights of the Iran plateau are visible, and Artyk where water is abundant although slightly brackish.

The train then traverses the oasis of the Atek, which is an important tributary of the Caspian. Verdure and trees are everywhere. This oasis justifies its name, and would not disgrace the Sahara. It extends to the station of Douchak at the six hundred and sixtieth verst, which we reach at six o'clock in the morning.

We stop here two hours, that is to say, there are two hours for us to walk about. I am off to look at Douchak with Major Noltitz as my cicerone.

A traveler precedes us out of the railway station; I recognize Sir Francis Trevellyan. The major makes me notice that this gentleman's face is more sullen than usual, his lip more scornful, his attitude more Anglo-Saxon.

"And do you know why, Monsieur Bombarnac? Because this station at Douchak might be the terminus of a line from British India through the Afghan frontier, Kandahar, the Bolan Pass and the Pendjeh oasis, that would unite the two systems."

"And how long would the line be?"

"About six hundred miles. But the English will not meet the Russians in a friendly way. But if we could put Calcutta within twelve days of London, what an advantage that would be for their trade!"

Talking in this way the major and I "did" Douchak. Some years ago it was foreseen how important this village would be. A branch line unites it with Teheran in Persia, while there has, as yet, been no survey for a line to India. While gentlemen cast in the mould of Sir Francis Trevellyan are in the majority in the United Kingdom, the Asiatic network of railways will never be complete.

I was led to question the major regarding the safety of the Grand Transasiatic across the provinces of Central Asia.

In Turkestan, he told me, the safety is well assured. The Russian police keep constant watch over it; there is a regular police force at the stations, and as the stations are not far apart, I don't think the travelers have much to fear from the nomad tribes. Besides, the Turkomans are kept in their place by the Russian administration. During the years the Transcaspian has been at work, there has been no attack to hinder the train service.

"That is comforting, Major Noltitz. And as to the section between the frontier and Pekin?"

"That is another matter," replied the major. "Over the Pamir plateau, up to Kachgar, the road is carefully guarded; but beyond that, the Grand Transasiatic is under Chinese control, and I have not much confidence in that."

"Are the stations very far from each other?" I asked.

"Very far, sometimes."

"And the Russians in charge of the train are replaced by Chinese, are they not?"

"Yes, with the exception of Popof, who goes through with us."

"So that we shall have Chinese engine drivers and stokers? Well, major, that seems rather alarming, and the safety of the travelers—"

"Let me undeceive you, Monsieur Bombarnac. These Chinese are just as clever as we are. They are excellent mechanics, and it is the same with the engineers who laid out the line through the Celestial Empire. They are certainly a very intelligent race, and very fit for industrial progress."

"I think, major, that they will one day become masters of the world—after the Slavs, of course!"

"I do not know what the future may have in store," said Major Noltitz, with a smile. "But, returning to the Chinese, I say that they are of quick comprehension, with an astonishing facility of assimilation. I have seen them at work, and I speak from experience."

"Agreed," said I; "but if there is no danger under this head, are there not a lot of scoundrels prowling about Mongolia and Northern China?"

"And you think these scoundrels will be daring enough to attack the train?"

"Exactly, major, and that is what makes me feel easy."

"What? Makes you feel easy?"

"Quite so, for my sole anxiety is that our journey may not be devoid of incident."

"Really, Mr. Special Correspondent, I admire you. You must have incidents—"

"As a doctor must have patients. Now a real good adventure—"

"Well, Monsieur Bombarnac, I am afraid you will be disappointed, as I have heard that the company has treated several chiefs of the robber bands—"

"As the Greek Government treated Hadji Stavros in About's romance."

"Precisely; and who knows that if in their wisdom—"

"I don't believe it."

"Why not? It would be quite in the modern style, this way of assuring the safety of the trains during the run through the Celestial Empire. Anyhow, there is one of these highwaymen, who has retained his independence and liberty of action, a certain Ki-Tsang."

"Who is he?"

"A bold bandit chief, half-Chinaman, half-Mongol. Having for some time been a terror to Yunnan, he was being too closely pursued, and has now moved into the northern provinces. His presence has ever been reported in that part of Mongolia served by the Grand Transasiatic."

"Well, he ought to furnish a few paragraphs."

"The paragraphs Ki-Tsang will furnish you with may cost you too dearly."

61

"Bah! major, the *Twentieth Century* is quite rich enough to pay for its glory."

"To pay with its money, perhaps, but we may have to pay with our lives! Luckily our companions have not heard you talk in this way, or they might come in a body and demand your expulsion from the train. So be careful, and keep a guard on your desires as a newspaper man in quest of adventures. Above all, don't have anything to do with this Ki-Tsang. It would be all the better in the interest of the passengers."

"But not of the passage, major."

We returned towards the station. The stoppage at Douchak had another half hour to last. As I walked on the quay, I observed something going on which would change the make-up of our train.

Another van had arrived from Teheran by the branch line to Mesphed, which puts the Persian capital in communication with the Transcaspian.

This van was bolted and barred, and accompanied by a squad of Persian police, whose orders seemed to be not to lose sight of it.

I don't know what made me think so, but it seemed as though this van had something mysterious about it, and as the major had left me, I went and spoke to Popof, who was watching over the proceedings.

"Popof, where is that van going?"

"To Pekin."

"And what has it got in it?"

"What has it got in it? An exalted personage."

"An exalted personage?"

"Are you surprised?"

"I am. In this van?"

"It is his own idea."

"Well, Popof, when this exalted personage gets out perhaps you will let me know?"

"He Will not get out."

"Why not?"

"Because he is dead."

"Dead?"

"Yes, and it is his body they are taking to Pekin, where he will be interred with all the honors due to him."

So that we were to have an important personage in our train—in the shape of a corpse, it is true. Never mind! I asked Popof to discover the name of the defunct. He ought to be some mandarin of mark. As soon as I knew it I would send a telegram to the *Twentieth Century*.

While I was looking at this van, a new passenger came up and examined it with no less curiosity than I did.

This traveler was a fine-looking man of about forty, wearing gracefully the costume of the richer Mongols, a tall fellow, with rather a gloomy look, a military moustache, tawny complexion, and eyes that never shut.

"Here is a splendid fellow," I said to myself. "I don't know if he will turn out the hero of the drama I am in search of, but, anyhow, I will number him twelve in my traveling troupe."

This leading star, I soon learned from Popof, bore the name of Faruskiar. He was accompanied by another Mongol, of inferior rank, of about the same age, whose name was Ghangir. As they looked at the van being attached to the tail of the train in front of the luggage van, they exchanged a few words. As soon as the arrangements were complete the Persians took their places in the second-class car, which preceded the mortuary van, so as to have the precious corpse always under their surveillance.

At this moment there was a shout on the station platform I recognized the voice. It was the Baron Weissschnitzerdoerfer shouting:

"Stop! stop!"

This time it was not a train on the start, but a hat in distress. A sudden gust had swept through the station and borne off the baron's hat—a helmet-shaped hat of a bluish color. It rolled on the platform, it rolled on the rails, it skimmed the enclosure and went out over the wall, and its owner ran his hardest to stop it.

At the sight of this wild pursuit the Caternas held their sides, the young Chinaman, Pan Chao, shouted with laughter, while Dr. Tio-King remained imperturbably serious.

The German purple, puffling and panting, could do no more. Twice he had got his hand on his hat, and twice it had escaped him, and now suddenly he fell full length with his head lost under the folds of his overcoat; whereupon Caterna began to sing the celebrated air from "Miss Helyett":

"Ah! the superb point of view—ew—ew—ew!
Ah! the view unexpected by you—you—you—you!"

I know nothing more annoying than a hat carried away by the wind, which bounds hither and thither, and spins and jumps, and glides, and slides, and darts off just as you think you are going to catch it. And if that should happen to me I will forgive those who laugh at the comic endeavor.

But the baron was in no mood for forgiveness. He bounded here, and bounded there, he jumped on to the line. They shouted to him, "Look out! look out!" for the Merv was coming in at some speed. It brought death to the hat, the engine smashed it pitilessly, and it was only a torn rag when it was handed to the baron. And then began again a series of imprecations on the Grand Transasiatic.

The signal is given. The passengers, old and new, hurry to their places. Among the new ones I notice three Mongols, of forbidding appearance, who get into the second-class car.

As I put my foot on the platform I hear the young Chinese say to his companion:

"Well, Dr. Tio-King, did you see the German with his performing hat? How I laughed!"

And so Pan Chao speaks French. What do I say? Better than French—he speaks Persian! Most extraordinary! I must have a talk with him.

CHAPTER IX

We started to time. The baron could not complain this time. After all, I understood his impatience; a minute's delay might cause him to lose the mail boat from Tien Tsin to Japan.

The day looked promising, that is to say, there might have been a wind strong enough to put out the sun as if it were a candle, such a hurricane as sometimes stops the locomotives of the Grand Transasiatic, but to-day it is blowing from the west, and will be supportable, as it blows the train along. We can remain out on the platforms.

I want to enter into conversation with Pan Chao. Popof was right; he must be the son of some family of distinction who has been spending some years in Paris for education and amusement. He ought to be one of the most regular visitors at the *Twentieth Century* "five o'clocks."

Meanwhile I will attend to other business. There is that man in the case. A whole day will elapse before I can relieve his anxiety. In what a state he must be! But as it would be unwise for me to enter the van during the day, I must wait until night.

I must not forget that an interview with the Caternas is included in the programme. There will be no difficulty in that, apparently.

What will not be so easy is to get into conversation with my No. 12, his superb lordship Faruskiar. He seems rather stiff, does this Oriental.

Ah! There is a name I must know as soon as possible, that of the mandarin returning to China in the form of a mortuary parcel. With a little ingenuity Popof may manage to ascertain it from one of the Persians in charge of his Excellency. If it would only be that of some grand functionary, the Pao-Wang, or the Ko-Wang, or the viceroy of the two Kiangs, the Prince King in person!

For an hour the train is running through the oasis. We shall soon be in the open desert. The soil is formed of alluvial beds extending up to the environs of Merv. I must get accustomed to this monotony of the journey which will last up to the frontier of Turkestan. Oasis and desert, desert and oasis. As we approach the Pamir the scenery will change a little. There are picturesque bits of landscape in that orographic knot which the Russians have had to cut as Alexander cut the gordian knot that was worth something to the Macedonian conqueror of Asia. Here is a good augury for the Russian conquest.

But I must wait for this crossing of the Pamir and its varied scenery. Beyond lay the interminable plains of Chinese Turkestan, the immense sandy desert of Gobi, where the monotony of the journey will begin again.

It is half-past ten. Breakfast will soon be served in the dining car. Let us take a walk through the length of the train.

Where is Ephrinell? I do not see him at his post by the side of Miss Horatia Bluett, whom I questioned on the subject after saluting her politely.

"Mr. Ephrinell has gone to give an eye to his cases," she replies.

In the rear of the second car Faruskiar and Ghangir have installed themselves; they are alone at this moment, and are talking together in a low tone.

As I return I meet Ephrinell, who is coming back to his traveling companion. He shakes my hand Yankee fashion. I tell him that Miss Horatia Bluett has given me news of him.

"Oh!" says he, "what a woman yonder! What a splendid saleswoman! One of those English—"

"Who are good enough to be Americans!" I add.

"Wait a bit!" he replies, with a significant smile.

As I am going put, I notice that the two Chinamen are already in the dining car, and that Dr. Tio-King's little book is on the table.

65

I do not consider it too much of a liberty for a reporter to pick up this little book, to open it and to read the title, which is as follows:

The temperate and regular life,
Or the art of living long in perfect health.
Translated from the italian of
LOUIS CORNARO, A VENETIAN NOBLE.
To which is added the way of correcting a bad constitution,
And enjoying perfect felicity to the most advanced years.
And to die only from the using up of the original humidity
In extreme old age.
Salerno,
1782.

And this is the favorite reading of Dr. Tio-King! And that is why his disrespectful pupil occasionally gives him the nickname of Cornaro!

I have not time to see anything else in this volume than *Abstinentia adjicit vitam;* but this motto of the noble Venetian I have no intention of putting in practice, at least at breakfast time.

There is no change in the order in which we sit down to table. I find myself close to Major Noltitz, who is looking attentively at Faruskiar and his companion, placed at the extremity of the table. We are asking ourselves who this haughty Mongol could be.

"Ah!" said I, laughing at the thought which crossed my mind, "if that is—"

"Who?" asked the major.

"The chief of the brigands, the famous Ki-Tsang."

"Have your joke, Monsieur Bombarnac, but under your breath, I advise you!"

"You see, major, he would then be an interesting personage and worth a long interview!"

We enjoyed our meal as we talked. The breakfast was excellent, the provisions having come freshly on board at Askhabad and Douchak. For drink we had tea, and Crimean wine, and Kazan beer; for meat we had mutton cutlets and excellent preserves; for dessert a melon with pears and grapes of the best quality.

After breakfast I went to smoke my cigar on the platform behind the dining car. Caterna almost immediately joins me. Evidently the estimable comedian has seized the opportunity to enter into conversation with me.

His intelligent eyes, his smooth face, his cheeks accustomed to false whiskers, his lips accustomed to false moustaches, his head accustomed to wigs red, black, or gray, bald or hairy, according to his part, everything denoted the actor made for the life of the boards. But he had such an open, cheery face, such an honest look, so frank an attitude, that he was evidently a really good fellow.

"Sir," said he to me, "are two Frenchmen going all the way from Baku to Pekin without making each other's acquaintance?"

"Sir," I replied, "when I meet a compatriot—"

"Who is a Parisian—"

"And consequently a Frenchman twice over," I added, "I am only too glad to shake hands with him! And so, Monsieur Caterna—"

"You know my name?"

"As you know mine, I am sure."

"Of course, Monsieur Claudius Bombarnac, correspondent of the *Twentieth Century*."

"At your service, believe me."

"A thousand thanks, Monsieur Bombarnac, and even ten thousand, as they say in China, whither Madame Caterna and I are bound."

"To appear at Shanghai in the French troupe at the residency as—"

"You know all that, then?"

"A reporter!"

"Quite so."

"I may add, from sundry nautical phrases I have noticed, that you have been to sea."

"I believe you, sir. Formerly coxswain of Admiral de Boissondy's launch on board the *Redoubtable*."

"Then I beg to ask why you, a sailor, did not go by way of the sea?"

"Ah, there it is, Monsieur Bombarnac. Know that Madame Caterna, who is incontestably the first leading lady of the provinces, and there is not one to beat her as a waiting maid or in a man's part, cannot stand the sea. And when I heard of the Grand Transasiatic, I said to her, 'Be easy, Caroline! Do not worry yourself about the perfidious element. We will cross Russia, Turkestan, and China, without leaving *terra firma!*' And that pleased her, the little darling, so brave and so devoted, so—I am at a loss for a word—well, a lady who will play the duenna in case of need, rather than leave the manager in a mess! An artiste, a true artiste!"

It was a pleasure to listen to Caterna; he was in steam, as the engineer says, and the only thing to do was to let him blow off. Surprising as it may seem, he adored his wife, and I believe she was equally fond of him. A well-matched couple, evidently, from what I learned from my comedian, never embarrassed, very wide awake, content with his lot, liking nothing so much as the theater—above all the provincial theater—where he and his wife had played in drama, vaudeville, comedy, operetta, opera comique, opera, spectacle, pantomime, happy in the entertainment which began at five o'clock in the afternoon and ended at one o'clock in the morning, in the grand theaters of the chief cities, in the saloon of the mayor, in the barn of the village, without boots, without patches, without orchestra, sometimes even without spectators—thus saving the return of the money—professionals fit for anything, no matter what.

As a Parisian, Caterna must have been the wag of the forecastle when he was at sea. As clever with his instrument of brass or wood, he possessed a most varied and complete assortment of jokes, songs, monologues, and dialogues. This he told me with an immense amount of attitude and gesture, now here, now there, legs, arms, hands, and feet all going together. I should never feel dull in the company of such a merry companion.

"And where were you before you left France?" I asked.

"At La Ferte-sous-Jouarre, where Madame Caterna achieved a genuine success as Elsa in 'Lohengrin,' which we played without music. But it is an interesting piece, and it was well done."

"You must have been a good deal about the world, Monsieur Caterna?"

"I believe you; Russia, England, both Americas. Ah! Monsieur Claudius."

He already called me Claudius.

"Ah! Monsieur Claudius, there was a time when I was the idol of Buenos Ayres, and the pet of Rio Janeiro! Do not think I would tell you an untruth! No! I know myself. Bad at Paris, I am excellent in the provinces. In Paris you play for yourself; in the provinces you play for the others! And then what a repertory!"

"My compliments, my dear compatriot!"

"I accept them, Monsieur Claudius, for I like my trade. What would you have? All the world cannot expect to be a senator or—a special correspondent."

"There, that is wicked, Monsieur Caterna," said I, with a laugh.

"No; it is the last word."

And while the unwearied actor ran on in this way, stations appeared one after the other between the shrieks of the whistle, Kulka, Nisachurch, Kulla Minor and others, not particularly cheerful to look at; then Bairam Ali at the seven hundred and ninety-fifth verst and Kourlan Kala at the eight hundred and fifteenth.

"And to tell you the truth," continued Caterna, "we have made a little money by going about from town to town. At the bottom of our boxes are a few Northern debentures, of which I think a good deal, and take much care, and they have been honestly got, Monsieur Claudius.

Although we live under a democratic government, the rule of equality, the time is still far off when you will see the noble father dining beside the prefect at the table of the judge of appeal, and the actress open the ball with the prefect at the house of the general-in-chief! Well! We can dine and dance among ourselves—"

"And be just as happy, Monsieur Caterna."

"Certainly no less, Monsieur Claudius," replied the future premier comic of Shanghai, shaking an imaginary frill with the graceful ease of one of Louis XV.'s noblemen.

At this point, Madame Caterna came up. She was in every way worthy of her husband, sent into the world to reply to him in life as on the stage, one of those genial theater folks, born one knows not where or how, but thoroughly genuine and good-natured.

"I beg to introduce you to Caroline Caterna," said the actor, in much the same tone as he would have introduced me to Patti or Sarah Bernhardt.

"Having shaken hands with your husband," said I, "I shall be happy to shake hands with you, Madame Caterna."

"There you are, then," said the actress, "and without ceremony, foot to the front, and no prompting."

"As you see, no nonsense about her, and the best of wives—"

"As he is the best of husbands."

"I believe I am, Monsieur Claudius," said the actor, "and why? Because I believe that marriage consists entirely in the precept to which husbands should always conform, and that is, that what the wife likes the husband should eat often."

It will be understood that it was touching to see this honest give-and-take, so different from the dry business style of the two commercials who were in conversation in the adjoining car.

But here is Baron Weissschnitzerdoerfer, wearing a traveling cap, coming out of the dining car, where I imagine he has not spent his time consulting the time-table.

"The good man of the hat trick!" said Caterna, after the baron went back into the car without favoring us with a salute.

"He is quite German enough!" said Madame Caterna.

"And to think that Henry Heine called those people sentimental oaks!" I added.

"Then he could not have known that one!" said Caterna. "Oak, I admit, but sentimental—"

"Do you know why the baron has patronized the Grand Transasiatic?" I asked.

"To eat sauerkraut at Pekin!" said Caterna.

"Not at all. To rival Miss Nelly Bly. He is trying to get around the world in thirty-nine days."

"Thirty-nine days!" exclaimed Gaterna. "You should say a hundred and thirty-nine!"

And in a voice like a husky clarinet the actor struck up the well-known air from the Cloches de Corneville:

"I thrice have been around the world."

Adding, for the baron's benefit:

"He will not do the half."

Chapter X

At a quarter-past twelve our train passed the station of Kari Bata, which resembles one of the stations on the line from Naples to Sorrento, with its Italian roofs. I noticed a vast Asiatico-Russian camp, the flags waving in the fresh breeze. We have entered the Mervian oasis, eighty miles long and eight wide, and containing about six hundred thousand hectares—there is nothing like being precise at the finish. Right and left are cultivated fields, clumps of fine trees, an uninterrupted succession of villages, huts among the thickets, fruit gardens between the houses, flocks of sheep and herds of cattle among the pastures. All this rich country is watered by the Mourgab—the White Water—or its tributaries, and pheasants swarm like crows on the plains of Normandy. At one o'clock in the afternoon the train stopped at Merv Station, over five hundred miles from Uzun Ada.

The town has been often destroyed and rebuilt. The wars of Turkestan have not spared it. Formerly, it seems, it was a haunt of robbers and bandits, and it is a pity that the renowned Ki-Tsang did not live in those days. Perhaps he would have become a Genghis Khan?

Major Noltitz told me of a Turkoman saying to the following effect: "If you meet a Mervian and a viper, begin by killing the Mervian and leave the viper till afterwards."

I fancy it would be better to begin with killing the viper now that the Mervian has become a Russian.

We have seven hours to stop at Merv. I shall have time to visit this curious town. Its physical and moral transformation has been profound, owing to the somewhat arbitrary proceedings of the Russian administration. It is fortunate that its fortress, five miles round, built by Nour Verdy in 1873, was not strong enough to prevent its capture by the czar, so that the old nest of malefactors has become one of the most important cities of the Transcaspian.

I said to Major Noltitz:

"If it is not trespassing on your kindness, may I ask you to go with me?"

"Willingly," he answered; "and as far as I am concerned, I shall be very pleased to see Merv again."

We set out at a good pace.

"I ought to tell you," said the major, "that it is the new town we are going to see."

"And why not the old one first? That would be more logical and more chronological."

"Because old Merv is eighteen miles away, and you will hardly see it as you pass. So you must refer to the accurate description given of it by your great geographer Elisee Reclus."

And certainly readers will not lose anything by the change.

The distance from the station to new Merv is not great. But what an abominable dust! The commercial town is built on the left of the river—a town in the American style, which would please Ephrinell, wide streets straight as a line crossing at right angles; straight boulevards with rows of trees; much bustle and movement among the merchants in Oriental costume, in Jewish costume, merchants of every kind; a number of camels and dromedaries, the latter much in request for their powers of withstanding fatigue and which differ in their hinder parts from their African congeners. Not many women along the sunny roads which seem white hot. Some of the feminine types are, however, sufficiently remarkable, dressed out in a quasi-military costume, wearing soft boots and a cartouche belt in the Circassian style. You must take care of the stray dogs, hungry brutes with long hair and disquieting fangs, of a breed reminding one of the dogs of the Caucasus, and these animals—according to Boulangier the engineer—have eaten a Russian general.

"Not entirely," replies the major, confirming the statement. "They left his boots."

In the commercial quarter, in the depths of the gloomy ground floors, inhabited by the Persians and the Jews, within the miserable shops are sold carpets of incredible fineness, and colors artistically combined, woven mostly by old women without any Jacquard cards.

On both banks of the Mourgab the Russians have their military establishment. There parade the Turkoman soldiers in the service of the czar. They wear the blue cap and the white epaulettes with their ordinary uniform, and drill under the orders of Russian officers.

A wooden bridge, fifty yards long, crosses the river. It is practicable not only for foot-passengers, but for trains, and telegraph wires are stretched above its parapets.

On the opposite bank is the administrative town, which contains a considerable number of civil servants, wearing the usual Russian cap.

In reality the most interesting place to see is a sort of annexe, a Tekke village, in the middle of Merv, whose inhabitants have retained the villainous characteristics of this decaying race, the muscular bodies, large ears, thick lips, black beard. And this gives the last bit of local color to be found in the new town.

At a turning in the commercial quarter we met the commercials, American and English.

"Mr. Ephrinell," I said, "there is nothing curious in this modern Merv."

"On the contrary, Mr. Bombarnac, the town is almost Yankee, and it will soon see the day when the Russians will give it tramways and gaslights!"

"That will come!"

"I hope it will, and then Merv will have a right to call itself a city."

"For my part, I should have preferred a visit to the old town, with its mosque, its fortress, and its palace. But that is a little too far off, and the train does not stop there, which I regret."

"Pooh!" said the Yankee. "What I regret is, that there is no business to be done in these Turkoman countries! The men all have teeth—"

"And the women all have hair," added Horatia Bluett.

"Well, miss, buy their hair, and you will not lose your time."

"That is exactly what Holmes-Holme of London will do as soon as we have exhausted the capillary stock of the Celestial Empire."

And thereupon the pair left us.

I then suggested to Major Noltitz—it was six o'clock—to dine at Merv, before the departure of the train. He consented, but he was wrong to consent. An ill-fortune took us to the Hotel Slav, which is very inferior to our dining car—at least as regards its bill of fare. It contained, in particular, a national soup called "borchtch," prepared with sour milk, which I would carefully refrain from recommending to the gourmets of the *Twentieth Century*.

With regard to my newspaper, and that telegram relative to the mandarin our train is "conveying" in the funereal acceptation of the word? Has Popof obtained from the mutes who are on guard the name of this high personage?

Yes, at last! And hardly are we within the station than he runs up to me, saying:

"I know the name."

"And it is?"

"Yen Lou, the great mandarin Yen Lou of Pekin."

"Thank you, Popof."

I rush to the telegraph office, and from there I send a telegram to the *Twentieth Century*.

"MERV, 16TH MAY, 7 P.M.

"Train, Grand Transasiatic, just leaving Merv. Took from Douchak the body of the great mandarin Yen Lou coming from Persia to Pekin."

It cost a good deal, did this telegram, but you will admit it was well worth its price.

The name of Yen Lou was immediately communicated to our fellow travelers, and it seemed to me that my lord Faruskiar smiled when he heard it.

We left the station at eight o'clock precisely. Forty minutes afterwards we passed near old Merv, and the night being dark I could see nothing of it. There was, however, a fortress with square towers and a wall of some burned bricks, and ruined tombs, and a palace and remains of mosques, and a collection of archaeological things, which would have run to quite two hundred lines of small text.

"Console yourself," said Major Noltitz. "Your satisfaction could not be complete, for old Merv has been rebuilt four times. If you had seen the fourth town, Bairam Ali of the Persian period, you would not have seen the third, which was Mongol, still less the Musalman village of the second epoch, which was called Sultan Sandjar Kala, and still less the town of the first epoch. That was called by some Iskander Kala, in honor of Alexander the Macedonian, and by others Ghiaour Kala, attributing its foundation to Zoroaster, the founder of the Magian religion, a thousand years before Christ. So I should advise you to put your regrets in the waste-paper basket."

And that is what I did, as I could do no better with them.

Our train is running northeast. The stations are twenty or thirty versts apart. The names are not shouted, as we make no stop, and I have to discover them on my time-table. Such are Keltchi, Ravina—why this Italian name in this Turkoman province?—Peski, Repetek, etc. We cross the desert, the real desert without a thread of water, where artesian wells have to be sunk to supply the reservoirs along the line.

The major tells me that the engineers experienced immense difficulty in fixing the sandhills on this part of the railway. If the palisades had not been sloped obliquely, like the barbs of a feather, the line would have been covered by the sand to such an extent as to stop the running of the trains. As soon as this region of sandhills had been passed we were again on the level plain on which the rails had been laid so easily.

Gradually my companions go to sleep, and our carriage is transformed into a sleeping car.

I then return to my Roumanian. Ought I to attempt to see him to-night? Undoubtedly; and not only to satisfy a very natural curiosity, but also to calm his anxiety. In fact, knowing his secret is known to the person who spoke to him through the panel of his case, suppose the idea occurred to him to get out at one of the stations, give up his journey, and abandon his attempt to rejoin Mademoiselle Zinca Klork, so as to escape the company's pursuit? That is possible, after all, and my intervention may have done the poor fellow harm—to say nothing of my losing No. 11, one of the most valuable in my collection.

I am resolved to visit him before the coming dawn. But, in order to be as careful as possible, I will wait until the train has passed Tchardjoui, where it ought to arrive at twenty-seven past two in the morning. There we shall stop a quarter of an hour before proceeding towards the Amu-Daria. Popof will then retire to his den, and I shall be able to slip into the van, without fear of being seen.

How long the hours appear! Several times I have almost fallen asleep, and twice or thrice I have had to go out into the fresh air on the platform.

The train enters Tchardjoui Station to the minute. It is an important town of the Khanate of Bokhara, which the Transcaspian reached towards the end of 1886, seventeen months after the first sleeper was laid. We are not more than twelve versts from the Amu-Daria, and beyond that river I shall enter on my adventure.

I have said that the stop at Tchardjoui ought to last a quarter of an hour. A few travelers alight, for they have booked to this town which contains about thirty thousand inhabitants. Others get in to proceed to Bokhara and Samarkand, but these are only second-class passengers. This produces a certain amount of bustle on the platform.

I also get out and take a walk up and down by the side of the front van, and I notice the door silently open and shut. A man creeps out on to the platform and slips away through the station, which is dimly lighted by a few petroleum lamps.

It is my Roumanian. It can be no one else. He has not been seen, and there he is, lost among the other travelers. Why this escape? Is it to renew his provisions at the refreshment bar? On the contrary, is not his intention, as I am afraid it is, to get away from us?

Shall I stop him? I will make myself known to him; promise to help him. I will speak to him in French, in English, in German, in Russian— as he pleases. I will say to him: "My friend, trust to my discretion; I will not betray you. Provisions? I will bring them to you during the night. Encouragements? I will heap them on you as I will the refreshments. Do not forget that Mademoiselle Zinca Klork, evidently the most lovely of Roumanians, is expecting you at Pekin, etc."

Behold me then following him without appearing to do so. Amid all this hurry to and fro he is in little danger of being noticed. Neither Popof nor any of the company's servants would suspect him to be a swindler. Is he going towards the gate to escape me?

No! He only wants to stretch his legs better than he can do in the van. After an imprisonment which has lasted since he left Baku—that is to say, about sixty hours—he has earned ten minutes of freedom.

He is a man of middle height, lithe in his movements, and with a gliding kind of walk. He could roll himself up like a cat and find quite room enough in his case. He wears an old vest, his trousers are held up by a belt, and his cap is a fur one—all of dark color.

I am at ease regarding his intentions. He returns towards the van, mounts the platform, and shuts the door gently behind him. As soon as the train is on the move I will knock at the panel, and this time—

More of the unexpected. Instead of waiting at Tchardjoui one-quarter of an hour we have to wait three. A slight injury to one of the brakes of the engine has had to be repaired, and, notwithstanding the German baron's remonstrances, we do not leave the station before half-past three, as the day is beginning to dawn.

It follows from this that if I cannot visit the van I shall at least see the Amou-Daria.

The Amou-Daria is the Oxus of the Ancients, the rival of the Indus and the Ganges. It used to be a tributary of the Caspian, as shown on the maps, but now it flows into the Sea of Aral. Fed by the snows and rains of the Pamir plateau, its sluggish waters flow between low clay cliffs and banks of sand. It is the River-Sea in the Turkoman tongue, and it is about two thousand five hundred kilometres long.

The train crosses it by a bridge a league long, the line being a hundred feet and more above its surface at low water, and the roadway trembles on the thousand piles which support it, grouped in fives between each of the spans, which are thirty feet wide.

In ten months, at a cost of thirty-five thousand roubles, General Annenkof built this bridge, the most important one on the Grand Transasiatic.

The river is of a dull-yellow color. A few islands emerge from the current here and there, as far as one can see.

Popof pointed out the stations for the guards on the parapet of the bridge.

"What are they for?" I asked.

"For the accommodation of a special staff, whose duty it is to give the alarm in case of fire, and who are provided with fire-extinguishers."

This is a wise precaution. Not only have sparks from the engines set it on fire in several places, but there are other disasters possible. A large number of boats, for the most part laden with petroleum, pass up and down the Amou-Daria, and it frequently happens that these become fire-ships. A constant watch is thus only too well justified, for if the bridge were destroyed, its reconstruction would take a year, during which the transport of passengers from one bank to the other would not be without its difficulties.

At last the train is going slowly across the bridge. It is broad daylight. The desert begins again at the second station, that of Karakoul. Beyond can be seen the windings of an affluent of the Amou-Daria, the Zarafchane, "the river that rolls with gold," the course of which extends up to the valley of the Sogd, in that fertile oasis on which stands the city of Samarkand.

At five o'clock in the morning the train stops at the capital of the Khanate of Bokhara, eleven hundred and seven versts from Uzun Ada.

CHAPTER XI

The Khanates of Bokhara and Samarkand used to form Sogdiana, a Persian satrapy inhabited by the Tadjiks and afterwards by the Usbegs, who invaded the country at the close of the fifteenth century. But another invasion, much more modern, is to be feared, that of the sands, now that the saksaouls intended to bring the sandhills to a standstill, have almost completely disappeared.

Bokhara, the capital of the Khanate, is the Rome of Islam, the Noble City, the City of Temples, the revered centre of the Mahometan religion. It was the town with the seven gates, which an immense wall surrounded in the days of its splendor, and its trade with China has always been considerable. Today it contains eighty thousand inhabitants.

I was told this by Major Noltitz, who advised me to visit the town in which he had lived several times. He could not accompany me, having several visits to pay. We were to start again at eleven o'clock in the morning. Five hours only to wait and the town some distance from the railway station! If the one were not connected with the other by a De-cauville—a French name that sounds well in Sogdiana—time would fail for having even a slight glimpse of Bokhara.

It is agreed that the major will accompany me on the Decauville; and when we reach our destination he will leave me to attend to his private affairs. I cannot reckon on him. Is it possible that I shall have to do without the company of any of my numbers?

Let us recapitulate. My Lord Faruskiar? Surely he will not have to worry himself about the mandarin Yen Lou, shut up in this traveling catafalque! Fulk Ephrinell and Miss Horatia Bluett? Useless to think of them when we are talking about palaces, minarets, mosques and other archaeological inutilities. The actor and the actress? Impossible, for Madame Caterna is tired, and Monsieur Caterna will consider it his duty to stay with her. The two Celestials? They have already left the railway station. Ah! Sir Francis Trevellyan. Why not? I am not a Russian, and it is the Russians he cannot stand. I am not the man who conquered Central Asia. I will try and open this closely shut gentleman.

I approach him; I bow; I am about to speak. He gives me a slight inclination and turns on his heel and walks off! The animal!

But the Decauville gives its last whistle. The major and I occupy one of the open carriages. Half an hour afterwards we are through the

77

Dervaze gate, the major leaves me, and here am I, wandering through the streets of Bokhara.

If I told the readers of the *Twentieth Century* that I visited the hundred schools of the town, its three hundred mosques—almost as many mosques as there are churches in Rome, they would not believe me, in spite of the confidence that reporters invariably receive. And so I will confine myself to the strict truth.

As I passed along the dusty roads of the city, I entered at a venture any of the buildings I found open. Here it was a bazaar where they sold cotton materials of alternate colors called "al adjas," handkerchiefs as fine as spider webs, leather marvelously worked, silks the rustle of which is called "tchakhtchukh," in Bokhariot, a name that Meilhac and Halevy did wisely in not adopting for their celebrated heroine. There it was a shop where you could buy sixteen sorts of tea, eleven of which are green, that being the only kind used in the interior of China and Central Asia, and among these the most sought after, the "louka," one leaf of which will perfume a whole teapot.

Farther on I emerged on the quay of the Divanbeghi, reservoirs, bordering one side of a square planted with elms. Not far off is the Arche, which is the fortified palace of the emir and has a modern clock over the door. Arminius Vambery thought the palace had a gloomy look, and so do I, although the bronze cannon which defend the entrance appear more artistic than destructive. Do not forget that the Bokhariot soldiers, who perambulate the streets in white breeches, black tunics, astrakan caps, and enormous boots, are commanded by Russian officers freely decorated with golden embroidery.

Near the palace to the right is the largest mosque of the town, the mosque of Mesjidi Kelan, which was built by Abdallah Khan Sheibani. It is a world of cupolas, clock towers, and minarets, which the storks appear to make their home, and there are thousands of these birds in the town.

Rambling on at a venture I reach the shores of the Zarafchane on the northeast of the town. Its fresh limpid waters fill its bed once or twice a fortnight. Excellent this for health! When the waters appear men, women, children, dogs, bipeds, quadrupeds, bathe together in tumultuous promiscuousness, of which I can give no idea, nor recommend as an example.

Going northwest towards the centre of the city, I came across groups of dervishes with pointed hats, a big stick in their hands, their hair straggling in the breeze, stopping occasionally to take their part in a dance which would not have disgraced the fanatics of the Elysee

Montmartre during a chant, literally vociferated, and accentuated by the most characteristic steps.

Let us not forget that I went through the book market. There are no less than twenty-six shops where printed books and manuscripts are sold, not by weight like tea or by the box like vegetables, but in the ordinary way. As to the numerous "medresses," the colleges which have given Bokhara its renown as a university—I must confess that I did not visit one. Weary and worn I sat down under the elms of the Divanbeghi quay. There, enormous samovars are continually on the boil, and for a "tenghe," or six pence three farthings, I refreshed myself with "shivin," a tea of superior quality which only in the slightest degree resembles that we consume in Europe, which has already been used, so they say, to clean the carpets in the Celestial Empire.

That is the only remembrance I retain of the Rome of Turkestan. Besides, as I was not able to stay a month there, it was as well to stay there only a few hours.

At half-past ten, accompanied by Major Noltitz, whom I found at the terminus of the Decauville, I alighted at the railway station, the warehouses of which are crowded with bales of Bokhariot cotton, and packs of Mervian wool.

I see at a glance that all my numbers are on the platform, including my German baron. In the rear of the train the Persians are keeping faithful guard round the mandarin Yen Lou. It seems that three of our traveling companions are observing them with persistent curiosity; these are the suspicious-looking Mongols we picked up at Douchak. As I pass near them I fancy that Faruskiar makes a signal to them, which I do not understand. Does he know them? Anyhow, this circumstance rather puzzles me.

The train is no sooner off than the passengers go to the dining car. The places next to mine and the major's, which had been occupied since the start, are now vacant, and the young Chinaman, followed by Dr. Tio-King, take advantage of it to come near us. Pan Chao knows I am on the staff of the *Twentieth Century*, and he is apparently as desirous of talking to me as I am of talking to him.

I am not mistaken. He is a true Parisian of the boulevard, in the clothes of a Celestial. He has spent three years in the world where people amuse themselves, and also in the world where they learn. The only son of a rich merchant in Pekin, he has traveled under the wing of this Tio-King, a doctor of some sort, who is really the most stupid of baboons, and of whom his pupil makes a good deal of fun.

79

Dr. Tio-King, since he discovered Cornaro's little book on the quays of the Seine, has been seeking to make his existence conform to the "art of living long in perfect health." This credulous Chinaman of the Chinese had become thoroughly absorbed in the study of the precepts so magisterially laid down by the noble Venetian. And Pan Chao is always chaffing him thereupon, though the good man takes no notice.

We were not long before we had a few specimens of his monomania, for the doctor, like his pupil, spoke very good French.

"Before we begin," said Pan Chao, "tell me, doctor, how many fundamental rules there are for finding the correct amounts of food and drink?"

"Seven, my young friend," replied Tio-King with the greatest seriousness. "The first is to take only just so much nourishment as to enable you to perform the purely spiritual functions."

"And the second?"

"The second is to take only such an amount of nourishment as will not cause you to feel any dullness, or heaviness, or bodily lassitude. The third—"

"Ah! We will wait there, to-day, if you don't mind, doctor," replied Pan Chao. "Here is a certain maintuy, which seems rather good, and—"

"Take care, my dear pupil! That is a sort of pudding made of hashed meat mixed with fat and spices. I fear it may be heavy—"

"Then, doctor, I would advise you not to eat it. For my part, I will follow these gentlemen."

And Pan Chao did—and rightly so, for the maintuy was delicious— while Doctor Tio-King contented himself with the lightest dish on the bill of fare. It appeared from what Major Noltitz said that these maintuys fried in fat are even more savory. And why should they not be, considering that they take the name of "zenbusis," which signifies "women's kisses?"

When Caterna heard this flattering phrase, he expressed his regret that zenbusis did not figure on the breakfast table. To which his wife replied by so tender a look that I ventured to say to him:

"You can find zenbusis elsewhere than in Central Asia, it seems to me."

"Yes," he replied, "they are to be met with wherever there are lovable women to make them."

And Pan Chao added, with a laugh:

"And it is again at Paris that they make them the best."

He spoke like a man of experience, did my young Celestial.

I looked at Pan Chao; I admired him.

How he eats! What an appetite! Not of much use to him are the observations of the doctor on the immoderate consumption of his radical humidity.

The breakfast continued pleasantly. Conversation turned on the work of the Russians in Asia. Pan Chao seemed to me well posted up in their progress. Not only have they made the Transcaspian, but the Transsiberian, surveyed in 1888, is being made, and is already considerably advanced. For the first route through Iscim, Omsk, Tomsk, Krasnojarsk, Nijni-Ufimsk, and Irkutsk, a second route has been substituted more to the south, passing by Orenburg, Akmolinsk, Minoussinsk, Abatoni and Vladivostock. When these six thousand kilometres of rails are laid, Petersburg will be within six days of the Japan Sea. And this Transsiberian, which will exceed in length the Transcontinental of the United States, will cost no more than seven hundred and fifty millions.

It will be easily imagined that this conversation on the Russian enterprise is not very pleasing to Sir Francis Trevellyan. Although he says not a word and does not lift his eyes from the plate, his long face flushes a little.

"Well, gentlemen," said I, "what we see is nothing to what our nephews will see. We are traveling to-day on the Grand Transasiatic. But what will it be when the Grand Transasiatic is in connection with the Grand Transafrican."

"And how is Asia to be united by railway with Africa?" asked Major Noltitz.

"Through Russia, Turkey, Italy, France and Spain. Travelers will go from Pekin to the Cape of Good Hope without change of carriage."

"And the Straits of Gibraltar?" asked Pan Chao.

At this Sir Francis Trevellyan raised his ears.

"Yes, Gibraltar?" said the major.

"Go under it!" said I. "A tunnel fifteen kilometres long is a mere nothing! There will be no English Parliament to oppose it as there is to oppose that between Dover and Calais! It will all be done some day, all—and that will justify the vein:

"*Omnia jam fieri quae posse negabam.*"

My sample of Latin erudition was only understood by Major Noltitz, and I heard Caterna say to his wife:

"That is volapuk."

"There is no doubt," said Pan Chap, "that the Emperor of China has been well advised in giving his hand to the Russians instead of the English. Instead of building strategic railways in Manchouria, which would never have had the approbation of the czar, the Son of Heaven has preferred to continue the Transcaspian across China and Chinese Turkestan."

81

"And he has done wisely," said the major. "With the English it is only the trade of India that goes to Europe, with the Russians it is that of the whole Asiatic continent."

I look at Sir Francis Trevellyan. The color heightens on his cheeks, but he makes no movement. I ask if these attacks in a language he understands perfectly will not oblige him to speak out. And yet I should have been very much embarrassed if I had had to bet on or against it.

Major Noltitz then resumed the conversation by pointing out the incontestable advantages of the Transasiatic with regard to the trade between Grand Asia and Europe in the security and rapidity of its communications. The old hatreds will gradually disappear under European influence, and in that respect alone Russia deserves the approbation of every civilized nation. Is there not a justification for those fine words of Skobeleff after the capture of Gheok Tepe, when the conquered feared reprisals from the victors: "In Central Asian politics we know no outcasts?"

"And in that policy," said the major, "lies our superiority over England."

"No one can be superior to the English."

Such was the phrase I expected from Sir Francis Trevellyan—the phrase I understand English gentlemen always use when traveling about the world. But he said nothing. But when I rose to propose a toast to the Emperor of Russia and the Russians, and the Emperor of China and the Chinese, Sir Francis Trevellyan abruptly left the table. Assuredly I was not to have the pleasure of hearing his voice to-day.

I need not say that during all this talk the Baron Weissschnitzerdoerfer was fully occupied in clearing dish after dish, to the extreme amazement of Doctor Tio-King. Here was a German who had never read the precepts of Cornaro, or, if he had read them, transgressed them in the most outrageous fashion.

For the same reason, I suppose, neither Faruskiar nor Ghangir took part in it, for they only exchanged a few words in Chinese.

But I noted rather a strange circumstance which did not escape the major.

We were talking about the safety of the Grand Transasiatic across Central Asia, and Pan Chao had said that the road was not so safe as it might be beyond the Turkestan frontier, as, in fact, Major Noltitz had told me. I was then led to ask if he had ever heard of the famous Ki Tsang before his departure from Europe.

"Often," he said, "for Ki Tsang was then in the Yunnan provinces. I hope we shall not meet him on our road."

My pronunciation of the name of the famous bandit was evidently incorrect, for I hardly understood Pan Chao when he repeated it with the accent of his native tongue.

But one thing I can say, and that is that when he uttered the name of Ki Tsang, Faruskiar knitted his brows and his eyes flashed. Then, with a look at his companion, he resumed his habitual indifference to all that was being said around him.

Assuredly I shall have some difficulty in making the acquaintance of this man. These Mongols are as close as a safe, and when you have not the word it is difficult to open them.

The train is running at high speed. In the ordinary service, when it stops at the eleven stations between Bokhara and Samarkand, it takes a whole day over the distance. This time it took but three hours to cover the two hundred kilometres which separate the two towns, and at two o'clock in the afternoon it entered the illustrious city of Tamerlane.

Chapter XII

Samarkand is situated in the rich oasis watered by the Zarafchane in the valley of Sogd. A small pamphlet I bought at the railway station informs me that this great city is one of the four sites in which geographers "agree" to place the terrestrial paradise. I leave this discussion to the exegetists of the profession.

Burned by the armies of Cyrus in B.C. 329, Samarkand was in part destroyed by Genghis Khan, about 1219. When it had become the capital of Tamerlane, its position, which certainly could not be improved upon, did not prevent its being ravaged by the nomads of the eighteenth century. Such alternations of grandeur and ruin have been the fate of all the important towns of Central Asia.

We had five hours to stop at Samarkand during the day, and that promised something pleasant and several pages of copy. But there was no time to lose. As usual, the town is double; one half, built by the Russians, is quite modern, with its verdant parks, its avenues of birches, its palaces, its cottages; the other is the old town, still rich in magnificent remains of its splendor, and requiring many weeks to be conscientiously studied.

This time I shall not be alone. Major Noltitz is free; he will accompany me. We had already left the station when the Caternas presented themselves.

"Are you going for a run round the town, Monsieur Claudius?" asked the actor, with a comprehensive gesture to show the vast surroundings of Samarkand.

"Such is our intention."

"Will Major Noltitz and you allow me to join you?"

"How so?"

"With Madame Caterna, for I do nothing without her."

"Our explorations will be so much the more agreeable," said the major, with a bow to the charming actress.

"And," I added, with a view to save fatigue and gain time, "my dear friends, allow me to offer you an arba."

"An arba!" exclaimed Caterna, with a swing of his hips. "What may that be, an arba?"

"One of the local vehicles."

"Let us have an arba."

We entered one of the boxes on wheels which were on the rank in front of the railway station. Under promise of a good "silao," that is to say, something to drink, the yemtchik or coachman undertook to give wings to his two doves, otherwise his two little horses, and we went off at a good pace.

On the left we leave the Russian town, arranged like a fan, the governor's house, surrounded by beautiful gardens, the public park and its shady walks, then the house of the chief of the district which is just on the boundary of the old town.

As we passed, the major showed us the fortress, round which our arba turned. There are the graves of the Russian soldiers who died in the attack in 1868, near the ancient palace of the Emir of Bokhara.

From this point, by a straight narrow road, our arba reached the Righistan square, which, as my pamphlet says, "must not be confounded with the square of the same name at Bokhara."

It is a fine quadrilateral, perhaps a little spoiled by the fact that the Russians have paved it and ornamented it with lamps—which would certainly, please Ephrinell, if he decides upon visiting Samarkand. On three sides of the square are the well-preserved ruins of three medresses, where the mollahs give children a good education. These medresses—there are seventeen of these colleges at Samarkand, besides eighty-five mosques—are called Tilla-Kari, Chir Dar and Oulong Beg.

In a general way they resemble each other; a portico in the middle leading to interior courts, built of enameled brick, tinted pale blue or pale yellow, arabesques designed in gold lines on a ground of turquoise blue, the dominant color; leaning minarets threatening to fall and never falling, luckily for their coating of enamel, which the intrepid traveller Madame De Ujfalvy-Bourdon, declares to be much superior to the finest of our crackle enamels—and these are not vases to put on a mantelpiece or on a stand, but minarets of good height.

These marvels are still in the state described by Marco Polo, the Venetian traveler of the thirteenth century.

"Well, Monsieur Bombarnac," asked the major, "do you not admire the square?"

"It is superb," I say.

"Yes," says the actor, "what a splendid scene it would make for a ballet, Caroline! That mosque, with a garden alongside, and that other one with a court—"

"You are right, Adolphe," said his wife; "but we would have to put those towers up straight and have a few luminous fountains."

"Excellent notion, Caroline! Write us a drama, Monsieur Claudius, a spectacle piece, with a third act in this square. As for the title—"

"Tamerlane is at once suggested!" I reply. The actor made a significant grimace. The conqueror of Asia seemed to him to be wanting in actuality. And leaning toward his wife, Caterna hastened to say:

"As a scene, I have seen a better at the Porte-Saint Martin, in the *Fils de la Nuit*—"

"And I have at the Chatelet in *Michael Strogoff*."

We cannot do better than leave our comedians alone. They look at everything from the theatrical point of view. They prefer the air gauze and the sky-blue foliage, the branches of the stage trees, the agitated canvas of the ocean waves, the prospectives of the drop scene, to the sites the curtain represents, a set scene by Cambon or Rube or Jambon to no matter what landscape; in short, they would rather have art than nature. And I am not the man to try and change their opinions on the subject.

As I have mentioned the name of Tamerlane, I asked Major Noltitz if we were going to visit the tomb of the famous Tartar. The major replied that we would see it as we returned; and our itinerary brought us in front of the Samarkand bazaar.

The arba stopped at one of the entrances to this vast rotunda, after taking us in and out through the old town, the houses of which consist of only one story, and seem very comfortless.

Here is the bazaar in which are accumulated enormous quantities of woollen stuffs, velvet-pile carpets in the brightest of colors, shawls of graceful patterns, all thrown anyhow on the counters of the shops. Before these samples the sellers and buyers stand, noisily arriving at the lowest price. Among the fabrics is a silk tissue known as Kanaous, which is held in high esteem by the Samarkand ladies, although they are very far from appreciating the similar product of Lyons manufacture, which it excels neither in quality nor appearance.

Madame Caterna appeared extraordinarily tempted, as if she were among the counters of the *Bon Marche* or the *Louvre.*

"That stuff would do well for my costume in the *Grande Duchesse!*" she said.

"And those slippers would suit me down to the ground as Ali Bajou in the *Caid!*" said Caterna.

And while the actress was investing in a remnant of Kanaous, the actor paid for a pair of those green slippers which the Turkomans wear when they enter a mosque. But this was not without recourse to the kindness of the major, who acted as interpreter between the Caternas and the merchant, whose "Yoks! Yoks!" sounded like a lot of crackers in his large mouth.

The arba started again and went off toward the square of Ribi-Khanym, where stands the mosque of that name which was that of one of Tamerlane's wives. If the square is not as regular as that of Righistan, it is in my opinion rather more picturesque. There are strangely grouped ruins, the remains of arcades, half-unroofed cupolas, columns without capitals, the shafts of which have retained all the brightness of their enamelling; then a long row of elliptical porticoes closing in one side of the vast quadrilateral. The effect is really grand, for these old monuments of the splendor of Samarkand stand out from a background of sky and verdure that you would seek in vain, even at the Grand Opera, if our actor does not object. But I must confess we experienced a deeper impression when, toward the northeast of the town, our arba deposited us in front of the finest of the mosques of Central Asia, which dates from the year 795 of the Hegira (1392 of our era).

I cannot, writing straight away, give you an idea of this marvel. If I were to thread the words, mosaics, pediments, spandrels, bas-reliefs, niches, enamels, corbels, all on a string in a sentence, the picture would still be incomplete. It is strokes of the brush that are wanted, not strokes of the pen. Imagination remains abashed at the remains of the most splendid architecture left us by Asiatic genius.

It is in the farthest depths of this mosque that the faithful go to worship at the tomb of Kassimben-Abbas, a venerated Mussulman saint, and we are told that if we open the tomb a living man will come forth from it in all his glory. But the experiment has not been made as yet, and we prefer to believe in the legend.

We had to make an effort to throw off our contemplative mood; and fortunately the Caternas did not trouble our ecstasy by evoking any of their recollections of the theater. Doubtless they had shared in our impressions.

We resumed our seats in the arba, and the yemtchik took us at the gallop of his doves along shady roads which the Russian administration keeps up with care.

Along these roads we met and passed many figures worthy of notice. Their costumes were varied enough, "Khalats," in startling colors, and their heads enturbaned most coquettishly. In a population of forty thousand there was, of course, a great mingling of races. Most of them seemed to be Tadjiks of Iranian origin. They are fine strong fellows, whose white skin has disappeared beneath the tan of the open air and the unclouded sun. Here is what Madame de Ujfalvy-Bourdon says of them in her interesting book: "Their hair is generally black, as is also their beard, which is very abundant. Their eyes are never turned up at the corners, and are almost always brown. The nose is very handsome, the lips are not thick, the teeth are small. The forehead is high, broad, and the general shape of the face is oval."

And I cannot refrain from mentioning a note of approval from Caterna when he saw one of these Tadjiks superbly draped in his many-colored Khalat.

"What a splendid lead! What an admirable Melingue! You can see him in Richepins's *Nana Sahib* or Meurice's *Schamyl*."

"He would make a lot of money! replied Madame Caterna.

"He just would—I believe you, Caroline!" replied the enthusiastic actor.

And for him, as for all other theatrical folks, is not the money the most serious and the least disputable manifestation of the dramatic art?

It was already five o clock, and in this incomparable city of Samarkand scene succeeded scene. There! I am getting into that way of looking at it now. Certainly the spectacle should finish before midnight. But as we start at eight o'clock, we shall have to lose the end of the piece. But as I considered that, for the honor of special correspondents in general, it would never do to have been at Samarkand without seeing Tamerlane's tomb, our arba returned to the southwest, and drew up near the mosque of Gour Emir, close to the Russian town. What a sordid neighborhood, what a heap of mud huts and straw huts, what an agglomeration of miserable hovels we have just been through!

The mosque has a grand appearance. It is crowned with its dome, in which the raw blue of the turquoise is the chief color, and which looks like a Persian cap; and on its only minaret, which has now lost its head, there glitter the enamelled arabesques which have retained their ancient purity.

We visited the central hall beneath the cupola. There stands the tomb of the lame Timour the Conqueror. Surrounded by the four tombs of his sons and his patron saint, beneath a stone of black jade covered with inscriptions, whiten the bones of Tamerlane, in whose name is gathered the whole fourteenth century of Asiatic history. The walls of the hall are covered with slabs of jade, on which are engraven innumerable scrolls of foliage, and in the southwest stands a little column marking the direction of Mecca. Madame De Ujfalvy-Bourdon has justly compared this part of the mosque of Gour Emir to a sanctuary, and we had the same impression. This impression took a still more religious tone when, by a dark and narrow stairway, we descended to the crypt in which are the tombs of Tamerlane's wives and daughters.

"But who was this Tamerlane?" asked Caterna. "This Tamerlane everybody is talking about."

"Tamerlane," replied Major Noltitz, "was one of the greatest conquerors of the world, perhaps the greatest, if you measure greatness by the extent of the conquests. Asia to the east of the Caspian Sea, Persia and the provinces to the north of it, Russia to the Sea of Azof, India, Syria, Asia Minor, China, on which he threw two hundred thousand men—he had a whole continent as the theater of his wars."

"And he was lame!" said Madame Caterna.

"Yes, madame, like Genseric, like Shakespeare, like Byron, like Walter Scott, like Talleyrand, but that did not hinder his getting along in the world. But how fanatic and bloodthirsty he was! History affirms that at Delhi he massacred a hundred thousand captives, and at Bagdad he erected an obelisk of eighty thousand heads."

"I like the one in the Place de la Concorde better," said Caterna, "and that is only in one piece."

At this observation we left the mosque of Gour Emir, and as it was time to "hurry up," as our actor said, the arba was driven briskly toward the station.

For my part, in spite of the observations of the Caternas, I was fully in tone with the local color due to the marvels of Samarkand, when I was roughly shaken back into modern reality.

In the streets—yes—in the streets near the railway station, in the very center of Tamerlane's capital, I passed two bicyclists.

"Ah!" exclaimed Caterna. "Messrs. Wheeler!"

And they were Turkomans!

After that nothing more could be done than leave a town so dishonored by the masterpiece of mechanical locomotion, and that was what we did at eight o'clock.

Chapter XIII

We dined an hour after the train left. In the dining car were several newcomers, among others two negroes whom Caterna began to speak of as darkies.

None of these travelers, Popof told me, would cross the Russo-Chinese frontier, so that they interested me little or not at all.

During dinner, at which all my numbers were present—I have twelve now, and I do not suppose I shall go beyond that—I noticed that Major Noltitz continued to keep his eye on his lordship Faruskiar. Had he begun to suspect him? Was it of any importance in his opinion that this Mongol seemed to know, without appearing to do so, the three second-class travelers, who were also Mongols? Was his imagination working with the same activity as mine, and was he taking seriously what was only a joke on my part? That I, a man of letters, a chronicler in search of scenes and incidents, should be pleased to see in his personage a rival of the famous Ki Tsang, or Ki Tsang himself, could be understood; but that he, a serious man, doctor in the Russian army, should abandon himself to such speculations no one would believe. Never mind now, we shall have something more to say about it by and by.

As for me, I had soon forgotten all about the Mongol for the man in the case. Tired as I am after that long run through Samarkand, if I get a chance to visit him to-night I will.

Dinner being over, we all begin to make ourselves comfortable for the night, with the intention of sleeping till we reach Tachkend.

The distance from Samarkand to Tachkend is three hundred kilometres. The train will not get in there before seven o'clock in the morning. It will stop three times at small stations for water and fuel—circumstances favorable to the success of my project. I add that the night is dark, the sky overcast, no moon, no stars. It threatens rain; the wind is freshening. It is no time for walking on platforms, and nobody walks there. It is important to choose the moment when Popof is sound asleep.

It is not necessary for the interview to be a long one. That the gallant fellow should be reassured—that is the essential point—and he will be, as soon as I have made his acquaintance. A little information concerning him, concerning Mademoiselle Zinca Klork, whence he comes, why he is going to Pekin, why he chose such a mode of transport, his provisions for the journey, how he gets into the case, his age, his trade, his birthplace, what he has done in the past, what he hopes to do in the future, etc., etc., and I have done all that a conscientious reporter can do. That is what I want to know; that is what I will ask him. It is not so very much.

And in the first place let us wait until the car is asleep. That will not be long, for my companions are more or less fatigued by the hours they have spent in Samarkand. The beds were ready immediately after dinner. A few of the passengers tried a smoke on the platform, but the gust drove them in very quickly. They have all taken up their places under the curtained lamps, and toward half-past ten the respiration of some and the snoring of others are blended with the continued grinding of the train on the steel rails.

I remained outside last of all, and Popof exchanged a few words with me.

"We shall not be disturbed to-night," he said to me, "and I would advise you to make the most of it. To-morrow night we shall be running through the defiles of the Pamir, and we shall not travel so quietly, I am afraid."

"Thanks, Popof, I will take your advice, and sleep like a marmot."

Popof wished me good night and went into his cabin.

I saw no use in going back into the car, and remained on the platform. It was impossible to see anything either to the left or right of the line. The oasis of Samarkand had already been passed, and the rails were now laid across a long horizontal plain. Many hours would elapse before the train reached the Syr Daria, over which the line passes by a bridge like that over the Amou-Daria, but of less importance.

It was about half-past eleven when I decided to open the door of the van, which I shut behind me.

I knew that the young Roumanian was not always shut up in his box, and the fancy might just have taken him to stretch his limbs by walking from one end to the other of the van.

The darkness is complete. No jet of light filters through the holes of the case. That seems all the better for me. It is as well that my No. 11 should not be surprised by too sudden an apparition. He is doubtless asleep. I will give two little knocks on the panel, I will awake him, and we will explain matters before he can move.

I feel as I go. My hand touches the case; I place my ear against the panel and I listen.

There is not a stir, not a breath! Is my man not here? Has he got away? Has he slipped out at one of the stations without my seeing him? Has my news gone with him? Really, I am most uneasy; I listen attentively.

No! He has not gone. He is in the case. I hear distinctly his regular and prolonged respiration. He sleeps. He sleeps the sleep of the innocent, to which he has no right, for he ought to sleep the sleep of the swindler of the Grand Transasiatic.

I am just going to knock when the locomotive's whistle emits its strident crow, as we pass through a station. But the train is not going to stop, I know, and I wait until the whistling has ceased.

I then give a gentle knock on the panel.

There is no reply.

However, the sound of breathing is not so marked as before.

I knock more loudly.

This time it is followed by an involuntary movement of surprise and fright.

"Open, open!" I say in Russian.

There is no reply.

"Open!" I say again. "It is a friend who speaks. You have nothing to fear!"

If the panel is not lowered, as I had hoped, there is the crack of a match being lighted and a feeble light appears in the case.

I look at the prisoner through the holes in the side.

There is a look of alarm on his face; his eyes are haggard. He does not know whether he is asleep or awake.

"Open, my friend, I say, open and have confidence. I have discovered your secret. I shall say nothing about it. On the other hand, I may be of use to you."

The poor man looks more at ease, although he does not move.

"You are a Roumanian, I think," I add, "and I am a Frenchman."

"Frenchman? You are a Frenchman?"

And this reply was given in my own language, with a foreign accent.

One more bond between us.

The panel slips along its groove, and by the light of a little lamp I can examine my No. 11, to whom I shall be able to give a less arithmetical designation.

"No one can see us, nor hear us?" he asked in a half-stifled voice.

"No one."

"The guard?"

"Asleep."

My new friend takes my hands, he clasps them. I feel that he seeks a support. He understands he can depend on me. And he murmurs:

"Do not betray me—do not betray me."

"Betray you, my boy? Did not the French newspapers sympathize with that little Austrian tailor, with those two Spanish sweethearts, who sent themselves by train in the way you are doing? Were not subscriptions opened in their favor? And can you believe that I, a journalist—"

"You are a journalist?"

"Claudius Bombarnac, special correspondent of the *Twentieth Century*."

"A French journal—"

"Yes, I tell you."

"And you are going to Pekin?"

"Through to Pekin."

"Ah! Monsieur Bombarnac, Providence has sent you onto my road."

"No, it was the managers of my journal, and they delegated to me the powers they hold from Providence, courage and confidence. Anything I can do for you I will."

"Thanks, thanks."

"What is your name?"

"Kinko."

"Kinko? Excellent name!"

"Excellent?"

"For my articles! You are a Roumanian, are you not?"

"Roumanian of Bucharest."

"But you have lived in France?"

"Four years in Paris, where I was apprentice to an upholsterer in the Faubourg Saint Antoine."

"And you went back to Bucharest?"

"Yes, to work at my trade there until the day came when it was impossible for me to resist the desire to leave—"

"To leave? Why?"

"To marry!"

"To marry—Mademoiselle Zinca—"

"Zinca?"

"Yes, Mademoiselle Zinca Klork, Avenue Cha-Coua, Pekin, China!"

"You know?"

"Certainly. The address is on the box."

"True."

"As to Mademoiselle Zinca Klork—"

"She is a young Roumanian. I knew her in Paris, where she was learning the trade of a milliner. Oh, charming—"

"I am sure upon it. You need not dwell on that."

"She also returned to Bucharest, until she was invited to take the management of a dressmaker's at Pekin. We loved, monsieur; she went—and we were separated for a year. Three weeks ago she wrote to me. She was getting on over there. If I could go out to her, I would do well. We should get married without delay. She had saved something. I would soon earn as much as she had. And here I am on the road—in my turn—for China."

"In this box?"

"What would you have, Monsieur Bombarnac?" asked Kinko, reddening. "I had only money enough to buy a packing case, a few provisions, and get myself sent off by an obliging friend. It costs a thousand francs to go from Tiflis to Pekin. But as soon as I have gained them, the company will be repaid, I assure you."

"I believe you, Kinko, I believe you; and on your arrival at Pekin?"

"Zinca has been informed. The box will be taken to Avenue Cha-Coua, and she—"

"Will pay the carriage?"

"Yes."

"And with pleasure, I will answer for it."

"You may be sure of it, for we love each other so much."

"And besides, Kinko, what would one not do for a sweetheart who consents to shut himself up in a box for a fortnight, and arrives labelled 'Glass,' 'Fragile,' 'Beware of damp—'"

"Ah, you are making fun of a poor fellow."

"Not at all; and you may rest assured I will neglect nothing which will enable you to arrive dry and in one piece at Mademoiselle Zinca Klork's—in short, in a perfect state of preservation!"

"Again I thank you," said Kinko, pressing my hands. "Believe me, you will not find me ungrateful."

"Ah! friend Kinko, I shall be paid, and more than paid!"

"And how?"

"By relating, as soon as I can do so without danger to you, the particulars of your journey from Tiflis to Pekin. Think now—what a heading for a column:

A Lover in a Box!
ZINCA AND KINKO!!
1,500 Leagues Through Central Asia in a Luggage Van!!!'"

The young Roumanian could not help smiling.

"You need not be in too much of a hurry!" he said.

"Never fear! Prudence and discretion, as they say at the matrimonial agencies."

Then I went to the door of the van to see that we were in no danger of surprise, and then the conversation was resumed. Naturally, Kinko asked me how I had discovered his secret. I told him all that had passed on the steamer during the voyage across the Caspian. His breathing had betrayed him. The idea that at first I took him for a wild beast seemed to amuse him. A wild beast! A faithful poodle, rather! Then with a sneeze he went up the animal scale to human rank.

"But," said he to me, lowering his voice, "two nights ago I thought all was lost. The van was closed. I had just lighted my little lamp, and had begun my supper when a knock came against the panel—"

"I did that, Kinko, I did that. And that night we should have become acquainted if the train had not run into a dromedary."

"It was you! I breathe again!" said Kinko. "In what dreams I have lived! It was known that some one was hidden in this box. I saw myself discovered, handed over to the police, taken to prison at Merv or Bokhara, and my little Zinca waiting for me in vain; and never should I see her again, unless I resumed the journey on foot. Well, I would have resumed, yes, I would."

And he said it with such an air of resolution that it was impossible not to see that the young Roumanian had unusual spirit.

"Brave Kinko!" I answered. "I am awfully sorry to have caused you such apprehensions. Now you are at ease again, and I fancy your chances have improved now we have made friends."

I then asked Kinko to show me how he managed in his box.

Nothing could be simpler or better arranged. At the bottom was a seat on which he sat with the necessary space for him to stretch his legs when he placed them obliquely; under the seat, shut in by a lid, were a few provisions, and table utensils reduced to a simple pocket knife and metal mug; an overcoat and a rug hung from a nail, and the little lamp he used at nighttime was hooked onto one of the walls.

The sliding panel allowed the prisoner to leave his prison occasionally. But if the case had been placed among other packages, if the porters had not deposited it with the precautions due to its fragility, he would not have been able to work the panel, and would have had to make a friend somehow before the end of the journey. Fortunately, there is a special Providence for lovers, and divine intervention in favor of Kinko and Zinca Klork was manifested in all its plenitude. He told me that very night he had taken a walk either in the van or else on the station platform where the train had stopped.

"I know that, Kinko. That was at Bokhara. I saw you!"

"You saw me?"

"Yes, and I thought you were trying to get away. But if I saw you, it was because I knew of your presence in the van, and I was there watching you, no one else having an idea of spying on you. Nevertheless, it was dangerous; do not do it again; let me replenish your larder when I get an opportunity."

"Thank you, Monsieur Bombarnac, thank you! I do not believe I am in danger of being discovered, unless at the Chinese frontier—or rather at Kachgar."

"And why?"

"The custom house is very keen on goods going into China. I am afraid they will come round the packages, and that my box—"

"In fact, Kinko," I replied, "there are a few difficult hours for you."

"If they find me out?"

"I shall be there, and I will do all I can to prevent anything unpleasant happening."

"Ah! Monsieur Bombarnac!" exclaimed Kinko, in a burst of gratitude. "How can I repay you?"

"Very easily, Kinko."

"And in what way?"

"Ask me to your marriage with the lovely Zinca."

"I will! And Zinca will embrace you."

"She will be only doing her duty, friend Kinko, and I shall be only doing mine in returning two kisses for one."

We exchanged a last grip of the hand; and, really, I think there were tears in the good fellow's eyes when I left him. He put out his lamp, he pushed back the panel, then through the case I heard one more "thanks" and an *au revoir.*

I came out of the van, I shut the door, I assured myself that Popof was still asleep. In a few minutes, after a breath or two of the night air, I go into my place near Major Noltitz.

And before I close my eyes my last thought is that, thanks to the appearance of the episodic Kinko, the journey of their energetic "Special" will not be displeasing to my readers.

❦

Chapter XIV

In 1870 the Russians endeavored without success to establish a fair at Tachkend which would rival that at Nijni-Novgorod. Some twenty years later the attempt would have succeeded, and as a matter of fact the fair now exists, owing to the making of the Transcaspian to unite Samarkand and Tachkend.

And now not only do merchants with their merchandise crowd into this town, but pilgrims with their pilgrimage outfits. And there will be quite a procession, or rather an exodus, when the time comes for the Mussulman faithful to ride to Mecca by railway.

Meanwhile we are at Tachkend, and the time-table shows that we stop here two hours and a half.

Of course I shall not have time to visit the town, which would be worth my while to do. But I must confess that these cities of Turkestan are very much alike, and to have seen one is to have seen another, unless we can go into details.

Crossing a fertile region where poplars like distaffs rise gracefully erect, skirting fields bristling with vines, running by gardens where fruit trees abound, our train stops at the new town.

As is inevitable since the Russian conquest, there are two towns side by side at Tachkend as at Samarkand, as at Bokhara, as at Merv. Here the old town has tortuous streets, houses of mud and clay, bazaars of poor appearance, caravanserais built of bricks dried in the sun, a few mosques, and schools as numerous as if the czar had decreed by ukase that everything French should be imitated. It is true that the scholars are wanting, but there is no want of schools.

The population of Tachkend does not differ very much from that met with in other parts of Turkestan. It comprises Sarthes, Usbegs, Tadjiks, Khirgizes, Nogais, Israelites, a few Afghans and Hindoos and—as may be naturally supposed—a fair supply of Russians.

It is perhaps at Tachkend that the Jews are gathered in the greatest numbers. And from the day that the town passed under Russian administration their situation has considerably improved. From that epoch dates the complete civil and political liberty they now enjoy.

I have only two hours to spare in visiting the town, and I do my work in true reporter style. You should have seen me dashing through the grand bazaar, a mere wooden building, which is crammed with Oriental stuffs, silk goods, metal ware, specimens of Chinese manufacture, including some very fine examples of porcelain.

In the streets of old Tachkend a certain number of women are to be met with. I need hardly say that there are no slaves in this country, much to the displeasure of the Mussulmans. Nowadays woman is free—even in her household.

"An old Turkoman," said Major Noltitz, "once told me that a husband's power is at an end now that he cannot thrash his wife without being threatened with an appeal to the czar; and that marriage is at an end!"

I do not know if the fair sex is still beaten, but the husbands know what they may expect if they knock their wives about. Will it be believed that these peculiar Orientals can see no progress in this prohibition to beat their wives? Perhaps they remember that the Terrestrial Paradise is not far off—a beautiful garden between the Tigris and Euphrates, unless it was between the Amou and the Syr-Daria. Perhaps they have not forgotten that mother Eve lived in this preadamite garden, and that if she had been thrashed a little before her first fault, she would probably not have committed it. But we need not enlarge on that.

I did not hear, as Madam Ujfalvy-Bourdon did, the band playing the *Pompiers de Nanterre* in the governor-general's garden. No! On this occasion they were playing *Le Pere la Victoire*, and if these are not national airs they are none the less agreeable to French ears.

We left Tachkend at precisely eleven o'clock in the morning. The country through which the Grand Transasiatic is now running is not so monotonous. The plain begins to undulate, for we are approaching the outer ramifications of the eastern orographic system. We are nearing the tableland of the Pamirs. At the same time we continue at normal speed along this section of a hundred and fifty kilometres which separates us from Khodjend.

97

As soon as we are on the move I begin to think of Kinko. His little love romance has touched me to the heart. This sweetheart who sent himself off—this other sweetheart who is going to pay the expenses—I am sure Major Noltitz would be interested in these two turtle doves, one of which is in a cage; he would not be too hard on this defrauder of the company, he would be incapable of betraying him. Consequently I have a great desire to tell him of my expedition into the baggage van. But the secret is not mine. I must do nothing that might get Kinko into trouble.

And so I am silent, and to-night I will, if possible, take a few provisions to my packing case—to my snail in his shell, let us say. And is not the young Roumanian like a snail in his shell, for it is as much as he can do to get out of it?

We reach Khodjend about three in the afternoon. The country is fertile, green, carefully cultivated. It is a succession of kitchen gardens, which seem to be well-kept immense fields sown with clover, which yield four or five crops a year. The roads near the town are bordered with long rows of mulberry trees, which diversify the view with eccentric branches.

Again, this pair of cities, old and new. Both of them had only thirty thousand inhabitants in 1868 and they have from forty-five to fifty thousand now. Is it the influence of the surroundings which produces the increase of the birth rate? Is the province affected by the prolific example of the Celestial Empire? No! It is the progress of trade, the concentration of merchants of all nations onto these new markets.

Our halt at Khodjend has lasted three hours. I have made my professional visit and walked on the banks of the Syr-Dana. This river, which bathes the foot of the high mountains of Mogol-Taou, is crossed by a bridge, the middle section of which gives passage to ships of moderate tonnage.

The weather is very warm. The town being protected by its shelter of mountains, the breezes of the steppe cannot reach it, and it is one of the hottest places in Turkestan.

I met the Caternas, delighted with their excursion. The actor said to me in a tone of the best humor:

"Never shall I forget Khodjend, Monsieur Claudius."

"And why will you never forget Khodjend, Monsieur Caterna?"

"Do you see these peaches?" he asked, showing me the fruit he was carrying.

"They are magnificent—"

"And not dear! A kilo for four kopeks—that is to say, twelve centimes!"

"Eh!" I answer. "That shows that peaches are rather common in this country. That is the Asiatic apple and it was one of those apples that Mrs. Adam took a bite at—"

"Then I excuse her!" said Madame Caterna, munching away at one of these delicious peaches.

After leaving Tachkend the railway had curved toward the south, so as to reach Khodjend; but after leaving town it curved to the east in the direction of Kokhan. It is at Tachkend that it is nearest to the Transsiberian, and a branch line is being made to Semipalatinsk to unite the railway systems of Central and Northern Asia.

Beyond we shall run due east, and by Marghelan and Och pass through the gorges of the Pamirs so as to reach the Turkesto-Chinese frontier.

The train had only just started when the travelers took their seats at the table, where I failed to notice any fresh arrival. We shall not pick up any more until we reach Kachgar. There the Russian cookery will give place to the Chinese, and although the name does not recall the nectar and ambrosia of Olympus, it is probable that we shall not lose by the change.

Ephrinell is in his usual place. Without going as far as familiarity, it is obvious that a close intimacy, founded on a similarity in tastes and aptitudes exists between Miss Horatia Bluett and the Yankee. There is no doubt, in our opinion, but what it will end in a wedding as soon as the train arrives. Both will have their romance of the rail. Frankly, I like that of Kinko and Zinca Klork much better. It is true the pretty Roumanian is not here!

We are all very friendly, and by "we" I mean my most sympathetic numbers, the major, the Caternas, young Pan Chao, who replies with very Parisian pleasantries to the actor's fooleries.

The dinner is a pleasant one and a good one. We learn what is the fourth rule formulated by Cornaco, that Venetian noble, and with the object of determining the right amount for drinking and eating. Pan Chao pressed the doctor on this subject, and Tio-King replied, with a seriousness truly buddhic:

"The rule is founded on the quantity of nourishment proportionate for each temperament as regards the difference of ages, and the strength and the food of various kinds."

"And for your temperament, doctor?" asked Caterna, "what is the right quantity?"

"Fourteen ounces of solid or liquid—"

"An hour?"

"No, sir, a day," replied Tio-King. "And it was in this manner that the illustrious Cornaro lived from the age of thirty-six, so as to leave himself enough strength of body and mind to write his fourth treatise when he was eighty-five, and to live to a hundred and two."

"In that case, give me my fifth cutlet," said Pan Ghao, with a burst of laughter.

There is nothing more agreeable than to talk before a well-served table; but I must not forget to complete my notes regarding Kokham. We were not due there till nine o'clock, and that would be in the nighttime. And so I asked the major to give me some information regarding this town, which is the last of any importance in Russian Turkestan.

"I know it all the better," said the major, "from having been in garrison there for fifteen months. It is a pity you have not time to visit it, for it remains very Asiatic, and there has not been time yet for it to grow a modern town. There is a square there unrivalled in Asia, a palace in great style, that of the old Khan of Khondajar, situated on a mound about a hundred yards high, and in which the governor has left his Sarthe artillery. It is considered wonderful, and there is good reason for it. You will lose by not going there a rare opportunity of bringing in the high-flown words of your language in description: the reception hall transformed into a Russian church, a labyrinth of rooms with the floors of the precious Karagatch wood, the rose pavilion, in which visitors receive a truly Oriental hospitality, the interior court of Moorish decoration recalling the adorable architectural fancies of the Alhambra, the terraces with their splendid views, the harem where the thousand wives of the Sultan—a hundred more than Solomon—live in peace together, the lacework of the fronts, the gardens with their shady walks under the ancient vines—that is what you would have seen—"

"And which I have already seen with your eyes, dear major," said I. "My readers will not complain. Pray tell me if there are any bazaars in ."

"A Turkestan town without bazaars would be like London without its docks."

"And Paris without its theaters!" said the actor.

"Yes; there are bazaars at Kokhan, one of them on the Sokh bridge, the two arms of which traverse the town and in it the finest fabrics of Asia are sold for tillahs of gold, which are worth three roubles and sixty kopeks of our money."

"I am sure, major, that you are going to mention mosques after bazaars."

"Certainly."

"And medresses?"

"Certainly; but you must understand that some of them are as good as the mosques and medresses of Samarkand of Bokhara."

I took advantage of the kindness of Major Noltitz and thanks to him, the readers of the *Twentieth Century* need not spend a night in Kokhan. I will leave my pen inundated with the solar rays of this city of which I could only see a vague outline.

The dinner lasted till rather late, and terminated in an unexpected manner by an offer from Caterna to recite a monologue.

I need scarcely say that the offer was gladly accepted.

Our train more and more resembled a small rolling town It had even its casino, this dining-car in which we were gathered at the moment. And it was thus in the eastern part of Turkestan, four hundred kilometres from the Pamir plateau, at dessert after our excellent dinner served in a saloon of the Grand Transasiatic, that the *Obsession* was given with remarkable talent by Monsieur Caterna, grand premier comique, engaged at Shanghai theater for the approaching season.

"Monsieur," said Pan Chao, "my sincere compliments. I have heard young Coquelin—"

"A master, monsieur; a master!" said Caterna.

"Whom you approach—"

"Respectfully—very respectfully!"

The bravos lavished on Caterna had no effect on Sir Francis Trevellyan, who had been occupying himself with onomatopic exclamations regarding the dinner, which he considered execrable. He was not amused—not even sadly, as his countrymen have been for four hundred years, according to Froissart. And yet nobody took any notice of this grumbling gentleman's recriminations.

Baron Weissschnitzerdoerfer had not understood a single word of this little masterpiece, and had he understood it, he would not have been able to appreciate this sample of Parisian monologomania.

As to my lord Faruskiar and his inseparable Ghangir, it seemed that in spite of their traditional reserve, the surprising grimaces, the significant gestures, the comical intonations, had interested them to a certain extent.

The actor had noticed it, and appreciated this silent admiration.

As he rose from the table he said to me:

"He is magnificent, this seigneur! What dignity! What a presence! What a type of the farthest East! I like his companion less—a third-rate fellow at the outside! But this superb Mongol! Caroline, cannot you imagine him as 'Morales' in the *Pirates of the Savannah?*"

"Not in that costume, at any rate," said I.

"Why not, Monsieur Claudius? One day at Perpignan I played 'Colonel de Monteclin' in the *Closerie des Genets* in the costume of a Japanese officer—"

"And he was applauded!" added Madame Caterna.

During dinner the train had passed Kastakos station, situated in the center of a mountainous region. The road curved a good deal, and ran over viaducts and through tunnels—as we could tell by the noise.

A little time afterward Popof told us that we were in the territory of Ferganah, the name of the ancient khanate of Kokhan, which was annexed by Russia in 1876, with the seven districts that compose it. These districts, in which Sarthes are in the majority, are administered by prefects, sub-prefects, and mayors. Come, then, to Ferganah, to find all the machinery of the constitution of the year VIII.

Beyond there is an immense steppe, extending before our train. Madame de Ujfalvy-Bourdon has justly compared it to a billiard table, so perfect in its horizontality. Only it is not an ivory ball which is rolling over its surface, but an express of the Grand Transasiatic running at sixty kilometres an hour.

Leaving the station of Tchontchai behind, we enter station at nine o'clock in the evening. The stoppage is to last two hours. We get out onto the platform.

As we are leaving the car I am near Major Noltitz, who asks young Pan Chao:

"Have you ever heard of this mandarin Yen Lou, whose body is being taken to Pekin?"

"Never, major."

"But he ought to be a personage of consideration, to be treated with the honor he gets."

"That is possible," said Pan Chao; "but we have so many personages of consideration in the Celestial Empire."

"And so, this mandarin, Yen Lou?"

"I never heard him mentioned."

Why did Major Noltitz ask the Chinaman this question? What was he thinking about?

CHAPTER XV

Kokhan, two hours to stop. It is night. The majority of the travelers have already taken up their sleeping quarters in the car, and do not care to alight.

Here am I on the platform, walking the deck as I smoke. This is rather an important station, and from the engine house comes a more powerful locomotive than those which have brought the train along since we left Uzun Ada. These early engines were all very well as long as the line lay over an almost horizontal plain. But now we are among the gorges of the Pamir plateau, there are gradients of such steepness as to require more engine power.

I watch the proceedings, and when the locomotive has been detached with its tender, the baggage van—with Kinko in—is at the head of the train.

The idea occurs to me that the young Roumanian may perhaps venture out on the platform. It would be an imprudence for he runs the risk of being seen by the police, the "gardovois," who move about taking a good look at the passengers. What my No. 11 had better do is to remain in his box, or at least in his van. I will go and get a few provisions, liquid and solid, and take them to him, even before the departure of the train, if it is possible to do so without fear of being noticed.

The refreshment room at the station is open, and Popof is not there. If he was to see me making purchases he would be astonished, as the dining car contains everything we might want.

At the bar I get a little cold meat, some bread, and a bottle of vodka.

The station is not well lighted. A few lamps give only a feeble light. Popof is busy with one of the railway men. The new engine has not yet been attached to the train. The moment seems favorable. It is useless to wait until we have left. If I can reach Kinko I shall be able to sleep through the night—and that will be welcome, I admit.

I step onto the train, and after assuring myself that no one is watching me, I enter the baggage van, saying as I do so:

"It is I."

In fact it is as well to warn Kinko in case he is out of his box.

But he had not thought of getting out, and I advise him to be very careful.

He is very pleased at the provisions, for they are a change to his usual diet.

"I do not know how to thank you, Monsieur Bombarnac," he says to me.

"If you do not know, friend Kinko," I reply, "do not do it; that is very simple."

"How long do we stop at ?"

"Two hours."

"And when shall we be at the frontier?"

"To-morrow, about one in the afternoon."

"And at Kachgar?"

"Fifteen hours afterward, in the night of the nineteenth."

"There the danger is, Monsieur Bombarnac."

"Yes, Kinko; for if it is difficult to enter the Russian possessions, it is no less difficult to get out of them, when the Chinese are at the gates. Their officials will give us a good look over before they will let us pass. At the same time they examine the passengers much more closely than they do their baggage. And as this van is reserved for the luggage going through to Pekin, I do not think you have much to fear. So good night. As a matter of precaution, I would rather not prolong my visit."

"Good night, Monsieur Bombarnac, good night."

I have come out, I have regained my couch, and I really did not hear the starting signal when the train began to move.

The only station of any importance which the railway passed before sunrise, was that of Marghelan, where the stoppage was a short one.

Marghelan, a populous town—sixty thousand inhabitants—is the real capital of Ferganah. That is owing to the fact that does not enjoy a good reputation for salubrity. It is of course, a double town, one town Russian, the other Turkoman. The latter has no ancient monuments, and no curiosities, and my readers must pardon my not having interrupted my sleep to give them a glance at it.

Following the valley of Schakhimardan, the train has reached a sort of steppe and been able to resume its normal speed.

At three o'clock in the morning we halt for forty-five minutes at Och station.

There I failed in my duty as a reporter, and I saw nothing. My excuse is that there was nothing to see.

Beyond this station the road reaches the frontier which divides Russian Turkestan from the Pamir plateau and the vast territory of the Kara-Khirghizes.

This part of Central Asia is continually being troubled by Plutonian disturbances beneath its surface. Northern Turkestan has frequently suffered from earthquake—the terrible experience of 1887 will not have been forgotten—and at Tachkend, as at Samarkand, I saw the traces of these commotions. In fact, minor oscillations are continually being observed, and this volcanic action takes place all along the fault, where lay the stores of petroleum and naphtha, from the Caspian Sea to the Pamir plateau.

In short, this region is one of the most interesting parts of Central Asia that a tourist can visit. If Major Noltitz had never been beyond Och station, at the foot of the plateau, he knew the district from having studied it on the modern maps and in the most recent books of travels. Among these I would mention those of Capus and Bonvalot—again two French names I am happy to salute out of France. The major is, nevertheless, anxious to see the country for himself, and although it is not yet six o'clock in the morning, we are both out on the gangway, glasses in hand, maps under our eyes.

The Pamir, or Bam-i-Douniah, is commonly called the "Roof of the World." From it radiate the mighty chains of the Thian Shan, of the Kuen Lun, of the Kara Korum, of the Himalaya, of the Hindoo Koosh. This orographic system, four hundred kilometres across, which remained for so many years an impassable barrier, has been surmounted by Russian tenacity. The Sclav race and the Yellow race have come into contact.

We may as well have a little book learning on the subject; but it is not I that speak, but Major Noltitz.

The travelers of the Aryan people have all attempted to explore the plateau of the Pamir. Without going back to Marco Polo in the thirteenth century, what do we find? The English with Forsyth, Douglas, Biddulph, Younghusband, and the celebrated Gordon who died on the Upper Nile; the Russians with Fendchenko, Skobeleff, Prjevalsky, Grombtchevsky, General Pevtzoff, Prince Galitzin, the brothers Groum-Grjimailo; the French with Auvergne, Bonvalot, Capus, Papin, Breteuil, Blanc, Ridgway, O'Connor, Dutreuil de Rhins, Joseph Martin, Grenard, Edouard Blanc; the Swedes with Doctor Swen-Hedin.

This Roof of the World, one would say that some devil on two sticks had lifted it up in his magic hand to let us see its mysteries. We know now that it consists of an inextricable entanglement of valleys, the mean altitude of which exceeds three thousand metres; we know that it is dominated by the peaks of Gouroumdi and Kauffmann, twenty-two thousand feet high, and the peak of Tagarma, which is twenty-seven thousand feet; we know that it sends off to the west the Oxus and the Amou Daria, and to the east the Tarim; we know that it chiefly consists of primary rocks, in which are patches of schist and quartz, red sands of secondary age, and the clayey, sandy loess of the quaternary period which is so abundant in Central Asia.

The difficulties the Grand Transasiatic had in crossing this plateau were extraordinary. It was a challenge from the genius of man to nature, and the victory remained with genius. Through the gently sloping passes which the Kirghizes call "bels," viaducts, bridges, embankments, cuttings, tunnels had to be made to carry the line. Here are sharp curves, gradients which require the most powerful locomotives, here and there stationary engines to haul up the train with cables, in a word, a herculean labor, superior to the works of the American engineers in the defiles of the Sierra Nevada and the Rocky Mountains.

The desolate aspect of these territories makes a deep impression on the imagination. As the train gains the higher altitudes, this impression is all the more vivid. There are no towns, no villages—nothing but a few scattered huts, in which the Pamirian lives a solitary existence with his family, his horses, his herds of yaks, or "koutars," which are cattle with horses' tails, his diminutive sheep, his thick-haired goats. The moulting of these animals, if we may so phrase it, is a natural consequence of the climate, and they change the dressing gown of winter for the white fur coat of summer. It is the same with the dog, whose coat becomes whiter in the hot season.

As the passes are ascended, wide breaks in the ranges yield frequent glimpses of the more distant portions of the plateau. In many places are clumps of birches and junipers, which are the principal trees of the Pamir, and on the undulating plains grow tamarisks and sedges and mugwort, and a sort of reed very abundant by the sides of the saline pools, and a dwarf labiate called "terskenne" by the Kirghizes.

The major mentioned certain animals which constitute a somewhat varied fauna on the heights of the Pamir. It is even necessary to keep an eye on the platforms of the cars in case a stray panther or bear might seek a ride without any right to travel either first or second class. During the day our companions were on the lookout from both ends of the cars. What shouts arose when plantigrades or felines capered along the line with intentions that certainly seemed suspicious! A few revolver shots were discharged, without much necessity perhaps, but they amused as well as reassured the travelers. In the afternoon we were witnesses of a magnificent shot, which killed instantly an enormous panther just as he was landing on the side step of the third carriage.

"It is thine, Marguerite!" exclaimed Caterna. And could he have better expressed his admiration than in appropriating the celebrated reply of Buridan to the Dauphine's wife—and not the queen of France, as is wrongly stated in the famous drama of the *Tour de Nesle?*

It was our superb Mongol to whom we were indebted for this marksman's masterpiece.

"What a hand and what an eye!" said I to the major, who continued to look on Faruskiar with suspicion.

Among the other animals of the Pamirian fauna appeared wolves and foxes, and flocks of those large wild sheep with gnarled and gracefully curved horns, which are known to the natives as arkars. High in the sky flew the vultures, bearded and unbearded, and amid the clouds of white vapor we left behind us were many crows and pigeons and turtledoves and wagtails.

The day passed without adventure. At six o'clock in the evening we crossed the frontier, after a run of nearly two thousand three hundred kilometres, accomplished in four days since leaving Uzun Ada. Two hundred and fifty kilometres beyond we shall be at Kachgar. Although we are now in Chinese Turkestan, it will not be till we reach that town that we shall have our first experience of Chinese administration.

Dinner over about nine o'clock, we stretched ourselves on our beds, in the hope, or rather the conviction, that the night will be as calm as the preceding one.

It was not to be so.

At first the train was running down the slopes of the Pamir at great speed. Then it resumed its normal rate along the level.

It was about one in the morning when I was suddenly awakened.

At the same time Major Noltitz and most of our companions jumped up.

There were loud shouts in the rear of the train.

What had happened?

Anxiety seized upon the travelers—that confused, unreasonable anxiety caused by the slightest incident on a railroad.

"What is the matter? What is the matter?"

These words were uttered in alarm from all sides and in different languages.

My first thought was that we were attacked. I thought of the famous Ki-Tsang, the Mongol pirate, whose help I had so imprudently called upon—for my chronicle.

In a moment the train began to slow, evidently preparing to stop.

Popof came into the van, and I asked him what had happened.

"An accident," he replied.

"Serious?"

"No, a coupling has broken, and the two last vans are left behind."

As soon as the train pulls up, a dozen travelers, of whom I am one, get out onto the track.

By the light of the lantern it is easy to see that the breakage is not due to malevolence. But it is none the less true that the two last vans, the mortuary van and the rear van occupied by the goods guard, are missing. How far off are they? Nobody knows.

You should have heard the shouts of the Persian guards engaged in escorting the remains of Yen Lou, for which they were responsible! The travelers in their van, like themselves, had not noticed when the coupling broke. It might be an hour, two hours, since the accident.

What ought to be done was clear enough. The train must be run backward and pick up the lost vans.

Nothing could be more simple. But—and this surprised me—the behavior of my lord Faruskiar seemed very strange. He insisted in the most pressing manner that not a moment should be lost. He spoke to Popof, to the driver, to the stoker, and for the first time I discovered that he spoke Russian remarkably well.

There was no room for discussion. We were all agreed on the necessity of a retrograde movement.

Only the German baron protested. More delays! A waste of time for the sake of a mandarin—and a dead mandarin!

He had to walk about and bear it. As to Sir Francis Trevellyan, he merely shrugged his shoulders, as much as to say: "What management! What couplings! We should not get this sort of thing on an Anglo-Indian line!"

Major Noltitz was as much struck as I was at the behavior of my lord Faruskiar. This Mongol, usually so calm, so impassible, with his cool look beneath his motionless eyelid, had become a prey to a sort of furious anxiety which he appeared incapable of controlling. His companion was as excited as he was. But what was there in these two missing vans which could be of interest to them? They had not even any luggage in the rear van! Was it the mandarin, Yen Lou? Was it for that reason that at Donchak they had so carefully watched the van which contained the corpse? I could see clearly enough that the major thought it all very suspicious.

The train began to run back as soon as we had taken our places. The German baron attempted to curse, but Faruskiar gave him such a look that he did not care to get another, and stowed himself away in the corner.

Dawn appeared in the east when the two wagons were found a kilometre off, and the train gently slowed up to them after an hour's run.

Faruskiar and Ghangir went to help in coupling on the vans, which was done as firmly as possible. Major Noltitz and I noticed that they exchanged a few words with the other Mongols. After all, there was nothing astonishing in that, for they were countrymen of theirs.

We resume our seats in the train, and the engineer tries to make up for lost time.

Nevertheless, the train does not arrive at Kachgar without a long delay, and it is half-past four in the morning when we enter the capital of Chinese Turkestan.

Chapter XVI

Kachgaria is Oriental Turkestan which is gradually being metamorphosed into Russian Turkestan.

The writers in the *New Review* have said: "Central Asia will only be a great country when the Muscovite administration have laid hands on Tibet, or when the Russians lord it at Kachgar."

Well, that is a thing half done! The piercing of the Pamir has joined the Russian railway with the Chinese line which runs from one frontier of the Celestial Empire to the other. The capital of Kachgaria is now as much Russian as Chinese. The Sclav race and the Yellow race have rubbed elbows and live in peace. How long will it last? To others leave the future; I am content with the present.

We arrive at half-past four; we leave at eleven. The Grand Transasiatic shows itself generous. I shall have time to see Kachgar, on condition of allowing myself an hour less than the time stated.

For what was not done at the frontier has to be done at Kachgar. Russians and Chinese are one as bad as the other when there are vexing formalities; papers to verify, passports to sign, etc., etc. It is the same sort of meddling, minute and over-fastidious, and we must put up with it. We must not forget the terrible threat of the formula the functionary of the Celestial Empire affixes to his acts—"Tremble and obey!" I am disposed to obey, and I am prepared to appear before the authorities of the frontier. I remember the fears of Kinko, and it is with regard to him that the trembling is to be done, if the examination of the travelers extends to their packages and luggage.

Before we reached Kachgar, Major Noltitz said to me:

"Do not imagine that Chinese Turkestan differs very much from Russian Turkestan. We are not in the land of pagodas, junks, flower boats, yamens, hongs and porcelain towers. Like Bokhara, Merv and Samarkand, Kachgar is a double town. It is with the Central Asian cities as it is with certain stars, only they do not revolve round one another."

The major's remark was very true. It was not so long ago since emirs reigned over Kachgaria, since the monarchy of Mohammed Yakoub extended over the whole of Turkestan, since the Chinese who wished to live here had to adjure the religion of Buddha and Confucius and become converts to Mahometanism, that is, if they wished to be respectable. What would you have? In these days we are always too late, and those marvels of the Oriental cosmorama, those curious manners, those masterpieces of Asiatic art, are either memories or ruins. The railways will end by bringing the countries they traverse down to the same level, to a mutual resemblance which will certainly be equality and may be fraternity. In truth, Kachgar is no longer the capital of Kachgaria; it is a station on the Grand Transasiatic, the junction between the Russian and Chinese lines, and the strip of iron which stretches for three thousand kilometres from the Caspian to this city runs on for nearly four thousand more to the capital of the Celestial Empire.

I return to the double town. The new one is Yangi-Chahr: the old one, three and a half miles off, is Kachgar. I have seen both, and I will tell you what they are like.

In the first place, both the old and the new towns are surrounded with a villainous earthen wall that does not predispose you in their favor. Secondly, it is in vain that you seek for any monument whatever, for the materials of construction are identical for houses as for palaces. Nothing but earth, and not even baked earth. It is not with mud dried in the sun that you can obtain regular lines, clean profiles and finely worked sculptures. Your architecture must be in stone or marble, and that is precisely what you do not get in Chinese Turkestan.

A small carriage quickly took the major and myself to Kachgar, which is three miles round. The Kizil-Sou, that is to say the Red River, which is really yellow, as a Chinese river ought to be, clasps it between its two arms, which are united by two bridges. If you wish to see a few ruins of some interest, you must go a short distance beyond the town, where there are the remains of fortifications dating from five hundred or two thousand years ago, according to the imagination of the archaeologist. What is certain is that Kachgar submitted to the furious assault of Tamerlane, and we will agree that without the exploits of this terrible cripple the history of Central Asia would be singularly monotonous. Since his time there have been fierce sultans, it is true—among others that Ouali-Khan-Toulla, who, in 1857, strangled Schlagintweit, one of the most learned and most daring explorers of the Asiatic continent. Two tablets of bronze, presented by the Geographical Societies of Paris and Petersburg, ornament his commemorative monument.

Kachgar is an important centre of trade, which is almost entirely in Russian hands. Khotan silks, cotton, felt, woolen carpets, cloth, are the principal articles in the markets, and these are exported beyond the frontier between Tachkend and Koulja, to the north of Oriental Turkestan.

Here, as the major told me, Sir Francis Trevellyan should have special cause for manifesting his ill humor. In fact, an English embassy under Chapman and Gordon in 1873 and 1874 had been sent from Kashmir to Kachgar by way of Kothan and Yarkand. At this time the English had reason to hope that commercial relations could be established to their advantage. But instead of being in communication with the Indian railways, the Russian railways are in communication with the Chinese, and the result of this junction has been that English influence has had to give place to Russian.

The population of Kachgar is Turkoman, with a considerable mixture of Chinese, who willingly fulfil the duties of domestics, artisans or porters. Less fortunate than Chapman and Gordon, Major Noltitz and I were not able to see the Kachgarian capital when the armies of the tumultuous emir filled its streets. There were none of those Djiguit foot soldiers who were mounted, nor of those Sarbaz who were not. Vanished had those magnificent bodies of Taifourchis, armed and disciplined in the Chinese manner, those superb lancers, those Kalmuck archers, bending bows five feet high, those "tigers" with their daubed shields and their matchlocks. All have disappeared, the picturesque warriors of Kachgaria and the emir with them.

At nine o'clock we are on our return to Yangi-Chahr. There, at the end of the streets near the citadel, what do we see? The Caternas in ecstatic admiration before a troop of musical dervishes.

Who says dervish says beggar, and who says beggar evokes the completest type of filth and laziness. But with what an extraordinary combination of gestures, with what attitudes in the management of the long-stringed guitar, with what acrobatic swingings of the body do they accompany their singing of their legends and poetry which could not be more profane. The instinct of the old actor was awakened in Caterna. He could not keep still; it was too much for him.

III

And so these gestures, these attitudes, these swingings he imitated there with the vigor of an old topman joined to that of a leading premier, and I saw him as he was figuring in this quadrille of dancing dervishes.

"Eh! Monsieur Claudius!" he said, "it is not difficult to copy the exercises of these gallant fellows! Make me a Turkestan operetta, let me act a dervish, and you will see if I don't do it to the very life."

"I do not doubt it, my dear Caterna," I replied; "but before you do that, come into the restaurant at the railway station and bid farewell to Turkestan cookery, for we shall soon be reduced to Chinese."

The offer is accepted all the more willingly, for the reputation of the Kachgarian cooks is well justified, as the major made us remark.

In fact, the Caternas, the major, young Pan Chao and I were astonished and enchanted at the quantity of dishes that were served us, as well as at their quality. Sweets alternated capriciously with roasts and grills. And as the Caternas could never forget—any more than they could forget the famous peaches of Khodjend—there are a few of these dishes which the English embassy wished to retain in remembrance, for they have given the composition in the story of their journey: pigs' feet dusted with sugar and browned in fat with a dash of pickles; kidneys fried with sweet sauce and served with fritters.

Caterna asked for the first twice, and for the other three times.

"I take my precautions," said he. "Who knows what the dining-car kitchen will give us on the Chinese railways? Let us beware of shark fins, which may perhaps be rather horny, and of swallows' nests which may not be quite fresh!"

It is ten o'clock when a stroke of the gong announces that the police formalities are about to begin. We leave the table after a parting glass of Choa-Hing wine, and a few minutes afterward are in the waiting room.

All my numbers are present, with the exception, of course, of Kinko, who would have done honor to our breakfast if it had been possible for him to take part in it. There was Doctor Tio-King, his *Cornaro* under his arm; Fulk Ephrinell and Miss Horatia Bluett, mingling their teeth and hair, figuratively, be it understood; Sir Francis Trevellyan, motionless and silent, intractable and stiff, smoking his cigar on the threshold; Faruskiar, accompanied by Ghangir; Russian, Turkoman, Chinese travelers—in all from sixty to eighty persons. Every one had in his turn to present himself at the table, which was occupied by two Celestials in uniform; a functionary speaking Russian fluently, an interpreter for German, French and English.

The Chinese was a man about fifty, with a bald head, a thick moustache, a long pigtail, and spectacles on his nose. Wrapped in a flowery robe, fat as if he belonged to the most distinguished people in the country, he had not a prepossessing face. After all, it was only a verification of our papers, and as ours were in order it did not much matter how repulsive he looked.

"What an air he has!" murmured Madame Caterna.

"The air of a Chinaman!" said her husband, "and frankly I do not want to have one like it."

I am one of the first to present my passport, which bears the visas of the consul at Tiflis and the Russian authorities at Uzun-Ada. The functionary looks at it attentively. When you are dealing with a mandarin, you should always be on the lookout. Nevertheless, the examination raises no difficulty, and the seal of the green dragon declares me all in order.

The same result with regard to the actor and actress. Nevertheless it was worth while looking at Caterna while his papers were being examined. He assumed the attitude of a criminal endeavoring to mollify a magistrate, he made the sheepiest of eyes, and smiled the most deprecating of smiles, and seemed to implore a grace or rather a favor, and yet the most obdurate of the Chinamen had not a word to say to him.

"Correct," said the interpreter.

"Thank you, my prince!" replied Caterna, with the accent of a Paris street boy.

As to Ephrinell and Miss Bluett, they went through like a posted letter. If an American commercial and an English ditto were not in order, who would be? Uncle Sam and John Bull are one as far as that goes.

The other travelers, Russian and Turkoman, underwent examination without any difficulty arising. Whether they were first-class or second-class, they had fulfilled the conditions required by the Chinese administration, which levies a rather heavy fee for each visa, payable in roubles, taels or sapeks.

Among the travelers I noticed an American clergyman bound to Pekin. This was the Reverend Nathaniel Morse, of Boston, one of those honest Bible distributors, a Yankee missionary, in the garb of a merchant, and very keen in business matters. At a venture I make him No. 13 in my notebook.

The verification of the papers of young Pan Chao and Doctor Tio-King gave rise to no difficulty, and on leaving they exchanged "ten thousand good mornings" with the more amiable of the Chinese representatives.

When it came to the turn of Major Noltitz, a slight incident occurred. Sir Francis Trevellyan, who came to the table at the same moment, did not seem inclined to give way. However, nothing resulted but haughty and provoking looks. The gentleman did not even take the trouble to open his mouth. It is evidently written above that I am not to hear the sound of his voice! The Russian and the Englishman each received the regulation visa, and the affair went no further.

My lord Faruskiar, followed by Ghangir, then arrived before the man in spectacles, who looked at him with a certain amount of attention. Major Noltitz and I watched him. How would he submit to this examination? Perhaps we were to be undeceived regarding him.

But what was our surprise and even our stupefaction at the dramatic outburst which at once took place!

After throwing a glance at the papers presented to him by Ghangir, the Chinese functionary rose and bowed respectfully to Faruskiar, saying:

"May the General Manager of the Grand Transasiatic deign to receive my ten thousand respects!"

General Manager, that is what he is, this lord Faruskiar! All is explained. During our crossing of Russian Turkestan he had maintained his *incognito* like a great personage in a foreign country; but now on the Chinese railways he resumed the rank which belonged to him.

And I—in a joke, it is true—had permitted myself to identify him with the pirate Ki-Tsang. And Major Noltitz, who had spent his time suspecting him! At last I have some one of note in our train—I have him, this somebody, I will make his acquaintance, I will cultivate it like a rare plant, and if he will only speak Russian I will interview him down to his boots!

Good! I am completely upset, and I could not help shrugging my shoulders, when the major whispers to me:

"Perhaps one of the bandit chiefs with whom the Grand Transasiatic had to make terms!"

"Come, major, be serious."

The visit was nearing its end when Baron Weissschnitzerdoerfer appeared.

He is preoccupied, he is troubled, he is anxious, he is confused, he is fidgety. Why is he shaking, and bending, and diving into his pockets like a man who has lost something valuable?

"Your papers!" demands the interpreter in German.

"My papers!" replies the baron, "I am looking for them. I have not got them; they were in my letter case."

And he dived again into his trousers pockets, his waistcoat pockets, his coat pockets, his great-coat pockets—there were twenty of them at the least—and he found nothing.

"Be quick—be quick!" said the interpreter. "The train cannot wait!"

"I object to its going without me!" exclaimed the baron. "These papers—how have they gone astray? I must have let them drop out of my case. They should have given them back to me—"

At this moment the gong awoke the echoes of the interior of the railway station.

"Wait! wait! Donner vetter! Can't you wait a few moments for a man who is going round the world in thirty-nine days—"

"The Grand Transasiatic does not wait," says the interpreter.

Without waiting for any more, Major Noltitz and I reach the platform, while the baron continues to struggle in the presence of the impassible Chinese functionaries.

I examine the train and see that its composition has been modified on account of there being fewer travelers between Kachgar and Pekin. Instead of twelve carriages, there are now only ten, placed in the following order: engine, tender, front van, two first-class cars, dining car, two second-class cars, the van with the defunct mandarin, rear van.

The Russian locomotives, which have brought us from Uzun-Ada, have been replaced by a Chinese locomotive, burning not naphtha but coal, of which there are large deposits in Turkestan, and stores at the chief stations along the line.

My first care is to look in at the front van. The custom-house officers are about to visit it, and I tremble for poor Kinko.

It is evident that the fraud has not been discovered yet, for there would have been a great stir at the news. Suppose the case is passed? Will its position be shifted? Will it be put hind side before or upside down? Kinko will not then be able to get out, and that would be a complication.

The Chinese officers have come out of the van and shut the door, so that I cannot give a glance into it. The essential point is that Kinko has not been caught in the act. As soon as possible I will enter the van, and as bankers say, "verify the state of the safe."

Before getting into our car, Major Noltitz asks me to follow him to the rear of the train.

The scene we witness is not devoid of interest; it is the giving over of the corpse of the mandarin Yen Lou by the Persian guards to a detachment of soldiers of the Green Standard, who form the Chinese gendarmerie. The defunct passes into the care of twenty Celestials, who are to occupy the second-class car in front of the mortuary van. They are armed with guns and revolvers, and commanded by an officer.

"Well," said I to the major, "this mandarin must be some very exalted personage if the Son of Heaven sends him a guard of honor—"

"Or of defence," replies the major.

Faruskiar and Ghangir assist at these proceedings, in which there is nothing surprising. Surely the general manager of the line ought to keep an eye on the illustrious defunct, entrusted to the care of the Grand Transasiatic?

The gong was struck for the last time; we hasten into our cars.

And the baron, what has become of him?

Here he comes out on to the platform like a whirlwind. He has found his papers at the bottom of his nineteenth pocket. He has obtained the necessary visa—and it was time.

"Passengers for Pekin, take your seats!" shouts Popof in a sonorous voice.

The train trembles, it starts, it has gone.

Chapter XVII

We are off on a Chinese railway, single line, the train drawn by a Chinese engine, driven by a Chinese driver. Let us hope we shall not be telescoped on the road, for among the passengers is one of the chief functionaries of the company in the person of Faruskiar.

After all, if an accident should happen it will break the monotony of the journey, and furnish me with an episode. I am forced to admit that up to the present my personages have not behaved as I expected. The drama does not run well, the action languishes. We want something startling to bring all the actors on—what Caterna would call "a good fourth act."

But then Ephrinell and Miss Bluett are all the time absorbed in their commercial tete-a-tete. Pan Chao and the doctor amused me for a time, but they are not equal to it now. The actor and the actress are of no use without opportunity. Kinko, Kinko himself, on whom I had built such hopes, has passed the frontier without difficulty, he will reach Pekin, he will marry Zinca Klork. Decidedly there is a want of excitement. I cannot get anything out of the corpse of Yen Lou! and the readers of the *Twentieth Century* who looked to me for something sensational and thrilling.

Must I have recourse to the German baron? No! he is merely ridiculous, stupidly ridiculous, and he has no interest for me.

I return to my idea: I want a hero, and up to the present no hero has appeared on the scene.

Evidently the moment has come to enter into more intimate relations with Faruskiar. Perhaps he will not now be so close in his incognito. We are under his orders, so to say. He is the mayor of our rolling town, and a mayor owes something to those he governs. Besides, in the event of Kinko's fraud being discovered I may as well secure the protection of this high functionary.

Our train runs at only moderate speed since we left Kachgar. On the opposite horizon we can see the high lands of the Pamir; to the southwest rises the Bolor, the Kachgarian belt from which towers the summit of Tagharma lost among the clouds.

I do not know how to spend my time. Major Noltitz has never visited the territories crossed by the Grand Transasiatic, and I am deprived of the pleasure of taking notes from his dictation. Dr. Tio-King does not lift his nose from his Cornaro, and Pan Chao reminds me more of Paris and France than of Pekin and China; besides, when he came to Europe he came by Suez, and he knows no more of Oriental Turkestan than he does of Kamtschatka. All the same, we talk. He is a pleasant companion, but a little less amiability and a little more originality would suit me better.

I am reduced to strolling from one car to another, lounging on the platforms, interrogating the horizon, which obstinately refuses to reply, listening on all sides.

Hello! there are the actor and his wife apparently in animated conversation. I approach. They sing in an undertone. I listen.

"*I'm fond of my turkeys—eys—eys,*" says Madame Caterna.

"*I'm fond of my wethers—ers—ers,*" says Monsieur Caterna, in any number of baritones.

It is the everlasting duet between Pipo and Bettina; and they are rehearsing for Shanghai. Happy Shanghai! They do not yet know the *Mascotte!*

Ephrinell and Miss Bluett are talking away with unusual animation, and I catch the end of the dialogue.

"I am afraid," said she, "that hair will be rising in Pekin—"

"And I," said he, "that teeth will be down. Ah! If a good war would only break out in which the Russians would give the Chinaman a smack on the jaw."

There now! Smack them on the jaw, in order that Strong, Bulbul & Co., of New York, might have a chance of doing a trade!

Really I do not know what to do, and we have a week's journey before us. To Jericho with the Grand Transasiatic and its monotonous security! The Great Trunk from New York to San Francisco has more life in it! At least, the redskins do sometimes attack the trains, and the chance of a scalping on the road cannot but add to the charm of the voyage!

But what is that I hear being recited, or rather intoned at the end of our compartment?

"There is no man, whoever he may be, who cannot prevent himself from eating too much, and avoid the evils due to repletion. On those who are intrusted with the direction of public affairs this is more incumbent than on others—"

It is Dr. Tio-King reading Cornaro aloud, in order that he may remember his principles better. Eh! after all, this principle is not to be despised. Shall I send it by telegram to our cabinet ministers? They might, perhaps, dine with more discretion after it.

During this afternoon I find by the guide-book that we shall cross the Yamanyar over a wooden bridge. This stream descends from the mountains to the west, which are at least twenty-five thousand feet high, and its rapidity is increased by the melting of the snows. Sometimes the train runs through thick jungles, amid which Popof assures me tigers are numerous. Numerous they may be, but I have not seen one. And yet in default of redskins we might get some excitement out of tiger-skins. What a heading for a newspaper, and what a stroke of luck for a journalist! TERRIBLE CATASTROPHE. A GRAND TRANSASIATIC EXPRESS ATTACKED BY TIGERS. FIFTY VICTIMS. AN INFANT DEVOURED BEFORE ITS MOTHER'S EYES—the whole thickly leaded and appropriately displayed.

Well, no! The Turkoman felidae did not give me even that satisfaction! And I treat them—as I treat any other harmless cats.

The two principal stations have been Yanghi-Hissar, where the train stops ten minutes, and Kizil, where it stops a quarter of an hour. Several blast furnaces are at work here, the soil being ferruginous, as is shown by the word "Kizil," which means red.

The country is fertile and well cultivated, growing wheat, maize, rice, barley and flax, in its eastern districts. Everywhere are great masses of trees, willows, mulberries, poplars. As far as the eye can reach are fields under culture, irrigated by numerous canals, also green fields in which are flocks of sheep; a country half Normandy, half Provence, were it not for the mountains of the Pamir on the horizon.

But this portion of Kachgaria was terribly ravaged by war when its people were struggling for independence. The land flowed with blood, and along by the railway the ground is dotted with tumuli beneath which are buried the victims of their patriotism. But I did not come to Central Asia to travel as if I were in France! Novelty! Novelty! The unforeseen! The appalling!

It was without the shadow of an accident, and after a particularly fine run, that we entered Yarkand station at four o'clock in the afternoon.

If Yarkand is not the administrative capital of eastern Turkestan, it is certainly the most important commercial city of the province.

"Again two towns together," said I to Major Noltitz. "That I have from Popof."

"But this time," said the major, "it was not the Russians who built the new one."

"New or old," I added, "I am afraid is like the others we have seen, a wall of earth, a few dozen gateways cut in the wall, no monuments or buildings of note, and the eternal bazaars of the East."

I was not mistaken, and it did not take four hours to visit both Yarkands, the newer of which is called Yanji-Shahr.

Fortunately, the Yarkand women are not forbidden to appear in the streets, which are bordered by simple mud huts, as they were at the time of the "dadkwahs," or governors of the province. They can give themselves the pleasure of seeing and being seen, and this pleasure is shared in by the farangis—as they call foreigners, no matter to what nation they may belong. They are very pretty, these Asiatics, with their long tresses, their transversely striped bodices, their skirts of bright colors, relieved by Chinese designs in Kothan silk, their high-heeled embroidered boots, their turbans of coquettish pattern, beneath which appear their black hair and their eyebrows united by a bar.

A few Chinese passengers alighted at Yarkand, and gave place to others exactly like them—among others a score of coolies—and we started again at eight o'clock in the evening.

During the night we ran the three hundred and fifty kilometres which separate Yarkand from Kothan.

A visit I paid to the front van showed me that the box was still in the same place. A certain snoring proved that Kinko was inside as usual, and sleeping peacefully. I did not care to wake him, and I left him to dream of his adorable Roumanian.

In the morning Popof told me that the train, which was now traveling about as fast as an omnibus, had passed Kargalik, the junction for the Kilian and Tong branches. The night had been cold, for we are still at an altitude of twelve hundred metres. Leaving Guma station, the line runs due east and west, following the thirty-seventh parallel, the same which traverses in Europe, Seville, Syracuse and Athens.

We sighted only one stream of importance, the Kara-kash, on which appeared a few drifting rafts, and files of horses and asses at the fords between the pebbly banks. The railroad crosses it about a hundred kilometres from Khotan, where we arrived at eight o'clock in the morning.

Two hours to stop, and as the town may give me a foretaste of the cities of China, I resolve to take a run through it.

It seems to be a Turkoman town built by the Chinese, or perhaps a Chinese town built by Turkomans. Monuments and inhabitants betray their double origin. The mosques look like pagodas, the pagodas look like mosques.

And I was not astonished when the Caternas, who would not miss this opportunity of setting foot in China, were rather disappointed.

"Monsieur Claudius," said the actor to me, "there is not a single scene here that would suit the *Prise de Pekin!*"

"But we are not at Pekin, my dear Caterna."

"That is true, and it has to be remembered, if we are to be thankful for little."

"'Thankful for very little,' as the Italians say."

"Well, if they say that, they are no fools."

As we were about to board the car again, I saw Popof running toward me, shouting:

"Monsieur Bombarnac!"

"What is the matter, Popof?"

"A telegraph messenger asked me if there was any one belonging to the *Twentieth Century* in the train."

"A telegraph messenger?"

"Yes, on my replying in the affirmative, he gave me this telegram for you."

"Give it me! give it me!"

I seize the telegram, which has been waiting for me for some days. Is it a reply to my wire sent from Merv, relative to the mandarin Yen Lou?

I open it. I read it. And it falls from my hand.

This is what it said:

"CLAUDIUS BOMBARNAC,
"*Correspondent,*
"*Twentieth Century.*
"*Khotan, Chinese Turkestan.*

"*It is not the corpse of a mandarin that the train is taking to Pekin, but the imperial treasure, value fifteen millions, sent from Persia to China, as announced in the Paris newspapers eight days ago; endeavor to be better informed for the future.*"

Chapter XVIII

"**M**illions—there are millions in that pretended mortuary van!" In spite of myself, this imprudent phrase had escaped me in such a way that the secret of the imperial treasure was instantly known to all, to the railway men as well as to the passengers. And so, for greater security, the Persian government, in agreement with the Chinese government, has allowed it to be believed that we were carrying the corpse of a mandarin, when we were really taking to Pekin a treasure worth fifteen million of francs.

Heaven pardon me, what a howler—pardonable assuredly—but what a howler I had been guilty of! But why should I have doubted what Popof told me, and why should Popof have suspected what the Persians had told him regarding this Yen Lou? There was no reason for our doubting their veracity.

I am none the less deeply humiliated in my self-esteem as a journalist, and I am much annoyed at the call to order which I have brought upon myself. I shall take very good care not to breathe a word of my misadventure, even to the major. Is it credible? In Paris the *Twentieth Century* is better informed of what concerns the Grand Transasiatic than I am! They knew that an imperial treasure is in the van, and I did not! Oh! the mistakes of special correspondents!

Now the secret is divulged, and we know that this treasure, composed of gold and precious stones, formerly deposited in the hands of the Shah of Persia, is being sent to its legitimate owner, the Son of Heaven.

That is why my lord Faruskiar, who was aware of it in consequence of his position as general manager of the company, had joined the train at Douchak so as to accompany the treasure to its destination. That is why he and Ghangir—and the three other Mongols—had so carefully watched this precious van, and why they had shown themselves so anxious when it had been left behind by the breakage of the coupling, and why they were so eager for its recovery. Yes, all is explained!

That is also why a detachment of Chinese soldiers has taken over the van at Kachgar, in relief of the Persians! That is why Pan-Chao never heard of Yen Lou, nor of any exalted personage of that name existing in the Celestial Empire!

We started to time, and, as may be supposed, our traveling companions could talk of nothing else but the millions which were enough to enrich every one in the train.

"This pretended mortuary van has always been suspicious to me," said Major Noltitz. "And that was why I questioned Pan-Chao regarding the dead mandarin."

"I remember," I said; "and I could not quite understand the motive of your question. It is certain now that we have got a treasure in tow."

"And I add," said the major, "that the Chinese government has done wisely in sending an escort of twenty well-armed men. From Kothan to Lan Teheou the trains will have two thousand kilometres to traverse through the desert, and the safety of the line is not as great as it might be across the Gobi."

"All the more so, major, as the redoubtable Ki-Tsang has been reported in the northern provinces."

"Quite so, and a haul of fifteen millions is worth having by a bandit chief."

"But how could the chief be informed of the treasure being sent?"

"That sort of people always know what it is their interest to know."

"Yes," thought I, "although they do not read the *Twentieth Century*."

Meanwhile different opinions were being exchanged on the gangways. Some would rather travel with the millions than carry a corpse along with them, even though it was that of a first-class mandarin. Others considered the carrying of the treasure a danger to the passengers. And that was the opinion of Baron Weissschnitzerdoerfer in a furious attack on Popof.

"You ought to have told us about it, sir, you ought to have told us about it! Those millions are known to be in the train, and they will tempt people to attack us. And an attack, even if repulsed, will mean delay, and delay I will not submit to! No, sir, I will not!"

"No one will attack us," replied Popof. "No one will dream of doing it!"

"And how do you know that? how do you know that?"

"Be calm, pray."

"I will not be calm; and if there is a delay, I will hold the company responsible!"

That is understood; a hundred thousand florins damages to Monsieur le Baron Tour de Monde.

Let us pass to the other passengers.

Ephrinell looked at the matter, of course, from a very practical point of view.

"There can be no doubt that our risks have been greatly increased by this treasure, and in case of accident on account of it, the *Life Travelers' Society*, in which I am insured, will, I expect, refuse to pay, so that the Grand Transasiatic Company will have all the responsibility."

"Of course," said Miss Bluett; "and if they had not found the missing van the company would have been in a serious difficulty with China. Would it not, Fulk?"

"Exactly, Horatia!"

Horatia and Fulk—nothing less.

The Anglo-American couple were right, the enormous loss would have had to be borne by the Grand Transasiatic, for the company must have known they were carrying a treasure and not a corpse—and thereby they were responsible.

As to the Caternas, the millions rolling behind did not seem to trouble them. The only reflection they inspired was, "Ah! Caroline, what a splendid theater we might build with all that money!"

But the best thing was said by the Reverend Nathaniel Morse, who had joined the train at Kachgar.

"It is never comfortable to be dragging a powder magazine after one!"

Nothing could be truer, and this van with its imperial treasure was a powder magazine that might blow up our train.

The first railway was opened in China about 1877 and ran from Shanghai to Fou-Tcheou. The Grand Transasiatic followed very closely the Russian road proposed in 1874 by Tachkend, Kouldja, Kami, Lan Tcheou, Singan and Shanghai. This railway did not run through the populous central provinces which can be compared to vast and humming hives of bees—and extaordinarily prolific bees. As before curving off to Lan Tcheou; it reaches the great cities by the branches it gives out to the south and southeast. Among others, one of these branches, that from Tai Youan to Nanking, should have put these two towns of the

Chan-Si and Chen-Toong provinces into communication. But at present the branch is not ready for opening, owing to an important viaduct not having finished building.

The completed portion gives me direct communication across Central Asia. That is the main line of the Transasiatic. The engineers did not find it so difficult of construction as General Annenkof did the Transcaspian. The deserts of Kara Koum and Gobi are very much alike; the same dead level, the same absence of elevations and depressions, the same suitability for the iron road. If the engineers had had to attack the enormous chain of the Kuen Lun, Nan Chan, Amie, Gangar Oola, which forms the frontier of Tibet, the obstacles would have been such that it would have taken a century to surmount them. But on a flat, sandy plain the railway could be rapidly pushed on up to Lan Tcheou, like a long Decauville of three thousand kilometres.

It is only in the vicinity of this city that the art of the engineer has had a serious struggle with nature in the costly and troublesome road through the provinces of Kan-Sou, Chan-Si and Petchili.

As we go along I must mention a few of the principal stations at which the train stops to take in coal and water. On the right-hand side the eye never tires of the distant horizon of mountains which bounds the tableland of Tibet to the north. On the left the view is over the interminable steppes of the Gobi. The combination of these territories constitutes the Chinese Empire if not China proper, and we shall only reach that when we are in the neighborhood of Lan Tcheou.

It would seem, therefore, as though the second part of the journey would be rather uninteresting, unless we are favored with a few startling incidents. But it seems to me that we are certainly in the possession of the elements out of which something journalistic can be made.

At eleven o'clock the train left Kothan station, and it was nearly two o'clock in the afternoon when it reached Keria, having left behind the small stations of Urang, Langar, Pola and Tschiria.

In 1889-90 this road was followed by Pevtsoff from Kothan to Lob-Nor at the foot of the Kuen Lun, which divides Chinese Turkestan from Tibet. The Russian traveler went by Keria, Nia, Tchertchen, as we are doing so easily, but then his caravan had to contend with much danger and difficulty—which did not prevent his reporting ten thousand kilometres of surveys, without reckoning altitude and longitude observations of the geographical points. It is an honor for the Russian government to have thus continued the work of Prjevalsky.

From Keria station you can see to the southwest the heights of Kara Korum and the peak of Dapsang, to which different geographers assign a height of eight thousand metres. At its foot extends the province of Kachmir. There the Indus rises in a number of inconsiderable sources which feed one of the greatest rivers of the Peninsula. Thence from the Pamir tableland extends the mighty range of the Himalaya, where rise the highest summits on the face of the globe.

Since we left Kothan we have covered a hundred and fifty kilometres in four hours. It is not a high rate of speed, but we cannot expect on this part of the Transasiatic the same rate of traveling we experienced on the Transcaspian. Either the Chinese engines are not so fast, or, thanks to their natural indolence, the engine drivers imagine that from thirty to forty miles an hour is the maximum that can be obtained on the railways of the Celestial Empire.

At five o'clock in the afternoon we were at another station, Nia, where General Pevtsoff established a meterological observatory. Here we stopped only twenty minutes. I had time to lay in a few provisions at the bar. For whom they were intended you can imagine.

The passengers we picked up were only Chinese, men and women. There were only a few for the first class, and these only went short journeys.

We had not started a quarter of an hour when Ephrinell, with the sferious manner of a merchant intent on some business, came up to me on the gangway.

"Monsieur Bombarnac," he said, "I have to ask a favor of you."

Eh! I thought, this Yankee knows where to find me when he wants me.

"Only too happy, I can assure you," said I. "What is it about?"

"I want you to be a witness—"

"An affair of honor? And with whom, if you please?"

"Miss Horatia Bluett."

"You are going to fight Miss Bluett!" I exclaimed, with a laugh.

"Not yet. I am going to marry her."

"Marry her?"

"Yes! a treasure of a woman, well acquainted with business matters, holding a splendid commission—"

"My compliments, Mr. Ephrinell! You can count on me—"

"And probably on M. Caterna?"

"He would like nothing better, and if there is a wedding breakfast he will sing at your dessert—"

"As much as he pleases," replied the American. "And now for Miss Bluett's witnesses."

"Quite so."

"Do you think Major Noltitz would consent?"

"A Russian is too gallant to refuse. I will ask him, if you like."

"Thank you in advance. As to the second witness, I am rather in a difficulty. This Englishman, Sir Francis Trevellyan—"

"A shake of the head is all you will get from him."

"Baron Weissschnitzerdoerfer?"

"Ask that of a man who is doing a tour of the globe, and who would never get through a signature of a name of that length!"

"Then I can only think of Pan-Chao, unless we try Popof—"

"Either would do it with pleasure. But there is no hurry, Mr. Ephrinell, and when you get to Pekin you will have no difficulty in finding a fourth witness."

"What! to Pekin? It is not at Pekin that I hope to marry Miss Bluett!"

"Where, then? At Sou Tcheou or Lan Tcheou, while we stop a few hours?"

"Wait a bit, Monsieur Bombarnac! Can a Yankee wait?"

"Then it is to be—"

"Here."

"In the train?"

"In the train."

"Then it is for me to say, Wait a bit!"

"Not twenty-four hours."

"But to be married you require—"

"An American minister, and we have the Reverend Nathaniel Morse."

"He consents?"

"As if he would not! He would marry the whole train if it asked him!"

"Bravo, Mr. Ephrinell! A wedding in a train will be delightful."

"We should never put off until to-morrow what we can do to-day."

"Yes, I know, time is money."

"No! Time is time, simply, and I do not care to lose a minute of it."

Ephrinell clasped my hand, and as I had promised, I went to take the necessary steps regarding the witnesses necessary for the nuptial ceremonial.

It needs not be said that the commercials were of full age and free to dispose of themselves, to enter into marriage before a clergyman, as is done in America, and without any of the fastidious preliminaries required in France and other formalistic countries. Is this an advantage or otherwise? The Americans think it is for the best, and, as Cooper says, the best at home is the best everywhere.

I first asked Major Noltitz, who willingly agreed to be Miss Bluett's witness.

"These Yankees are astonishing," he said to me.

"Precisely because they are astonished at nothing, major."

I made a similar proposition to Pan-Chao.

"Delighted, Monsieur Bombarnac," he replied. "I will be the witness of this adorable and adored Miss Bluett! If a wedding between an Englishwoman and an American, with French, Russian and Chinese witnesses, does not offer every guarantee of happiness, where are we likely to meet with it?"

And now for Caterna.

The actor would have consented for any number of weddings.

"What a notion for a vaudeville or an operetta!" he exclaimed. "We have the *Mariage au tambour*, the *Mariage aux olives*, the *Mariage aux lanternes*—well, this will be the *Mariage en railway*, or the Marriage by Steam! Good titles, all those, Monsieur Claudius! Your Yankee can reckon on me! Witness old or young, noble father or first lover, marquis or peasant, as you like, I am equal to it—"

"Be natural, please," said I. "It will have a good effect, considering the scenery."

"Is Madame Caterna to come to the wedding?"

"Why not—as bridesmaid!"

In all that concerns the traditional functions we must have no difficulties on the Grand Transasiatic.

It is too late for the ceremony to take place to-day. Ephrinell understood that certain conventionalities must be complied with. The celebration could take place in the morning. The passengers could all be invited, and Faruskiar might be prevailed on to honor the affair with his presence.

During dinner we talked of nothing else. After congratulating the happy couple, who replied with true Anglo-Saxon grace, we all promised to sign the marriage contract.

"And we will do honor to your signatures," said Ephrinell, in the tone of a tradesman accepting a bill.

The night came, and we retired, to dream of the marriage festivities of the morrow. I took my usual stroll into the car occupied by the Chinese soldiers, and found the treasure of the Son of Heaven faithfully guarded. Half the detachment were awake and half were asleep.

About one o'clock in the morning I visited Kinko, and handed him over my purchases at Nia. The young Roumanian was in high spirits. He anticipated no further obstacles, he would reach port safely, after all.

"I am getting quite fat in this box," he told me.

I told him about the Ephrinell-Bluett marriage, and how the union was to be celebrated next morning with great pomp.

"Ah!" said he, with a sigh. "They are not obliged to wait until they reach Pekin!"

"Quite so, Kinko; but it seems to me that a marriage under such conditions is not likely to be lasting! But after all, that is the couple's lookout."

At three o'clock in the morning we stopped forty minutes at Tchertchen, almost at the foot of the ramifications of the Kuen Lun. None of us had seen this miserable, desolate country, treeless and verdureless, which the railway was now crossing on its road to the northeast.

Day came; our train ran the four hundred kilometres between Tchertchen and Tcharkalyk, while the sun caressed with its rays the immense plain, glittering in its saline efflorescences.

Chapter XIX

When I awoke I seemed to have had an unpleasant dream. A dream in no way like those we interpret by the *Clef d'Or*. No! Nothing could be clearer. The bandit chief Ki Tsang had prepared a scheme for the seizure of the Chinese treasure; he had attacked the train in the plains of Gobi; the car is assaulted, pillaged, ransacked; the gold and precious stones, to the value of fifteen millions, are torn from the grasp of the Celestials, who yield after a courageous defence. As to the passengers, another two minutes of sleep would have settled their fate—and mine.

But all that disappeared with the vapors of the night. Dreams are not fixed photographs; they fade in the sun, and end by effacing themselves.

In taking my stroll through the train as a good townsman takes his stroll through the town, I am joined by Major Noltitz. After shaking hands, he showed me a Mongol in the second-class car, and said to me, "That is not one of those we picked up at Douchak when we picked up Faruskiar and Ghangir."

"That is so," said I; "I never saw that face in the train before."

Popof, to whom I applied for information, told me that the Mongol had got in at Tchertchen. "When he arrived," he said, "the manager spoke to him for a minute, from which I concluded that he also was one of the staff of the Grand Transasiatic."

I had not noticed Faruskiar during my walk. Had he alighted at one of the small stations between Tchertchen and Tcharkalyk, where we ought to have been about one o'clock in the afternoon?

No, he and Ghangir were on the gangway in front of our car. They seemed to be in animated conversation, and only stopped to take a good look toward the northeastern horizon. Had the Mongol brought some news which had made them throw off their usual reserve and gravity? And I abandoned myself to my imagination, foreseeing adventures, attacks of bandits, and so on, according to my dream.

I was recalled to reality by the Reverend Nathaniel Morse, who said to me, "It is fixed for to-day, at nine o'clock; do not forget."

That meant the marriage of Fulk Ephrinell and Horatia Bluett. Really, I was not thinking of it. It is time for me to go and dress for the occasion. All I can do will be to change my shirt. It is enough that one of the husband's witnesses should be presentable; the other, Caterna, will be sure to be magnificent!

In fact, the actor had gone into the luggage van—how I trembled for Kinko!—and there, with Popof's assistance, had got out of one of his boxes a somewhat free-and-easy costume, but one certain of success at a wedding: A primrose coat with metal buttons, and a buttonhole, a sham diamond pin in the cravat, poppy-colored breeches, copper buckles, flowered waistcoat, clouded stockings, thread gloves, black pumps, and white beaver hat. What a number of bridegrooms and uncles of bridegrooms our friend had been in this traditional attire! He looked superb, with his beaming face, his close-shaven chin, and blue cheeks, and his laughing eyes and rosy lips.

Madame Caterna was quite as glorious in her array. She had easily discovered a bridesmaid's costume in her wardrobe, bodice with intercrossing stripes, short petticoat in green woolen, mauve stockings, straw hat with artificial flowers, a suspicion of black on the eyelids and of rouge on the cheeks. There you have the provincial stage beauty, and if she and her husband like to play a village piece after the breakfast, I can promise them bravos enough.

It was at nine o'clock that this marriage was to take place, announced by the bell of the tender, which was to sound full clang as if it were a chapel bell. With a little imagination, we could believe we were in a village. But whither did this bell invite the witnesses and guests? Into the dining car, which had been conveniently arranged for the ceremony, as I had taken good care.

It was no longer a dining car; it was a hall car, if the expression is admissible. The big table had been taken away, and replaced by a small table which served as a desk. A few flowers bought at Tchertchen had been arranged in the corners of the car, which was large enough to hold nearly all who wished to be present—and those who could not get inside could look on from the gangways.

That all the passengers might know what was going on, we had put up a notice at the doors of the first and second-class cars, couched in the following terms:

"Mr. Fulk Ephrinell, of the firm of Messrs. Strong, Bulbul & Co., of New York City, has the honor to invite you to his wedding with Miss Horatia Bluett, of the firm of Messrs. Holmes-Holme, London, which will take place in the dining car on this the 22d of May, at nine o'clock precisely. The Reverend Nathaniel Morse, of Boston, U.S.A., will officiate.

"Miss Horatia Bluett, of the firm of Messrs. Holmes-Holme, of London, has the honor to invite you to her wedding with Mr. Fulk Ephrinell, of the firm of Messrs. Strong, Bulbul & Co., of New York City, etc., etc."

If I do not make half a dozen pars out of all this I am no newspaper man!

Meanwhile I learn from Popof the precise spot where the ceremony will take place.

Popof points it out on the map. It is a hundred and fifty kilometres from Tcharkalyk station, in the middle of the desert, amid the plains which are traversed by a little stream which flows into the Lob Nor. For twenty leagues there is no station, and the ceremony is not likely to be interrupted by any stoppage.

It need hardly be said that at half-past eight I and Caterna were ready for the call.

Major Noltitz and Pan-Chao had got themselves up in all due form for the solemnity. The major looked as serious as a surgeon who was going to cut off a leg. The Chinaman looked as gay as a Parisian at a village bridal.

Doctor Tio-King and Cornaro, one carrying the other, were to be at this little festivity. The noble Venetian was a bachelor, if I am not mistaken, but I do not think he gives any opinion on marriage, at least

I have no recollection of its being in the chapter headed "Safe and easy means of promptly remedying the different accidents that threaten life."

"And," added Pan-Chao, who has just quoted this Cornarian phrase, "I suppose marriage ought to be included among those accidents!"

A quarter to nine. No one has yet seen the happy couple. Miss Bluett is in one of the toilet cabinets in the first van, where she is probably preparing herself. Fulk Ephrinell is perhaps struggling with his cravat and giving a last polish to his portable jewelry. I am not anxious. We shall see them as soon as the bell rings.

I have but one regret, and that is that Faruskiar and Ghangir should be too busy to join us. Why do they continue to look out over the immense desert? Before their eyes there stretches not the cultivated steppe of the Lob Nor region, but the Gobi, which is barren, desolate and gloomy, according to the reports of Grjimailo, Blanc and Martin. It may be asked why these people are keeping such an obstinate lookout.

"If my presentiments do not deceive me," said Major Noltitz, "there is some reason for it."

What does he mean? But the bell of the tender, the tender bell, begins its joyous appeal. Nine o'clock; it is time to go into the dining car.

Caterna comes near me, and I hear him singing:

> *"It is the turret bell,*
> *Which sud-denly is sounding."*

While Madame Caterna replies to the trio of the *Dame Blanche* by the refrain of the *Dragons de Villars:*

> *"And it sounds, sounds, sounds,*
> *It sounds and resounds—"*

The passengers move in a procession, the four witnesses first, then the guests from the end of the village—I mean of the train; Chinese, Turkomans, Tartars, men and women, all curious to assist at the ceremony. The four Mongols remain on the last gangway near the treasure which the Chinese soldiers do not leave for an instant.

We reach the dining car.

The clergyman is seated at the little table, on which is the certificate of marriage he has prepared according to the customary form. He looks as though he was accustomed to this sort of thing, which is as much commercial as matrimonial.

The bride and bridegroom have not appeared.

"Ah!" said I to the actor, "perhaps they have changed their minds."

"If they have," said Caterna, laughing, "the reverend gentleman can marry me and my wife over again. We are in wedding garments, and it is a pity to have had all this fuss for nothing, isn't it, Caroline?"

"Yes, Adolphe—"

But this pleasing second edition of the wedding of the Caternas did not come off. Here is Mr. Fulk Ephrinell, dressed this morning just as he was dressed yesterday—and—detail to note—with a pencil behind the lobe of his left ear, for he has just been making out an account for his New York house.

Here is Miss Horatia Bluett, as thin, as dry, as plain as ever, her dust cloak over her traveling gown, and in place of jewelry a noisy bunch of keys, which hangs from her belt.

The company politely rise as the bride and bridegroom enter. They "mark time," as Caterna says. Then they advance toward the clergyman, who is standing with his hand resting on a Bible, open probably at the place where Isaac, the son of Abraham, espouses Rebecca, the daughter of Rachel.

We might fancy we were in a chapel if we only had a harmonium.

And the music is here! If it is not a harmonium, it is the next thing to it. An accordion makes itself heard in Caterna's hands. As an ancient mariner, he knows how to manipulate this instrument of torture, and here he is swinging out the andante from *Norma* with the most accordionesque expression.

It seems to give great pleasure to the natives of Central Asia. Never have their ears been charmed by the antiquated melody that the pneumatic apparatus was rendering so expressively.

But everything must end in this world, even the andante from *Norma*. and the Reverend Nathaniel Morse began to favor the young couple with the speech which had clone duty many times before under similar circumstances. "The two souls that blend together—Flesh of my flesh—Increase and multiply—"

In my opinion he had much better have got to work like a notary: "Before us, there has been drawn up a deed of arrangement regarding Messrs. Ephrinell, Bluett & Co.—"

My thought remained unfinished. There are shouts from the engine. The brakes are suddenly applied with a scream and a grind. Successive shocks accompany the stoppage of the train. Then, with a violent bump, the cars pull up in a cloud of sand.

What an interruption to the nuptial ceremony!

Everything is upset in the dining car, men, furniture, bride, bridegroom and witnesses. Not one kept his equilibrium. It is an indescribable pell-mell, with cries of terror and prolonged groans. But I hasten to point out that there was nothing serious, for the stoppage was not all at once.

"Quick!" said the major. "Out of the train!"

❧

Chapter XX

In a moment the passengers, more or less bruised and alarmed, were out on the track. Nothing but complaints and questions uttered in three or four different languages, amid general bewilderment.

Faruskiar, Ghangir and the four Mongols were the first to jump off the cars. They are out on the line, kandijar in one hand, revolver in the other. No doubt an attack has been organized to pillage the train.

The rails have been taken up for about a hundred yards, and the engine, after bumping over the sleepers, has come to a standstill in a sandhill.

"What! The railroad not finished—and they sold me a through ticket from Tiflis to Pekin? And I came by this Transasiatic to save nine days in my trip round the world!"

In these phrases, in German, hurled at Popof, I recognized the voice of the irascible baron. But this time he should have addressed his reproaches not to the engineers of the company, but to others.

We spoke to Popof, while Major Noltitz continued to watch Faruskiar and the Mongols.

"The baron is mistaken," said Popof, "the railway is completed, and if a hundred yards of rails have been lifted here, it has been with some criminal intention."

"To stop the train!" I exclaim.

"And steal the treasure they are sending to Pekin!" says Caterna.

"There is no doubt about that," says Popof. "Be ready to repulse an attack."

"Is it Ki-Tsang and his gang that we have to do with?" I asked.

Ki-Tsang! The name spread among the passengers and caused inexpressible terror.

The major said to me in a low voice: "Why Ki-Tsang? Why not my lord Faruskiar?"

"He—the manager of the Transasiatic?"

"If it is true that the company had to take several of these robber chiefs into its confidence to assure the safety of the trains—"

"I will never believe that, major."

"As you please, Monsieur Bombarnac. But assuredly Faruskiar knew that this pretended mortuary van contained millions."

"Come, major, this is no time for joking."

No, it was the time for defending, and defending one's self courageously.

The Chinese officer has placed his men around the treasure van. They are twenty in number, and the rest of the passengers, not counting the women, amount to thirty. Popof distributes the weapons which are carried in case of attack. Major Noltitz, Caterna, Pan-Chao, Ephrinell, driver and stoker, passengers, Asiatic and European, all resolve to fight for the common safety.

On the right of the line, about a hundred yards away, stretches a deep, gloomy thicket, a sort of jungle, in which doubtless are hidden the robbers, awaiting the signal to pounce upon us.

Suddenly there is a burst of shouting, the thicket has given passage to the gang in ambush—some sixty Mongols, nomads of the Gobi. If these rascals beat us, the train will be pillaged, the treasure of the Son of Heaven will be stolen, and, what concerns us more intimately, the passengers will be massacred without mercy.

And Faruskiar, whom Major Noltitz so unjustly suspected? I look at him. His face is no longer the same; his fine features have become pale, his height has increased, there is lightning in his eyes.

Well! If I was mistaken about the mandarin Yen Lou, at least I had not mistaken the general manager of the Transasiatic or the famous bandit of Yunnan.

However, as soon as the Mongols appeared, Popof hurried Madame Caterna, Miss Horatia Bluett, and the other women into the cars. We took every means for putting them in safety.

My only weapon was a six-shot revolver, and I knew how to use it.

Ah! I wanted incidents and accidents, and impressions of the journey! Well, the chronicler will not fail to chronicle, on condition that he emerges safe and sound from the fray, for the honor of reporting in general and the glory of the *Twentieth Century* in particular.

But is it not possible to spread trouble among the assailants, by beginning with blowing out Ki-Tsang's brains, if Ki-Tsang is the author of this ambuscade? That would bring matters to a crisis.

The bandits fire a volley, and begin brandishing their arms and shouting. Faruskiar, pistol in one hand, kandijar in the other, has rushed onto them, his eyes gleaming, his lips covered with a slight foam. Ghangir is at his side, followed by four Mongols whom he is exciting by word and gesture.

Major Noltitz and I throw ourselves into the midst of our assailants. Caterna is in front of us, his mouth open, his white teeth ready to bite, his eyes blinking, his revolver flourishing about. The actor has given place to the old sailor who has reappeared for the occasion.

"These beggars want to board us!" said he. "Forward, forward, for the honor of the flag! To port, there, fire! To starboard, there, fire! All together, fire!"

And it was with no property daggers he was armed, nor dummy pistols loaded with Edouard Philippe's inoffensive powder. No! A revolver in each hand, he was bounding along, firing, as he said, right and left and everywhere.

Pan-Chao also exposed himself bravely, a smile on his lips, gallantly leading on the other Chinese passengers. Popof and the railwaymen did their duty bravely. Sir Francis Trevellyan, of Trevellyan Hall, took matters very coolly, but Ephrinell abandoned himself to true Yankee fury, being no less irritated at the interruption to his marriage as to the danger run by his forty-two packages of artificial teeth.

And in short, the band of robbers met with a much more serious resistance than they expected.

And Baron Weissschnitzerdoerfer? Well, he is one of the most furious of us all. He sweats blood and water, his fury carries him away at the risk of his being massacred. Many times we have to rescue him. These rails lifted, this train stopped, this attack in the open Gobi desert, the delays that it will all occasion, the mailboat lost at Tientsin, the voyage round the world spoiled, his plan come to grief before he had half accomplished it! What a shock to his German self-esteem!

Faruskiar, my hero—I cannot call him anything else—displays extraordinary intrepidity, bearing himself the boldest in the struggle, and when he had exhausted his revolver, using his kandijar like a man who had often faced death and never feared it.

Already there were a few wounded on both sides, perhaps a few dead among the passengers who lay on the line. I have had my shoulder grazed by a bullet, a simple scratch I have hardly noticed. The Reverend Nathaniel Morse does not think that his sacred character compels him to cross his arms, and, from the way he works, one would not imagine that it was the first time he has handled firearms. Caterna has his hat shot through, and it will be remembered that it is his village bridegroom's hat, the gray beaver, with the long fur. He utters a gigantic maritime oath, something about thunder and portholes, and then, taking a most deliberate aim, quietly shoots stone dead the ruffian who has taken such a liberty with his best headgear.

For ten minutes or so the battle continues with most alarming alternations. The number of wounded on both sides increases, and the issue is still doubtful. Faruskiar and Ghangir and the Mongols have been driven back toward the precious van, which the Chinese guard have not left for an instant. But two or three of them have been mortally wounded, and their officer has just been killed by a bullet in the head. And my hero does all that the most ardent courage can do for the defence of the treasure of the Son of Heaven.

I am getting uneasy at the prolongation of the combat. It will continue evidently as long as the chief of the band—a tall man with a black beard—urges on his accomplices to the attack on the train. Up till now he has escaped unhurt, and, in spite of all we can do, he is gaining ground. Shall we be obliged to take refuge in the vans, as behind the walls of a fortress, to entrench ourselves, to fight until the last has succumbed? And that will not be long, if we cannot stop the retrograde movement which is beginning on our side.

To the reports of the guns there are now added the cries of the women, who in their terror are running about the gangways, although Miss Bluett and Madame Caterna are trying to keep them inside the cars. A few bullets have gone through the panels, and I am wondering if any of them have hit Kinko.

Major Noltitz comes near me and says: "This is not going well."

"No, it is not going well," I reply, "and I am afraid the ammunition will give out. We must settle their commander-in-chief. Come, major—"

But what we are about to do was done by another at that very instant.

This other was Faruskiar. Bursting through the ranks of the assailants, he cleared them off the line, in spite of the blows they aimed at him. He is in front of the bandit chief, he raises his arm, he stabs him full in the chest.

Instantly the thieves beat a retreat, without even carrying off their dead and wounded. Some run across the plain, some disappear in the thickets. Why pursue them, now that the battle has ended in our favor? And I must say that without the admirable valor of Faruskiar, I do not expect any of us would have lived to tell the story.

But the chief of the bandits is not dead, although the blood flows abundantly from his chest.

He has fallen with one knee on the ground, one hand up, with the other he is supporting himself.

Faruskiar stands over him, towering above him.

Suddenly he rises in a last effort, his arm threatens his adversary, he looks at him.

A last thrust of the kandijar is driven into his heart.

Faruskiar returns, and in Russian, with perfect calmness, remarks:

"Ki-Tsang is dead! So perish all who bear weapons against the Son of Heaven!"

Chapter XXI

And so it was Ki-Tsang who had just attacked the Grand Transasiatic on the plains of Gobi. The pirate of Vunnan had learned that a van containing gold and precious stones of enormous value had formed part of this train! And was there anything astonishing in that, considering that the newspapers, even those of Paris, had published the fact many days before? So Ki-Tsang had had time to prepare his attempt, and had lifted a portion of the rails, and would probably have succeeded in carrying off the treasure if Faruskiar had not brought him to his feet. That is why our hero had been so uneasy all the morning; if he had been looking out over the desert so persistently, it was because he had been warned of Ki-Tsang's plans by the last Mongol who had joined the train at Tchertchen! Under any circumstances we had now nothing to fear from Ki-Tsang. The manager of the company had done justice on the bandit—speedy justice, I admit. But we are in the midst of the deserts of Mongolia, where there are no juries as yet, which is a good thing for the Mongols.

"Well," said I to the major, "I hope you have abandoned your suspicions with regard to my lord Faruskiar?"

"To a certain extent, Monsieur Bombarnac!" Only to a certain extent? Evidently Major Noltitz is difficult to please.

But let us hasten on and count our victims. On our side there are three dead, including the Chinese officer, and more than twelve wounded, four of them seriously, the rest slightly, so that they can continue their journey to Pekin. Popof escaped without a scratch, Caterna with a slight graze which his wife insists on bathing.

The major has the wounded brought into the cars and does the best for them under the circumstances. Doctor Tio-King offers his services, but they seem to prefer the Russian army surgeon, and that I understand. As to those who have fallen it is best for us to take them on to the next station and there render them the last services.

The thieves had abandoned their dead. We covered them over with a little sand, and that is all we need say.

The place where we had been stopped was halfway between Tcharkalyk and Tchertchen, the only two stations from which we could procure help. Unfortunately they were no longer in telegraphic communication, Ki-Tsang having knocked down the posts at the same time as he lifted the rails.

Hence a discussion as to what was the best thing to be done, which was not of long duration.

As the engine had run off the rails, the very first thing to do was evidently to get it onto them again; then as there was a gap in the line, the simplest thing to do was to run back to Tchertchen, and wait there until the company's workmen had repaired the damage, which they could easily do in a couple of days.

We set to work without losing a moment. The passengers were only too glad to help Popof and the officials who had at their disposal a few tools, including jacks, levers and hammers, and in three hours the engine and tender were again on the line.

The most difficult business is over. With the engine behind we can proceed at slow speed to Tchertchen. But what lost time! What delays! And what recriminations from our German baron, what donnervetters and teufels and other German expletives!

I have omitted to say that immediately after the dispersal of the bandits we had in a body thanked Faruskiar. The hero received our thanks with all the dignity of an Oriental.

"I only did my duty as general manager of the company," he replied, with a truly noble modesty.

And then at his orders the Mongols had set to work, and I noticed that they displayed indefatigable ardor, for which they earned our sincere felicitations.

Meanwhile Faruskiar and Ghangir were often talking together in a whisper, and from these interviews arose a proposition which none of us expected.

"Guard," said Faruskiar, addressing Popof, "it is my opinion that we had much better run on to Tcharkalyk than go back; it would suit the passengers much better."

"Certainly, sir, it would be preferable," said Popof; "but the line is broken between here and Tcharkalyk, and we cannot get through."

"Not at present, but we could get the cars through if we could temporarily repair the line."

That was a proposal worth consideration, and we assembled to consider it, Major Noltitz, Pan-Chao, Fulk Ephrinell, Caterna, the clergyman, Baron Weissschnitzerdoerfer, and a dozen others—all who understood Russian.

Faruskiar spoke as follows:

"I have been looking at the portion of the line damaged by the band of Ki-Tsang. Most of the sleepers are still in place. As to the rails, the scoundrels have simply thrown them onto the sand, and by replacing them end to end it would be easy to get the train over to the uninjured track. It would not take a day to do this, and five hours afterward we should be at Tcharkalyk."

Excellent notion, at once approved of by Popof, the driver, the passengers, and particularly by the baron. The plan was possible, and if there were a few rails useless, we could bring to the front those we had already run over, and in this way get over the difficulty.

Evidently this Faruskiar is a man, he is our true chief, he is the personage I was in want of, and I will sound his name over the entire universe in all the trumpets of my chronicle!

And yet Major Noltitz is mistaken enough to see in him only a rival to this Ki-Tsang, whose crimes have just received their final punishment from his hand!

We set to work to replace the sleepers that had been shifted aside from where they had left their mark, and we continued our task without intermission.

Having no fear of being noticed amid the confusion which followed the attack, I went into the luggage van to assure myself that Kinko was safe and sound, to tell him what had passed, to caution him on no account to come put of his box. He promised me, and I was at ease regarding him.

It was nearly three o'clock when we began work. The rails had been shifted for about a hundred yards. As Faruskiar remarked, it was not necessary for us to fix them permanently. That would be the task of the workmen the company would send from Tcharkalyk when we reached that station, which is one of the most important on the line.

As the rails were heavy we divided ourselves into detachments. First-class and second-class, all worked together with good will. The baron displayed tremendous ardor. Ephrinell, who thought no more of his marriage than if he had never thought about it, devoted strict attention to business. Pan-Chao was second to nobody, and even Doctor Tio-King strove to make himself useful—in the fashion of the celebrated Auguste, the fly on the chariot wheel.

"It is hot, this Gobi sun!" said Caterna.

Alone sat Sir Francis Trevellyan of Trevellyanshire, calm and impassive in his car, utterly regardless of our efforts.

At seven o'clock thirty yards of the line had been repaired. The night was closing in. It was decided to wait until the morning. In half a day we could finish the work, and in the afternoon we could be off again.

We were in great want of food and sleep. After so rude a task, how rude the appetite! We met in the dining car without distinction of classes. There was no scarcity of provisions, and a large breach was made in the reserves. Never mind! We can fill up again at Tcharkalyk.

Caterna is particularly cheery, talkative, facetious, communicative, overflowing. At dessert he and his wife sang the air—appropriate to the occasion—from the *Voyage en Chine*, which we caught up with more power than precision:

> *"China is a charming land*
> *Which surely ought to please you."*

Oh! Labiche, could you ever have imagined that this adorable composition would one day charm passengers in distress on the Grand Transasiatic? And then our actor—a little fresh, I admit—had an idea. And such an idea! Why not resume the marriage ceremony interrupted by the attack on the train?

"What marriage?" asked Ephrinell.

"Yours, sir, yours," replied Caterna. "Have you forgotten it? That is rather too good!"

The fact is that Fulk Ephrinell, on the one part, and Horatia Bluett, on the other part, seemed to have forgotten that had it not been for the attack of Ki-Tsang and his band they would now have been united in the gentle bonds of matrimony.

But we were all too tired. The Reverend Nathaniel Morse was unequal to the task; he would not have strength enough to bless the pair, and the pair would not have strength enough to support his blessing.

The ceremony could be resumed on the day after to-morrow. Between Tcharkalyk and Lan Tcheou there was a run of nine hundred kilometres, and that was quite long enough for this Anglo-American couple to be linked together in.

And so we all went to our couches or benches for a little refreshing sleep. But at the same time the requirements of prudence were not neglected.

Although it appeared improbable, now that their chief had succumbed, the bandits might still make a nocturnal attack. There were always these cursed millions of the Son of Heaven to excite their covetousness, and if we are not on our guard—

But we feel safe. Faruskiar in person arranges for the surveillance of the train. Since the death of the officer he has taken command of the Chinese detachment. He and Ghangir are on guard over the imperial treasure, and according to Caterna, who is never in want of a quotation from some comic opera:

"This night the maids of honor will be guarded well."

And, in fact, the imperial treasure was much better guarded than the beautiful Athenais de Solange between the first and second acts of the *Mousquetaires de la Reine.*

At daybreak next morning we are at work. The weather is superb. The day will be warm. Out in the Asian desert on the 24th of May the temperature is such that you can cook eggs if you only cover them with a little sand.

Zeal was not wanting, and the passengers worked as hard as they had done the night before. The line was gradually completed. One by one the sleepers were replaced, the rails were laid end to end, and about four o'clock in the afternoon the gap was bridged.

At once the engine began to advance slowly, the cars following until they were over the temporary track and safe again. Now the road is clear to Tcharkalyk; what do I say? to Pekin.

We resume our places. Popof gives the signal for departure as Caterna trolls out the chorus of victory of the admiral's sailors in *Haydee.*

A thousand cheers reply to him. At ten o'clock in the evening the train enters Tcharkalyk station.

We are exactly thirty hours behind time. But is not thirty hours enough to make Baron Weissschnitzerdoerfer lose the mail from Tient-Tsin to Yokohama?

Chapter XXII

I who wanted an incident, have had one to perfection. I am thankful enough not to have been one of the victims. I have emerged from the fray safe and sound. All my numbers are intact, barring two or three insignificant scratches. Only No. 4 has been traversed by a bullet clean through—his hat.

At present I have nothing in view beyond the Bluett-Ephrinell marriage and the termination of the Kinko affair. I do not suppose that Faruskiar can afford us any further surprises. I can reckon on the casual, of course, for the journey has another five days to run. Taking into account the delay occasioned by the Ki-Tsang affair that will make thirteen days from the start from Uzun Ada.

Thirteen days! Heavens! And there are the thirteen numbers in my notebook! Supposing I were superstitious?

We remained three hours at Tcharkalyk. Most of the passengers did not leave their beds. We were occupied with declarations relative to the attack on the train, to the dead which the Chinese authorities were to bury, to the wounded who were to be left at Tcharkalyk, where they would be properly looked after. Pan-Chao told me it was a populous town, and I regret I was unable to visit it.

The company sent off immediately a gang of workmen to repair the line and set up the telegraph posts; and in a day everything would be clear again.

I need scarcely say that Faruskiar, with all the authority of the company's general manager, took part in the different formalities that were needed at Tcharkalyk. I do not know how to praise him sufficiently. Besides, he was repaid for his good offices by the deference shown him by the staff at the railway station.

At three in the morning we arrived at Kara Bouran, where the train stopped but a few minutes. Here the railway crosses the route of Gabriel Bonvalot and Prince Henri of Orleans across Tibet in 1889-90, a much more complete journey than ours, a circular trip from Paris to Paris, by Berlin, Petersburg, Moscow, Nijni, Perm, Tobolsk, Omsk, Semipalatinsk, Kouldja, Tcharkalyk, Batong, Yunnan, Hanoi, Saigon, Singapore, Ceylon, Aden, Suez, Marseilles, the tour of Asia, and the tour of Europe.

The train halts at Lob Nor at four o'clock and departs at six. This lake, the banks of which were visited by General Povtzoff in 1889, when he returned from his expedition to Tibet, is an extensive marsh with a few sandy islands, surrounded by two or three feet of water. The country through which the Tarim slowly flows had already been visited by Fathers Hue and Gabet, the explorers Prjevalski and Carey up to the Davana pass, situated a hundred and fifty kilometres to the south. But from that pass Gabriel Bonvalot and Prince Henri of Orleans, camping sometimes at fifteen thousand feet of altitude, had ventured across virgin territories to the foot of the superb Himalayan chain.

Our itinerary lay eastwards toward Kara Nor, skirting the base of the Nan Chan mountains, behind which lies the region of Tsaidam. The railway dare not venture among the mountainous countries of the Kou-Kou-Nor, and we were on our way to the great city of Lan Tcheou along, the base of the hills.

Gloomy though the country might be, there was no reason for the passengers to be so. This glorious sun, with its rays gilding the sands of the Gobi as far as we could see, announced a perfect holiday. From Lob Nor to Kara Nor there are three hundred and fifty kilometres to run, and between the lakes we will resume the interrupted marriage of Fulk Ephrinell and Horatia Bluett, if nothing occurs to again delay their happiness.

The dining car has been again arranged for the ceremony, the witnesses are ready to resume their parts, and the happy pair cannot well be otherwise than of the same mind.

The Reverend Nathaniel Morse, in announcing that the marriage will take place at nine o'clock, presents the compliments of Mr. Ephrinell and Miss Bluett.

Major Noltitz and I, Caterna and Pan-Chao are under arms at the time stated.

Caterna did not think it his duty to resume his costume, nor did his wife. They were dressed merely for the grand dinner party which took place at eight o'clock in the evening—the dinner given by Ephrinell to his witnesses and to the chief first-class passengers. Our actor, puffing out his left cheek, informed me that he had a surprise for us at dessert. What? I thought it wise not to ask.

A little before nine o'clock the bell of the tender begins to ring. Be assured it does not announce an accident. Its joyous tinkling calls us to the dining car, and we march in procession toward the place of sacrifice.

Ephrinell and Miss Bluett are already seated at the little table in front of the worthy clergyman, and we take our places around them.

On the platforms are grouped the spectators, anxious to lose nothing of the nuptial ceremony.

My lord Faruskiar and Ghangir, who had been the object of a personal invitation, had just arrived. The assembly respectfully rises to receive them. They will sign the deed of marriage. It is a great honor, and if it were my marriage I should be proud to see the illustrious name of Faruskiar figure among the signatures to the deed.

The ceremony begins, and this time the Reverend Nathaniel Morse was able to finish his speech, so regrettably interrupted on the former occasion.

The young people rise, mud the clergyman asks them if they are mutually agreed as to marriage.

Before replying, Miss Bluett turns to Ephrinell, and says:

"It is understood that Holmes-Holme will have twenty-five per cent. of the profits of our partnership."

"Fifteen," said Ephrinell, "only fifteen."

"That is not fair, for I agree to thirty per cent, from Strong, Bulbul & Co."

"Well, let us say twenty per cent., Miss Bluett."

"Be it so, Mr. Ephrinell."

"But that is a good deal for you!" whispered Caterna in my ear.

The marriage for a moment was in check for five per cent.!

But all is arranged. The interests of the two houses have been safeguarded. The Reverend Nathaniel Morse repeats the question.

A dry "yes" from Horatia Bluett, a short "yes" from Fulk Ephrinell, and the two are declared to be united in the bonds of matrimony.

The deed is then signed, first by them, then by the witnesses, then by Faruskiar, and the other signatures follow. At length the clergyman adds his name and flourish, and that closes the series of formalities according to rule.

"There they are, riveted for life," said the actor to me, with a little lift of his shoulder.

"For life—like two bullfinches," said the actress, who had not forgotten that these birds are noted for the fidelity of their armours.

"In China," said Pan-Chao, "it is not the bullfinch but the mandarin duck that symbolizes fidelity in marriage."

"Ducks or bullfinches, it is all one," said Caterna philosophically.

The ceremony is over. We compliment the newly married pair. We return to our occupation, Ephrinell to his accounts, Mrs. Ephrinell to her work. Nothing is changed in the train. There are only two more married people.

Major Noltitz, Pan-Chao and I go out and smoke on one of the platforms, leaving to their preparations the Caternas, who seem to be having a sort of rehearsal in their corner. Probably it is the surprise for the evening.

There is not much variety in the landscape. All along is this monotonous desert of Gobi with the heights of the Humboldt mountains on the right reaching on to the ranges of Nan Chan. The stations are few and far between, and consist merely of an agglomeration of huts, with the signal cabin standing up among them like a monument. Here the tender fills up with water and coal. Beyond the Kara Nor, where a few towns appear, the approach to China Proper, populous and laborious, becomes more evident.

This part of the desert of Gobi has little resemblance to the regions of Eastern Turkestan we crossed on leaving Kachgar. These regions are as new to Pan-Chao and Doctor Tio-King as to us Europeans.

I should say that Faruskiar no longer disdains to mingle in our conversation. He is a charming man, well informed and witty, with whom I shall become better acquainted when we reach Pekin. He has already invited me to visit him at his yamen, and I will then have an opportunity of putting him to the question—that is, to the interview. He has traveled a good deal, and seems to have an especially good opinion of French journalists. He will not refuse to subscribe to the *Twentieth Century*. I am sure—Paris, 48 francs, Departments, 56, Foreign, 76.

While the train is running at full speed we talk of one thing and another. With regard to Kachgaria, which had been mentioned, Faruskiar gave us a few very interesting details regarding the province, which had been so greatly troubled by insurrectionary movements. It was at this epoch that the capital, holding out against Chinese covetousness, had not yet submitted to Russian domination. Many times numbers of Celestials had been massacred in the revolts of the Turkestan chiefs, and the garrison had taken refuge in the fortress of Yanghi-Hissar.

Among these insurgent chiefs there was one, a certain Ouali-Khan-Toulla, whom I have mentioned with regard to the murder of Schlagintweit, and who for a time had become master of Kachgaria. He was a man of great intelligence, but of uncommon ferocity. And Faruskiar told us an anecdote giving us an idea of these pitiless Orientals.

"There was at Kachgar," he said, "an armorer of repute, who, wishing to secure the favors of Ouali-Khan-Toulla, made a costly sword. When he had finished his work he sent his son, a boy of ten, to present the sword, hoping to receive some recompense from the royal hand. He received it. The Khan admired the sword, and asked if the blade was of the first quality. 'Yes,' said the boy. 'Then approach!' said the Khan, and at one blow he smote off the head, which he sent back to the father with the price of the blade he had thus proved to be of excellent quality."

This story he told really well. Had Caterna heard it, he would have asked for a Turkestan opera on the subject.

The day passed without incident. The train kept on at its moderate speed of forty kilometres an hour, an average that would have been raised to eighty had they listened to Baron Weissschnitzerdoerfer. The truth is that the Chinese driver had no notion of making up the time lost between Tchertchen and Tcharkalyk.

At seven in the evening we reach Kara Nor, to stay there fifty minutes. This lake, which is not as extensive as Lob Nor, absorbs the waters of the Soule Ho, coming down from the Nan Chan mountains. Our eyes are charmed with the masses of verdure that clothe its southern bank, alive with the flight of numerous birds. At eight o'clock, when we left the station, the sun had set behind the sandhills, and a sort of mirage produced by the warming of the lower zones of the atmosphere prolonged the twilight above the horizon.

The dining car has resumed its restaurant appearance, and here is the wedding banquet, instead of the usual fare. Twenty guests have been invited to this railway love feast, and, first of them, my lord Faruskiar. But for some reason or other he has declined Ephrinell's invitation.

I am sorry for it, for I hoped that good luck would place me near him.

It occurred to me then that this illustrious name was worth sending to the office of the *Twentieth Century*, this name and also a few lines relative to the attack on the train and the details of the defense. Never was information better worth sending by telegram, however much it might cost. This time there is no risk of my bringing a lecture down on myself. There is no mistake possible, as in the case of that pretended mandarin, Yen-Lou, which I shall never forget—but then, it was in the country of the false Smerdis and that must be my excuse.

It is agreed that as soon as we arrive at Sou-Tcheou, the telegraph being repaired at the same time as the line, I will send off a despatch, which will reveal to the admiration of Europe the brilliant name of Faruskiar.

We are seated at the table. Ephrinell has done the thing as well as circumstances permit. In view of the feast, provisions were taken in at Tcharkalyk. It is not Russian cookery, but Chinese, and by a Chinese chef to which we do honor. Luckily we are not condemned to eat it with chopsticks, for forks are not prohibited at the Grand Transasiatic table.

I am placed to the left of Mrs. Ephrinell, Major Noltitz to the right of her husband. The other guests are seated as they please. The German baron, who is not the man to refuse a good dinner, is one of the guests. Sir Francis Trevellyan did not even make a sign in answer to the invitation that was tendered him.

To begin with, we had chicken soup and plovers' eggs, then swallows' nests cut in threads, stewed spawn of crab, sparrow gizzards, roast pig's feet and sauce, mutton marrow, fried sea slug, shark's fin—very gelatinous; finally bamboo shoots in syrup, and water lily roots in sugar, all the most out-of-the-way dishes, watered by Chao Hing wine, served warm in metal tea urns.

The feast is very jolly and—what shall I say?—very confidential, except that the husband takes no notice of the wife, and reciprocally.

What an indefatigable humorist is our actor? What a continuous stream of wheezes, unintelligible for the most part, of antediluvian puns, of pure nonsense at which he laughs so heartily that it is difficult not to laugh with him. He wanted to learn a few words of Chinese, and Pan-Chao having told him that "tching-tching" means thanks, he has been tching-tchinging at every opportunity, with burlesque intonation.

Then we have French songs, Russian songs, Chinese songs—among others the "Shiang-Touo-Tching," the *Chanson de la Reverie*, in which our young Celestial repeats that the flowers of the peach tree are of finest fragrance at the third moon, and those of the red pomegranate at the fifth.

The dinner lasts till ten o'clock. At this moment the actor and actress, who had retired during dessert, made their entry, one in a coachman's overcoat, the other in a nurse's jacket, and they gave us the *Sonnettes* with an energy, a go, a dash—well, it would only be fair to them if Claretie, on the recommendation of Meilhac and Halevy, offers to put them on the pension list of the Comedie Francaise.

At midnight the festival is over. We all retire to our sleeping places. We do not even hear them shouting the names of the stations before we come to Kan-Tcheou, and it is between four and five o'clock in the morning that a halt of forty minutes retains us at the station of that town.

The country is changing as the railway runs south of the fortieth degree, so as to skirt the eastern base of the Nan Shan mountains. The desert gradually disappears, villages are not so few, the density of the population increases. Instead of sandy flats, we get verdant plains, and even rice fields, for the neighboring mountains spread their abundant streams over these high regions of the Celestial Empire. We do not complain of this change after the dreariness of the Kara-Koum and the solitude of Gobi. Since

147

we left the Caspian, deserts have succeeded deserts, except when crossing the Pamir. From here to Pekin picturesque sites, mountain horizons, and deep valleys will not be wanting along the Grand Transasiatic.

We shall enter China, the real China, that of folding screens and porcelain, in the territory of the vast province of Kin-Sou. In three days we shall be at the end of our journey, and it is not I, a mere special correspondent, vowed to perpetual movement, who will complain of its length. Good for Kinko, shut up in his box, and for pretty Zinca Klork, devoured by anxiety in her house in the Avenue Cha-Coua!

We halt two hours at Sou-Tcheou. The first thing I do is to run to the telegraph office. The complaisant Pan-Chao offers to be my interpreter. The clerk tells us that the posts are all up again, and that messages can be sent through to Europe.

At once I favor the *Twentieth Century* with the following telegram:

"*Sou-Tcheou,*

25TH MAY, 2:25 P.M.

"*Train attacked between Tchertchen and Tcharkalyk by the gang of the celebrated Ki-Tsang; travelers repulsed the attack and saved the Chinese treasure; dead and wounded on both sides; chief killed by the heroic Mongol grandee Faruskiar, general manager of the company, whose name should be the object of universal admiration.*"

If this telegram does not gratify the editor of my newspaper, well— Two hours to visit Sou-Tcheou, that is not much.

In Turkestan we have seen two towns side by side, an ancient one and a modern one. Here, in China, as Pan-Chao points out, we have two and even three or four, as at Pekin, enclosed one within the other.

Here Tai-Tchen is the outer town, and Le-Tchen the inner one. It strikes us at first glance that both look desolate. Everywhere are traces of fire, here and there pagodas or houses half destroyed, a mass of ruins, not the work of time, but the work of war. This shows that Sou-Tcheou, taken by the Mussulmans and retaken by the Chinese, has undergone the horrors of those barbarous contests which end in the destruction of buildings and the massacre of their inhabitants of every age and sex.

It is true that population rapidly increases in the Celestial Empire; more rapidly than monuments are raised from their ruins. And so Sou-Tcheou has become populous again within its double wall as in the suburbs around. Trade is flourishing, and as we walked through the principal streets we noticed the well-stocked shops, to say nothing of the perambulating pedlars.

Here, for the first time, the Caternas saw pass along between the inhabitants, who stood at attention more from fear than respect, a mandarin on horseback, preceded by a servant carrying a fringed parasol, the mark of his master's dignity.

But there is one curiosity for which Sou-Tcheou is worth a visit. It is there that the Great Wall of China ends.

After descending to the southeast toward Lan-Tcheou, the wall runs to the northeast, covering the provinces of Kian-Sou, Chan-si, and Petchili to the north of Pekin. Here it is little more than an embankment with a tower here and there, mostly in ruins. I should have failed in my duty as a chronicler if I had not noticed this gigantic work at its beginning, for it far surpasses the works of our modern fortifications.

"Is it of any real use, this wall of China?" asked Major Noltitz.

"To the Chinese, I do not know," said I; "but certainly it is to our political orators for purposes of comparison, when discussing treaties of commerce. Without it, what would become of the eloquence of our legislators?"

Chapter XXIII

I have not seen Kinko for two days, and the last was only to exchange a few words with him to relieve his anxiety.

To-night I will try and visit him. I have taken care to lay in a few provisions at Sou-Tcheou.

We started at three o'clock. We have got a more powerful engine on. Across this undulating country the gradients are occasionally rather steep. Seven hundred kilometres separate us from the important city of Lan-Tcheou, where we ought to arrive to-morrow morning, running thirty miles an hour.

I remarked to Pan-Chao that this average was not a high one.

"What would you have?" he replied, crunching the watermelon seeds. "You will not change, and nothing will change the temperament of the Celestials. As they are conservatives in all things, so will they be conservative in this matter of speed, no matter how the engine may be improved. And, besides, Monsieur Bombarnac, that there are railways at all in the Middle Kingdom is a wonder to me."

"I agree with you, but where you have a railway you might as well get all the advantage out of it that you can."

"Bah!" said Pan-Chao carelessly.

"Speed," said I, "is a gain of time—and to gain time—"

"Time does not exist in China, Monsieur Bombarnac, and it cannot exist for a population of four hundred millions. There would not be enough for everybody. And so we do not count by days and hours, but always by moons and watches."

"Which is more poetical than practical," I remark.

"Practical, Mr. Reporter? You Westerners are never without that word in your mouth. To be practical is to be the slave of time, work, money, business, the world, everybody else, and one's self included. I confess that during my stay in Europe—you can ask Doctor Tio-King— I have not been very practical, and now I return to Asia I shall be less so. I shall let myself live, that is all, as the cloud floats in the breeze, the straw on the stream, as the thought is borne away by the imagination."

"I see," said I, "we must take China as it is."

"And as it will probably always be, Monsieur Bombarnac. Ah! if you knew how easy the life is—an adorable *dolce far niente* between folding screens in the quietude of the yamens. The cares of business trouble us little; the cares of politics trouble us less. Think! Since Fou Hi, the first emperor in 2950, a contemporary of Noah, we are in the twenty-third dynasty. Now it is Manchoo; what it is to be next what matters? Either we have a government or we have not; and which of its sons Heaven has chosen for the happiness of four hundred million subjects we hardly know, and we hardly care to know."

It is evident that the young Celestial is a thousand and ten times wrong, to use the numerative formula; but it is not for me to tell him so.

At dinner Mr. and Mrs. Ephrinell, sitting side by side, hardly exchanged a word. Their intimacy seems to have decreased since they were married. Perhaps they are absorbed in the calculation of their reciprocal interests, which are not yet perfectly amalgamated. Ah! they do not count by moons and watches, these Anglo-Saxons! They are practical, too practical!

We have had a bad night. The sky of purple sulphury tint became stormy toward evening, the atmosphere became stifling, the electrical tension excessive. It meant a "highly successful" storm, to quote Caterna, who assured me he had never seen a better one except perhaps in the second act of *Freyschuetz*. In truth the train ran through a zone, so to speak, of vivid lightning and rolling thunder, which the echoes of the mountains prolonged indefinitely. I think there must have been several lightning strokes, but the rails acted as conductors, and preserved the cars from injury. It was a fine spectacle, a little alarming, these fires in the sky that the heavy rain could not put out—these continuous discharges from the clouds, in which were mingled the strident whistlings of our locomotive as we passed through the stations of Yanlu, Youn Tcheng, Houlan-Sien and Da-Tsching.

By favor of this troubled night I was able to communicate with Kinko, to take him some provisions and to have a few minutes' conversation with him.

"Is it the day after to-morrow," he asked, "that we arrive at Pekin?"

"Yes, the day after to-morrow, if the train is not delayed."

"Oh, I am not afraid of delays! But when my box is in the railway station at Pekin, I have still to get to the Avenue Cha-Coua—"

"What does it matter, will not the fair Zinca Klork come and call for it?"

"No. I advised her not to do so."

"And why?"

"Women are so impressionable! She would want to see the van in-which I had come, she would claim the box with such excitement that suspicions would be aroused. In short, she would run the risk of betraying me."

"You are right, Kinko."

"Besides, we shall reach the station in the afternoon, very late in the afternoon perhaps, and the unloading of the packages will not take place until next morning—"

"Probably."

"Well, Monsieur Bombarnac, if I am not taking too great a liberty, may I ask a favor of you?"

"What is it?"

"That you will be present at the departure of the case, so as to avoid any mistake."

"I will be there, Kinko, I will be there. Glass fragile, I will see that they don't handle it too roughly. And if you like I will accompany the case to Avenue Cha-Coua—"

"I hardly like to ask you to do that—"

"You are wrong, Kinko. You should not stand on ceremony with a friend, and I am yours, Kinko. Besides, it will be a pleasure to me to make the acquaintance of Mademoiselle Zinca Klork. I will be there when they deliver the box, the precious box. I will help her to get the nails out of it—"

"The nails out of it, Monsieur Bombarnac? My panel? Ah, I will jump through my panel!"

A terrible clap of thunder interrupted our conversation. I thought the train had been thrown off the line by the commotion of the air. I left the young Roumanian and regained my place within the car.

In the morning—26th of May, 7 A.M.—we arrived at Lan-Tcheou. Three hours to stop, three hours only.

"Come, Major Noltitz, come, Pan-Chao, come, Caterna, we have not a minute to spare."

But as we are leaving the station we are stopped by the appearance of a tall, fat, gray, solemn personage. It is the governor of the town in a double robe of white and yellow silk, fan in hand, buckled belt, and a mantilla—a black mantilla which would have looked much better on the shoulders of a manola. He is accompanied by a certain number of globular mandarins, and the Celestials salute him by holding out their two fists, which they move up and down as they nod their heads.

"Ah! What is this gentleman going to do? Is it some Chinese formality? A visit to the passengers and their baggage? And Kinko, what about him?"

Nothing alarming, after all. It is only about the treasure of the Son of Heaven. The governor and his suite have stopped before the precious van, bolted and sealed, and are looking at it with that respectful admiration which is experienced even in China before a box containing many millions.

I ask Popof what is meant by the governor's presence, has it anything to do with us?

"Not at all," says Popof; "the order has come from Pekin to telegraph the arrival of the treasure. The governor has done so, and he is awaiting a reply as to whether he is to send it on to Pekin or keep it provisionally at Lan-Tcheou."

"That will not delay us?"

"I don't think so."

"Then come on," said I to my companions. But if the imperial treasure was a matter of indifference to us, it did not seem to be so to Faruskiar. But whether this van started or did not start, whether it was attached to our train or left behind, what could it matter to him? Nevertheless, he and Ghangir seemed to be much put about regarding it, although they tried to hide their anxiety, while the Mongols, talking together in a low tone, gave the governor anything but friendly glances.

Meanwhile the governor had just heard of the attack on the train and of the part that our hero had taken in defence of the treasure, with what courage he had fought, and how he had delivered the country from the terrible Ki-Tsang. And then in laudatory terms, which Pan-

Chao translated to us, he thanked Faruskiar, complimented him, and gave him to understand that the Son of Heaven would reward him for his services.

The manager of the Grand Transasiatic listened with that tranquil air that distinguished him, not without impatience, as, I could clearly see. Perhaps he felt himself superior to praises as well as recompenses, no matter from how great a height they might come. In that I recognized all the Mongol pride.

But we need not wait. The treasure van may remain here or go on to Pekin, but it makes no difference to us! Our business is to visit Lan-Tcheou.

What we did briefly I will more briefly tell.

There is an outer town and an inner one. No ruins this time. A very lively city, population swarming like ants and very active, familiarized by the railway with the presence of strangers whom they do not follow about with indiscreet curiosity as they used to do. Huge quarters occupy the right of the Hoang Ho, two kilometres wide. This Hoang Ho is the yellow river, the famous yellow river, which, after a course of four thousand four hundred kilometres, pours its muddy waters into the Gulf of Petchili.

"Is not its mouth near Tien Tsin, where the baron thinks of catching the mail for Yokohama?" asks the major.

"That is so," I reply.

"He will miss it," says the actor.

"Unless he trots, our globe-trotter."

"A donkey's trot does not last long," says Caterna, "and he will not catch the boat."

"He will catch it if the train is no later," said the major. "We shall be at Tien Tsin on the 23d at six o'clock in the morning, and the steamer leaves at eleven."

"Whether he misses the boat or not, my friends, do not let us miss our walk."

A bridge of boats crosses the river, and the stream is so swift that the footway rises and falls like the waves of the sea. Madame Caterna, who had ventured on it, began to turn pale.

"Caroline, Caroline," said her husband, "you will be seasick! Pull yourself together; pull yourself together!"

She "pulled herself together," and we went up towards a pagoda which rises over the town.

Like all the monuments of this kind, the pagoda resembles a pile of dessert dishes placed one on the other, but the dishes are of graceful form, and if they are in Chinese porcelain it is not astonishing.

We get an outside view of a cannon foundry, a rifle factory, the workmen being natives. Through a fine garden we reach the governor's house, with a capricious assemblage of bridges, kiosks, fountains and doors like vases. There are more pavilions and upturned roofs than there are trees and shady walks. Then there are paths paved with bricks, among them the remains of the base of the Great Wall.

It is ten minutes to ten when we return to the station, absolutely tired out; for the walk has been a rough one, and almost suffocating, for the heat is very great.

My first care is to look after the van with the millions. It is there as usual behind the train under the Chinese guard.

The message expected by the governor has arrived; the order to forward on the van to Pekin, where the treasure is to be handed over to the finance minister.

Where is Faruskiar? I do not see him. Has he given us the slip?

No! There he is on one of the platforms, and the Mongols are back in the car.

Ephrinell has been off to do a round of calls—with his samples, no doubt—and Mrs. Ephrinell has also been out on business, for a deal in hair probably. Here they come, and without seeming to notice one another they take their seats.

The other passengers are only Celestials. Some are going to Pekin; some have taken their tickets for intermediate stations like Si-Ngan, Ho Nan. Lou-Ngan, Tai-Youan. There are a hundred passengers in the train. All my numbers are on board. There is not one missing. Thirteen, always thirteen!

We were still on the platform, just after the signal of departure had been given, when Caterna asked his wife what was the most curious thing she had seen at Lan-Tcheou.

"The most curious thing, Adolphe? Those big cages, hung on to the walls and trees, which held such curious birds—"

"Very curious, Madame Caterna," said Pan-Chao. "Birds that talk—"

"What—parrots?"

"No; criminals' heads."

"Horrible!" said the actress, with a most expressive grimace.

"What would you have, Caroline?" said Caterna. "It is the custom of the country."

❦

Chapter XXIV

On leaving Lan-Tcheou, the railway crosses a well-cultivated country, watered by numerous streams, and hilly enough to necessitate frequent curves. There is a good deal of engineering work; mostly bridges, viaducts on wooden trestles of somewhat doubtful solidity, and the traveler is not particularly comfortable when he finds them bending under the weight of the train. It is true we are in the Celestial Empire, and a few thousand victims of a railway accident is hardly anything among a population of four hundred millions.

"Besides," said Pan-Chao, "the Son of Heaven never travels by railway."

So much the better.

At six o'clock in the evening we are at King-Tcheou, after skirting for some time the capricious meanderings of the Great Wall. Of this immense artificial frontier built between Mongolia and China, there remain only the blocks of granite and red quartzite which served as its base, its terrace of bricks with the parapets of unequal heights, a few old cannons eaten into with rust and hidden under a thick veil of lichens, and then the square towers with their ruined battlements. The interminable wall rises, falls, bends, bends back again, and is lost to sight on the undulations of the ground.

At six o'clock we halt for half an hour at King-Tcheou, of which I only saw a few pagodas, and about ten o'clock there is a halt of three-quarters of an hour at Si-Ngan, of which I did not even see the outline.

All night was spent in running the three hundred kilometres which separate this town from Ho Nan, where we had an hour to stop.

I fancy the Londoners might easily imagine that this town of Ho Nan was London, and perhaps Mrs. Ephrinell did so. Not because there was a Strand with its extraordinary traffic, nor a Thames with its prodigious movement of barges and steamboats. No! But because we were in a fog so thick that it was impossible to see either houses or pagodas.

The fog lasted all day, and this hindered the progress of the train. These Chinese engine-drivers are really very skilful and attentive and intelligent.

We were not fortunate in our last day's journey before reaching Tien Tsin! What a loss of copy! What paragraphs were melted away in these unfathomable vapors! I saw nothing of the gorges and ravines, through which runs the Grand Transasiatic; nothing of the valley of Lou-Ngan, where we stopped at eleven o'clock; nothing of the two hundred and thirty kilometres which we accomplished amid the wreaths of a sort of yellow steam, worthy of a yellow country, until we stopped about ten o'clock at night at Tai-Youan.

Ah! the disagreeable day.

Luckily the fog rose early in the evening. Now it is night—and a very dark night, too.

I go to the refreshment bar and buy a few cakes and a bottle of wine. My intention is to pay a last visit to Kinko. We will drink to his health, to his approaching marriage with the fair Roumanian. He has traveled by fraud, I know, and if the Grand Transasiatic only knew! But the Grand Transasiatic will not know.

During the stoppage Faruskiar and Ghangir are walking on the platform and looking at the train. But it is not the van at the rear that is attracting their attention, but the van in front, and they seem to be much interested in it.

Are they suspicious of Kinko? No! the hypothesis is unlikely. The driver and stoker seem to be the object of their very particular attention. They are two brave Chinamen who have just come on duty, and perhaps Faruskiar is not sorry to see men in whom he can trust, with this imperial treasure and a hundred passengers behind them!

The hour for departure strikes, and at midnight the engine begins to move, emitting two or three loud whistles.

As I have said, the night is very dark, without moon, without stars. Long clouds are creeping across the lower zones of the atmosphere. It will be easy for me to enter the van without being noticed. And I have not been too liberal in my visits to Kinko during these twelve days on the road.

At this moment Popof says to me:

"Are you not going to sleep to-night, Monsieur Bombarnac?"

"I am in no hurry," I reply; "after this foggy day, spent inside the car, I am glad of a breath of fresh air. Where does the train stop next?"

"At Fuen-Choo, when it has passed the junction with the Nanking line."

"Good night, Popof."

"Good night, Monsieur Bombarnac."

I am alone.

The idea occurs to me to walk to the rear of the train, and I stop for an instant on the gangway in front of the treasure van.

The passengers, with the exception of the Chinese guard, are all sleeping their last sleep—their last, be it understood, on the Grand Transasiatic.

Returning to the front of the train, I approach Popof's box, and find him sound asleep.

I then open the door of the van, shut it behind me, and signal my presence to Kinko.

The panel is lowered, the little lamp is lighted. In exchange for the cakes and wine I receive the brave fellow's thanks, and we drink to the health of Zinca Klork, whose acquaintance I am to make on the morrow.

It is ten minutes to one. In twelve minutes, so Popof says, we shall pass the junction with the Nanking branch. This branch is only completed for five or six kilometres, and leads to the viaduct over the Tjon valley. This viaduct is a great work—I have the details from Pan-Chao— and the engineers have as yet only got in the piers, which rise for a hundred feet above the ground.

As I know we are to halt at Fuen-Choo, I shake hands with Kinko, and rise to take my leave.

At this moment I seem to hear some one on the platform in the rear of the van.

"Look out, Kinko!" I say in a whisper.

The lamp is instantly extinguished, and we remain quite still.

I am not mistaken. Some one is opening the door of the van.

"Your panel," I whisper.

The panel is raised, the car is shut, and I am alone in the dark.

Evidently it must be Popof who has come in. What will he think to find me here? The first time I came to visit the young Roumanian I hid among the packages. Well, I will hide a second time. If I get behind Ephrinell's boxes it is not likely that Popof will see me, even by the light of his lantern.

I do so; and I watch.

It is not Popof, for he would have brought his lantern.

I try to recognize the people who have just entered. It is difficult. They have glided between the packages, and after opening the further door, they have gone out and shut it behind them.

They are some of the passengers, evidently; but why here—at this hour?

I must know. I have a presentiment that something is in the wind Perhaps by listening?

I approach the front door of the van, and in spite of the rumbling of the train I hear them distinctly enough—

Thousand and ten thousand devils! I am not mistaken! It is the voice of my lord Faruskiar. He is talking with Ghangir in Russian. It is indeed Faruskiar. The four Mongols have accompanied him. But what are they doing there? For what motive are they on the platform which is just behind the tender? And what are they saying?

What they are saying is this.

Of these questions and answers exchanged between my lord Faruskiar and his companions, I do not lose a word.

"When shall we be at the junction?"

"In a few minutes."

"Are you sure that Kardek is at the points?"

"Yes; that has been arranged."

What had been arranged? And who is this Kardek they are talking about?

The conversation continues.

"We must wait until we get the signal," says Faruskiar.

"Is that a green light?" asks Ghangir.

"Yes—it will show that the switch is over."

I do not know if I am in my right senses. The switch over? What switch?

A half minute elapses. Ought I not to tell Popof? Yes—I ought.

I was turning to go out of the van, when an exclamation kept me back.

"The signal—there is the signal!" says Ghangir.

"And now the train is on the Nanking branch!" replies Faruskiar.

The Nanking branch? But then we are lost. At five kilometres from here is the Tjon viaduct in course of construction, and the train is being precipitated towards an abyss.

Evidently Major Noltitz was not mistaken regarding my lord Faruskiar. I understand the scheme of the scoundrels. The manager of the Grand Transasiatic is a scoundrel of the deepest dye. He has entered the service of the company to await his opportunity for some extensive haul. The opportunity has come with the millions of the Son of Heaven I Yes! The whole abominable scheme is clear enough to me. Faruskiar has defended the imperial treasure against Ki-Tsang to keep it from the chief of the bandits who stopped the train, whose attack would have interfered with his criminal projects! That is why he had fought so bravely. That is why he had risked his life and behaved like a hero. And thou, poor beast of a Claudius, how thou hast been sold! Another howler! Think of that, my friend!

But somehow we ought to prevent this rascal from accomplishing his work. We ought to save the train which is running full speed towards the unfinished viaduct, we ought to save the passengers from a frightful catastrophe. As to the treasure Faruskiar and his accomplices are after, I care no more than for yesterday's news! But the passengers—and myself—that is another affair altogether.

I will go back to Popof. Impossible. I seem to be nailed to the floor of the van. My head swims—

Is it true we are running towards the abyss? No! I am mad. Faruskiar and his accomplices would be hurled over as well. They would share our fate. They would perish with us!

But there are shouts in front of the train. The screams of people being killed. There is no doubt now. The driver and the stoker are being strangled. I feel the speed of the train begin to slacken.

I understand. One of the ruffians knows how to work the train, and he is slowing it to enable them to jump off and avoid the catastrophe.

I begin to master my torpor. Staggering like a drunken man, I crawl to Kinko's case. There, in a few words, I tell him what has passed, and I exclaim:

"We are lost!"

"No—perhaps" he replies.

Before I can move, Kinko is out of his box. He rushes towards the front door; he climbs on to the tender.

"Come along! Come along!" he shouts.

I do not know how I have done it, but here I am at his side, on the foot-plate, my feet in the blood of the driver and stoker, who have been thrown off on to the line.

Faruskiar and his accomplices are no longer here.

But before they went one of them has taken off the brakes, jammed down the regulator to full speed, thrown fresh coals into the fire-box, and the train is running with frightful velocity.

In a few minutes we shall reach the Tjon viaduct.

Kinko, energetic and resolute, is as cool as a cucumber. But in vain he tries to move the regulator, to shut off the steam, to put on the brake. These valves and levers, what shall we do with them?

"I must tell Popof!" I shout.

"And what can he do? No; there is only one way—"

"And what is that?"

"Rouse up the fire," says Kinko, calmly; "shut down the safety valves, and blow up the engine."

And was that the only way—a desperate way—of stopping the train before it reached the viaduct?

Kinko scattered the coal on to the fire bars. He turned on the greatest possible draught, the air roared across the furnace, the pressure goes up, up, amid the heaving of the motion, the bellowings of the boiler, the beating of the pistons. We are going a hundred kilometres an hour.

"Get back!" shouts Kinko above the roar. "Get back into the van."

"And you, Kinko?"

"Get back, I tell you."

I see him hang on to the valves, and put his whole weight on the levers.

"Go!" he shouts.

I am off over the tender. I am through the van. I awake Popof, shouting with all my strength:

"Get back! Get back!"

A few passengers suddenly waking from sleep begin to run from the front car.

Suddenly there is an explosion and a shock. The train at first jumps back. Then it continues to move for about half a kilometre.

It stops.

Popof, the major, Caterna, most of the passengers are out on the line in an instant.

A network of scaffolding appears confusedly in the darkness, above the piers which were to carry the viaduct across the Tjon valley.

Two hundred yards further the train would have been lost in the abyss.

Chapter XXV

And I, who wanted "incident," who feared the weariness of a monotonous voyage of six thousand kilometres, in the course of which I should not meet with an impression or emotion worth clothing in type!

I have made another muddle of it, I admit! My lord Faruskiar, of whom I had made a hero—by telegraph—for the readers of the *Twentieth. Century*. Decidedly my good intentions ought certainly to qualify me as one of the best paviers of a road to a certain place you have doubtless heard of.

We are, as I have said, two hundred yards from the valley of the Tjon, so deep and wide as to require a viaduct from three hundred and fifty to four hundred feet long. The floor of the valley is scattered over with rocks, and a hundred feet down. If the train had been hurled to the bottom of that chasm, not one of us would have escaped alive. This memorable catastrophe—most interesting from a reporter's point of view—would have claimed a hundred victims. But thanks to the coolness, energy and devotion of the young Roumanian, we have escaped this terrible disaster.

All? No! Kinko has paid with his life for the safety of his fellow passengers.

Amid the confusion my first care was to visit the luggage van, which had remained uninjured. Evidently if Kinko had survived the explosion he would have got back into his box and waited till I put myself in communication with him.

Alas! The coffer is empty—empty as that of a company which has suspended payment. Kinko has been the victim of his sacrifice.

And so there has been a hero among our traveling companions, and he was not this Faruskiar, this abominable bandit hidden beneath the skin of a manager, whose name I have so stupidly published over the four corners of the globe! It was this Roumanian, this humble, this little, this poor fellow, whose sweetheart will wait for him in vain, and whom she will never again see! Well, I will do him justice! I will tell what he has done. As to his secret, I shall be sorry if I keep it. If he defrauded the Grand Transasiatic, it is thanks to that fraud that a whole train has been saved. We were lost, we should have perished in the most horrible of deaths if Kinko had not been there!

I went back on to the line, my heart heavy, my eyes full of tears.

Assuredly Faruskiar's scheme—in the execution of which he had executed his rival Ki-Tsang—had been cleverly contrived in utilizing this branch line leading to the unfinished viaduct. Nothing was easier than to switch off the train if an accomplice was at the points. And as soon as the signal was given that we were on the branch, all he had to do was to gain the foot-plate, kill the driver and stoker, slow the train and get off, leaving the steam on full to work up to full speed.

And now there could be no doubt that the scoundrels worthy of the most refined tortures that Chinese practice could devise were hastening down into the Tjon valley. There, amid the wreck of the train, they expected to find the fifteen millions of gold and precious stones, and this treasure they could carry off without fear of surprise when the night enabled them to consummate this fearful crime. Well! They have been robbed, these robbers, and I hope that they will pay for their crime with their lives, at the least. I alone know what has passed, but I will tell the story, for poor Kinko is no more.

Yes! My mind is made up. I will speak as soon as I have seen Zinca Klork. The poor girl must be told with consideration. The death of her betrothed must not come upon her like a thunderclap. Yes! To-morrow, as soon as we are at Pekin.

After all, if I do not say anything about Kinko, I may at least denounce Faruskiar and Ghangir and the four Mongols. I can say that I saw them go through the van, that I followed them, that I found they were talking on the gangway, that I heard the screams of the driver and stoker as they were strangled on the foot-plate, and that I then returned to the cars shouting: "Back! Back!" or whatever it was.

Besides, as will be seen immediately, there was somebody else whose just suspicions had been changed into certainty, who only awaited his opportunity to denounce Faruskiar.

We are now standing at the head of the train, Major Noltitz, the German baron, Caterna, Ephrinell, Pan-Chao, Popof, about twenty travelers in all. The Chinese guard, faithful to their trust, are still near the treasure which not one of them has abandoned. The rear guard has brought along the tail lamps, and by their powerful light we can see in what a state the engine is.

If the train, which was then running at enormous velocity, had not stopped suddenly—and thus brought about its destruction—it was because the boiler had exploded at the top and on the side. The wheels being undamaged, the engine had run far enough to come gradually to a standstill of itself, and thus the passengers had been saved a violent shock.

Of the boiler and its accessories only a few shapeless fragments remained. The funnel had gone, the dome, the steam chest; there was nothing but torn plates, broken, twisted tubes, split cylinders, and loose connecting rods—gaping wounds in the corpse of steel.

And not only had the engine been destroyed, but the tender had been rendered useless. Its tank had been cracked, and its load of coals scattered over the line. The luggage-van, curious to relate, had miraculously escaped without injury.

And looking at the terrible effects of the explosion, I could see that the Roumanian had had no chance of escape, and had probably been blown to fragments.

Going a hundred yards down the line I could find no trace of him—which was not to be wondered at.

At first we looked on at the disaster in silence; but eventually conversation began.

"It is only too evident," said one of the passengers, "that our driver and stoker have perished in the explosion."

"Poor fellows!" said Popof. "But I wonder how the train could have got on the Nanking branch without being noticed?"

"The night was very dark," said Ephrinell, "and the driver could not see the points."

"That is the only explanation possible," said Popof, "for he would have tried to stop the train, and, on the contrary, we were traveling at tremendous speed."

"But," said Pan-Chao, "how does it happen the Nanking branch was open when the Tjon viaduct is not finished? Had the switch been interfered with?"

"Undoubtedly," said Popof, "and probably out of carelessness."

"No," said Ephrinell, deliberately. "There has been a crime—a crime intended to bring about the destruction of the train and passengers—"

"And with what object?" asked Popof.

"The object of stealing the imperial treasure," said Ephrinell. "Do you forget that those millions would be a temptation to scoundrels? Was it not for the purpose of robbing the train that we were attacked between Tchertchen and Tcharkalyk?"

The American could not have been nearer the truth.

"And so," said Popof, "after Ki-Tsang's attempt, you think that other bandits—"

Up to now Major Noltitz had taken no part in the discussion. Now he interrupted Popof, and in a voice heard by all he asked:

"Where is Faruskiar?"

They all looked about and tried to discover what had become of the manager of the Transasiatic.

"And where is his friend Ghangir?" asked the major.

There was no reply.

"And where are the four Mongols who were in the rear van?" asked Major Noltitz.

And none of them presented themselves.

They called my lord Faruskiar a second time.

Faruskiar made no response.

Popof entered the car where this personage was generally to be found.

It was empty.

Empty? No. Sir Francis Trevellyan was calmly seated in his place, utterly indifferent to all that happened. Was it any business of his? Not at all. Was he not entitled to consider that the Russo-Chinese railways were the very apex of absurdity and disorder? A switch opened, nobody knew by whom! A train on the wrong line! Could anything be more ridiculous than this Russian mismanagement?

"Well, then!" said Major Noltitz, "the rascal who sent us on to the Nanking line, who would have hurled us into the Tjon valley, to walk off with the imperial treasure, is Faruskiar."

"Faruskiar!" the passengers exclaimed. And most of them refused to believe it.

"What!" said Popof. "The manager of the company who so courageously drove off the bandits and killed their chief Ki-Tsang with his own hand?"

Then I entered on the scene.

"The major is not mistaken. It was Faruskiar who laid this fine trap for us."

And amid the general stupefaction I told them what I knew, and what good fortune had enabled me to ascertain. I told them how I had overheard the plan of Faruskiar and his Mongols, when it was too late to stop it, but I was silent regarding the intervention of Kinko. The moment had not come, and I would do him justice in due time.

To my words there succeeded a chorus of maledictions and menaces.

What! This seigneur Faruskiar, this superb Mongol, this functionary we had seen at work! No! It was impossible.

But they had to give in to the evidence. I had seen; I had heard; I affirmed that Faruskiar was the author of this catastrophe in which all our train might have perished, was the most consummate bandit who had ever disgraced Central Asia!

"You see, Monsieur Bombarnac," said Major Noltitz, "that I was not mistaken in my first suspicion."

"It is only too true," I replied, without any false modesty, "that I was taken in by the grand manners of the abominable rascal."

"Monsieur Claudius," said Caterna, "put that into a romance, and see if anybody believes it likely."

Caterna was right; but unlikely as it may seem, it was. And, besides, I alone knew Kinko's secret. It certainly did seem as though it was miraculous for the locomotive to explode just on the verge of the abyss.

Now that all danger had disappeared we must take immediate measures for running back the cars on to the Pekin line.

"The best thing to do is for one of us to volunteer—"

"I will do that," said Caterna.

"What is he to do?" I asked.

"Go to the nearest station, that of Fuen Choo, and telegraph to Tai-Youan for them to send on a relief engine."

"How far is it to Fuen Choo?" asked Ephrinell.

"About six kilometres to Nanking junction, and about five kilometres beyond that."

"Eleven kilometres," said the major; "that is a matter of an hour and a half for good walkers. Before three o'clock the engine from Tai-Youan ought to be here. I am ready to start."

"So am I," said Popof! "I think several of us ought to go. Who knows if we may not meet Faruskiar and his Mongols on the road?"

"You are right, Popof," said Major Noltitz, "and we should be armed."

This was only prudent, for the bandits who ought to be on their way to the Tjon viaduct could not be very far off. Of course, as soon as they found that their attempt had failed, they would hasten to get away. How would they dare—six strong—to attack a hundred passengers, including the Chinese guard?

Twelve of us, including Pan-Chao, Caterna, and myself, volunteered to accompany Major Noltitz. But by common accord we advised Popof not to abandon the train, assuring him that we would do all that was necessary at Fuen Choo.

Then, armed with daggers and revolvers—it was one o'clock in the morning—we went along the line to the junction, walking as fast as the very dark night permitted.

In less than two hours we arrived at Fuen Choo station without adventure. Evidently Faruskiar had cleared off. The Chinese police would have to deal with the bandit and his accomplices. Would they catch him? I hoped so, but I doubted.

At the station Pan-Chao explained matters to the stationmaster, who telegraphed for an engine to be sent from Tai-Youan to the Nanking line.

At three o'clock, just at daybreak, we returned to wait for the engine at the junction. Three-quarters of an hour afterwards its whistle announced its approach, and it stopped at the bifurcation of the lines. We climbed up on to the tender, and half an hour later had rejoined the train.

The dawn had come on sufficiently for us to be able to see over a considerable distance. Without saying anything to anybody, I went in search of the body of my poor Kinko. And I could not find it among the wreck.

As the engine could not reach the front of the train, owing to their being only a single line, and no turning-table, it was decided to couple it on in the rear and run backwards to the junction. In this way the box, alas! without the Roumanian in it, was in the last carriage.

165

We started, and in half an hour we were on the main line again.

Fortunately it was not necessary for us to return to Tai-Youan, and we thus saved a delay of an hour and a half. At the junction the engine was detached and run for a few yards towards Pekin, then the vans and cars, one by one, were pushed on to the main line, and then the engine backed and the train proceeded, made up as before the accident. By five o'clock we were on our way across Petchili as if nothing had happened.

I have nothing to say regarding this latter half of the journey, during which the Chinese driver—to do him justice—in no way endeavored to make up for lost time. But if a few hours more or less were of no importance to us, it was otherwise with Baron Weissschnitzerdoerfer, who wanted to catch the Yokohama boat at Tien Tsin.

When we arrived there at noon the steamer had been gone for three-quarters of an hour; and when the German globe-trotter, the rival of Bly and Bisland, rushed on to the platform, it was to learn that the said steamer was then going out of the mouths of the Pei-Ho into the open sea.

Unfortunate traveler! We were not astonished when, as Gaterna said, the baron "let go both broadsides" of Teutonic maledictions. And really he had cause to curse in his native tongue.

We remained but a quarter of an hour at Tien Tsin. My readers must pardon me for not having visited this city of five hundred thousand inhabitants, the Chinese town with its temples, the European quarter in which the trade is concentrated, the Pei-Ho quays where hundreds of junks load and unload. It was all Faruskiar's fault, and were it only for having wrecked my reportorial endeavors he ought to be hanged by the most fantastic executioner in China.

Nothing happened for the rest of our run. I was very sorry at the thought that I was not bringing Kinko along with me, and that his box was empty. And he had asked me to accompany him to Mademoiselle Zinca Klork! How could I tell this unfortunate girl that her sweetheart would never reach Pekin station?

Everything ends in this world below, even a voyage of six thousand kilometres on the Grand Transasiatic; and after a run of thirteen days, hour after hour, our train stopped at the gates of the capital of the Celestial Empire.

CHAPTER XXVI

"Pekin!" shouted Popof. "All change here."

And Caterna replied with truly Parisian unction:

"I believe you, my boy!"

And we all changed.

It was four o'clock in the afternoon. For people fatigued with three hundred and twelve hours of traveling, it was no time for running about the town—what do I say?—the four towns inclosed one within the other. Besides, I had plenty of time. I was going to stop some weeks in this capital.

The important thing was to find a hotel in which one could live passably. From information received I was led to believe that the hotel of *Ten Thousand Dreams,* near the railway station, might be sufficiently in accord with Western notions.

As to Mademoiselle Klork, I will postpone my visit till to-morrow. I will call on her before the box arrives, and even then I shall be too soon, for I shall take her the news of Kinko's death.

Major Noltitz will remain in the same hotel as I do. I have not to bid him farewell, nor have I to part with the Caternas, who are going to stay a fortnight before starting for Shanghai. As to Pan-Chao and Dr. Tio-King, a carriage is waiting to take them to the yamen in which the young Chinaman's family live. But we shall see each other again. Friends do not separate at a simple good-by, and the grip of the hand I gave him as he left the car will not be the last.

Mr. and Mrs. Ephrinell lose no time in leaving the station on business, which obliges them to find a hotel in the commercial quarter of the Chinese town. But they do not leave without receiving my compliments. Major Noltitz and I go up to this amiable couple, and the conventional politenesses are reciprocally exchanged.

"At last," said I to Ephrinell, "the forty-two packages of Strong, Bulbul & Co. have come into port. But it is a wonder the explosion of our engine did not smash your artificial teeth."

"Just so," said the American, "my teeth had a narrow escape. What adventures they have had since we left Tiflis? Decidedly this journey has been less monotonous than I expected."

"And," added the major, "you were married on the way—unless I am mistaken!"

167

"Wait a bit!" replied the Yankee in a peculiar tone. "Excuse me; we are in a hurry."

"We will not keep you, Mr. Ephrinell," I replied, "and to Mrs. Ephrinell and yourself allow us to say au revoir!"

"Au revoir!" replied the Americanized lady, rather more dryly at her arrival than at her departure.

Then, turning, she said:

"I have no time to wait, Mr. Ephrinell."

"Nor have I, Mrs. Ephrinell," replied the Yankee.

Mr.! Mrs.! And not so long ago they were calling each other Fulk and Horatia.

And then, without taking each other's arm, they walked out of the station. I believe he turned to the right and she to the left; but that is their affair.

There remains my No. 8, Sir Francis Trevellyan, the silent personage, who has not said a word all through the piece—I mean all through the journey. I wanted to hear his voice, if it was only for one second.

Eh! If I am not mistaken, here is the opportunity at last.

There is the phlegmatic gentleman contemptuously looking up and down the cars. He has just taken a cigar from his yellow morocco case, but when he looks at his match-box he finds it empty.

My cigar—a particularly good one—is alight, and I am smoking it with the blessed satisfaction of one who enjoys it, and regretting that there is not a man in all China who has its equal.

Sir Francis Trevellyan has seen the light burning at the end of my cigar, and he comes towards me.

I think he is going to ask me for a light. He stretches out his hand, and I present him with my cigar.

He takes it between his thumb and forefinger, knocks off the white ash, lights up, and then, if I had not heard him ask for a light, I at least expected him to say, "Thank you, sir!"

Not at all! Sir Francis Trevellyan takes a few puffs at his own cigar, and then nonchalantly throws mine on to the platform. And then without even a bow, he walks leisurely off out of the railway station.

Did you say nothing? No, I remained astounded. He gave me neither a word nor a gesture. I was completely dumfounded at this ultra-Britannic rudeness, while Major Noltitz could not restrain a loud outburst of laughter.

Ah! If I should see this gentleman again. But never did I see again Sir Francis Trevellyan of Trevellyan Hall, Trevellyanshire.

Half an hour afterwards we are installed at the Hotel of *Ten Thousand Dreams*. There we are served with a dinner in Chinese style. The repast being over—towards the second watch—we lay ourselves on beds that are too narrow in rooms with little comfort, and sleep not the sleep of the just, but the sleep of the exhausted—and that is just as good.

I did not wake before ten o'clock, and I might have slept all the morning if the thought had not occurred to me that I had a duty to fulfil. And what a duty! To call in the Avenue Cha Coua before the delivery of the unhappy case to Mademoiselle Zinca Klork.

I arise. Ah! If Kinko had not succumbed, I should have returned to the railway station—I should have assisted, as I had promised, in the unloading of the precious package. I would have watched it on to the cart, and I would have accompanied it to the Avenue Cha Coua, I would even have helped in carrying him up to Mademoiselle Zinca Klork! And what a double explosion of joy there would have been when Kinko jumped through the panel to fall into the arms of the fair Roumanian!

But no! When the box arrives it will be empty—empty as a heart from which all the blood has escaped.

I leave the Hotel of *Ten Thousand Dreams* about eleven o'clock, I call one of those Chinese carriages, which look like palanquins on wheels, I give the address of Mademoiselle Klork, and I am on the way.

You know, that among the eighteen provinces of China Petchili occupies the most northerly position. Formed of nine departments, it has for its capital Pekin, otherwise known as Chim-Kin-Fo, an appellation which means a "town of the first order, obedient to Heaven."

I do not know if this town is really obedient to Heaven, but it is obedient to the laws of rectilineal geometry. There are four towns, square or rectangular, one within the other. The Chinese town, which contains the Tartar town, which contains the yellow town, or Houng Tching, which contains the Red Town, or Tsen-Kai-Tching, that is to say, "the forbidden town." And within this symmetrical circuit of six leagues there are more than two millions of those inhabitants, Tartars or Chinese, who are called the Germans of the East, without mentioning several thousands of Mongols and Tibetans. That there is much bustle in the streets, I can see by the obstacles my vehicle encounters at every step, itinerating peddlers, carts heavily laden, mandarins and their noisy following. I say nothing of those abominable wandering dogs, half jackals, half wolves, hairless and mangy, with deceitful eyes, threatening jaws, and having no other food than the filthy rubbish which foreigners detest. Fortunately I am not on foot, and I have no business in the Red Town, admittance to which is denied, nor in the yellow town nor even in the Tartar town.

The Chinese town forms, a rectangular parallelogram, divided north and south by the Grand Avenue leading from the Houn Ting gate to the Tien gate, and crossed east and west by the Avenue Cha-Coua, which runs from the gate of that name to the Cpuan-Tsa gate. With this indication nothing could be easier than to find the dwelling of Mademoiselle Zinca Klork, but nothing more difficult to reach, considering the block in the roads in this outer ring.

A little before twelve I arrived at my destination. My vehicle had stopped before a house of modest appearance, occupied by artisans as lodgings, and as the signboard said more particularly by strangers.

It was on the first floor, the window of which opened on to the avenue, that the young Roumanian lived, and where, having learned her trade as a milliner in Paris, she was engaged in it at Pekin.

I go up to the first floor. I read the name of Madame Zinca Klork on a door. I knock. The door is opened.

I am in the presence of a young lady who is perfectly charming, as Kinko said. She is a blonde of from twenty-two to twenty-three years old, with the black eyes of the Roumanian type, an agreeable figure, a pleasant, smiling face. In fact, has she not been informed that the Grand Transasiatic train has been in the station ever since last evening, in spite of the circumstances of the journey, and is she not awaiting her betrothed from one moment to another?

And I, with a word, am about to extinguish this joy. I am to wither that smile.

Mademoiselle Klork is evidently much surprised at seeing a stranger in her doorway. As she has lived several years in France, she does not hesitate to recognize me as a Frenchman, and asks to what she is indebted for my visit.

I must take care of my words, for I may kill her, poor child.

"Mademoiselle Zinca—" I say.

"You know my name?" she exclaims.

"Yes, mademoiselle. I arrived yesterday by the Grand Transasiatic."

The girl turned pale; her eyes became troubled. It was evident that she feared something. Had Kinko been found in his box? Had the fraud been discovered? Was he arrested? Was he in prison?

I hastened to add:

"Mademoiselle Zinca—certain circumstances have brought to my knowledge—the journey of a young Roumanian—"

"Kinko—my poor Kinko—they have found him?" she asks in a trembling voice.

"No—no—" say I, hesitating. "No one knows—except myself. I often visited him in the luggage-van at night; we were companions, friends. I took him a few provisions—"

"Oh! thank you, sir!" says the lady, taking me by the hands. "With a Frenchman Kinko was sure of not being betrayed, and even of receiving help! Thank you, thank you!"

I am more than ever afraid of the mission on which I have come.

"And no one suspected the presence of my dear Kinko?" she asks.

"No one."

"What would you have had us do, sir? We are not rich. Kinko was without money over there at Tiflis, and I had not enough to send him his fare. But he is here at last. He will get work, for he is a good workman, and as soon as we can we will pay the company—"

"Yes; I know, I know."

"And then we are going to get married, monsieur. He loves me so much, and I love him. We met one another in Paris. He was so kind to me. Then when he went back to Tiflis I asked him to come to me in that box. Is the poor fellow ill?"

"No, Mademoiselle Zinca, no."

"Ah! I shall be happy to pay the carriage of my dear Kinko."

"Yes—pay the carriage—"

"It will not be long now?"

"No; this afternoon probably."

I do not know what to say.

"Monsieur," says mademoiselle, "we are going to get married as soon as the formalities are complied with; and if it is not abusing your confidence, will you do us the honor and pleasure of being present?"

"At your marriage—certainly. I promised my friend Kinko I would."

Poor girl! I cannot leave her like this. I must tell her everything.

"Mademoiselle Zinca—Kinko—"

"He asked you to come and tell me he had arrived?"

"Yes—but—you understand—he is very tired after so long a journey—"

"Tired?"

"Oh! do not be alarmed—"

"Is he ill?"

"Yes—rather—rather ill—"

"Then I will go—I must see him—I pray you, sir, come with me to the station—"

"No; that would be an imprudence—remain here—remain—"

Zinca Klork looked at me fixedly.

"The truth, monsieur, the truth! Hide nothing from me—Kinko—"

"Yes—I have sad news—to give you." She is fainting. Her lips tremble. She can hardly speak.

"He has been discovered!" she says. "His fraud is known—they have arrested him—"

"Would to heaven it was no worse. We have had accidents on the road. The train was nearly annihilated—a frightful catastrophe—"

"He is dead! Kinko is dead!"

The unhappy Zinca falls on to a chair—and to employ the imaginative phraseology of the Chinese—her tears roll down like rain on an autumn night. Never have I seen anything so lamentable. But it will not do to leave her in this state, poor girl! She is becoming unconscious. I do not know where I am. I take her hands. I repeat:

"Mademoiselle Zinca! Mademoiselle Zinca!"

Suddenly there is a great noise in front of the house. Shouts are heard. There is a tremendous to do, and amid the tumult I hear a voice.

Good Heavens! I cannot be mistaken. That is Kinko's voice!

I recognize it. Am I in my right senses?

Zinca jumps up, springs to the window, opens it, and we look out.

There is a cart at the door. There is the case, with all its inscriptions: *This side up, this side down, fragile, glass, beware of damp,* etc., etc. It is there—half smashed. There has been a collision. The cart has been run into by a carriage, as the case was being got down. The case has slipped on to the ground. It has been knocked in. And Kinko has jumped out like a jack-in-the-box—but alive, very much alive!

I can hardly believe my eyes! What, my young Roumanian did not perish in the explosion? No! As I shall soon hear from his own mouth, he was thrown on to the line when the boiler went up, remained there inert for a time, found himself uninjured—miraculously—kept away till he could slip into the van unperceived. I had just left the van after looking for him in vain, and supposing that he had been the first victim of the catastrophe.

Then—oh! the irony of fate!—after accomplishing a journey of six thousand kilometres on the Grand Transasiatic, shut up in a box among the baggage, after escaping so many dangers, attack by bandits, explosion of engine, he was here, by the mere colliding of a cart and a carriage in a Pekin Street, deprived of all the good of his journey—fraudulent it may be—but really if—I know of no epithet worthy of this climax.

The carter gave a yell at the sight of a human being who had just appeared. In an instant the crowd had gathered, the fraud was discovered, the police had run up. And what could this young Roumanian do who did not know a word of Chinese, but explain matters in the sign language? And if he could not be understood, what explanation could he give?

Zinca and I ran down to him.

"My Zinca—my dear Zinca!" he exclaims, pressing the girl to his heart.

"My Kinko—my dear Kinko!" she replies, while her tears mingle with his.

"Monsieur Bombarnac!" says the poor fellow, appealing for my intervention.

"Kinko," I reply, "take it coolly, and depend on me. You are alive, and we thought you were dead."

"But I am not much better off!" he murmurs.

Mistake! Anything is better than being dead—even when one is menaced by prison, be it a Chinese prison. And that is what happens, in spite of the girl's supplications and my entreaties. And Kinko is dragged off by the police, amid the laughter and howls of the crowd.

But I will not abandon him! No, if I move heaven and earth, I will not abandon him.

Chapter XXVII

If ever the expression, "sinking in sight of port," could be used in its precise meaning, it evidently can in this case. And I must beg you to excuse me. But although a ship may sink by the side of the jetty, we must not conclude that she is lost. That Kinko's liberty is in danger, providing the intervention of myself and fellow passengers is of no avail, agreed. But he is alive, and that is the essential point.

But we must not waste an hour, for if the police is not perfect in China, it is at least prompt and expeditious. Soon caught, soon hanged— and it will not do for them to hang Kinko, even metaphorically.

I offer my arm to Mademoiselle Zinca, and I lead her to my carriage, and we return rapidly towards the *Hotel of the Ten Thousand Dreams*.

There I find Major Noltitz and the Caternas, and by a lucky chance young Pan-Chao, without Dr. Tio-King. Pan-Chao would like nothing better than to be our interpreter before the Chinese authorities.

And then, before the weeping Zinca, I told my companions all about Kinko, how he had traveled, how I had made his acquaintance on the journey. I told them that if he had defrauded the Transasiatic Company it was thanks to this fraud that he was able to get on to the train at Uzun Ada. And if he had not been in the train we should all have been engulfed in the abyss of the Tjon valley.

And I enlarged on the facts which I alone knew. I had surprised Faruskiar at the very moment he was about to accomplish his crime, but it was Kinko who, at the peril of his life, with coolness and courage superhuman, had thrown on the coals, hung on to the lever of the safety valves, and stopped the train by blowing up the engine.

What an explosion there was of exclamatory ohs and ahs when I had finished my recital, and in a burst of gratitude, somewhat of the theatrical sort, our actor shouted:

"Hurrah for Kinko! He ought to have a medal!"

Until the Son of Heaven accorded this hero a green dragon of some sort, Madame Caterna took Zinca's hand, drew her to her heart and embraced her—embraced her without being able to restrain her tears. Just think of a love story interrupted at the last chapter!

But we must hasten, and as Caterna says, "all on the scene for the fifth"—the fifth act, in which dramas generally clear themselves up.

"We must not let this brave fellow suffer!" said Major Noltitz; "we must see the Grand Transasiatic people, and when they learn the facts they will be the first to stop the prosecution."

"Doubtless," I said, "for it cannot be denied that Kinko saved the train and its passengers."

"To say nothing of the imperial treasure," added Caterna, "the millions of his majesty!"

"Nothing could be truer," said Pan-Chao. "Unfortunately Kinko has fallen into the hands of the police, and they have taken him to prison, and it is not easy to get out of a Chinese prison."

"Let us be off," I replied, "and see the company."

"See here," said Madame Caterna, "is there any need of a subscription to defray the cost of the affair?"

"The proposal does you honor, Caroline," said the actor, putting his hand in his pocket.

"Gentlemen," said pretty Zinca Klork, her eyes bathed in tears, "do save him before he is sentenced—"

"Yes, my darling," said Madame Caterna, "yes, my heart, we will save your sweetheart for you, and if a benefit performance—"

"Bravo, Caroline, bravo!" exclaimed Caterna, applauding with the vigor of the sub-chief of the claque.

We left the young Roumanian to the caresses, as exaggerated as they were sincere, of the worthy actress. Madame Caterna would not leave her, declaring that she looked upon her as her daughter, that she would protect her like a mother. Then Pan-Chao, Major Noltitz, Caterna, and I went off to the company's offices at the station.

The manager was in his office, and we were admitted.

He was a Chinese in every acceptation of the word, and capable of every administrative Chinesery—a functionary who functioned in a way that would have moved his colleagues in old Europe to envy.

Pan-Chao told the story, and, as he understood Russian, the major and I took part in the discussion.

Yes! There was a discussion. This unmistakable Chinaman did not hesitate to contend that Kinko's case was a most serious one. A fraud undertaken on such conditions, a fraud extending over six thousand kilometres, a fraud of a thousand francs on the Grand Transasiatic Company and its agents.

We replied to this Chinesing Chinee that it was all very true, but that the damage had been inconsiderable, that if the defrauder had not been in the train he could not have saved it at the risk of his life, and at the same time he could not have saved the lives of the passengers.

Well, would you believe it? This living China figure gave us to understand that from a certain point of view it would have been better to regret the deaths of a hundred victims—

Yes! We knew that! Perish the colonies and all the passengers rather than a principle!

In short, we got nothing. Justice must take its course against the fraudulent Kinko.

We retired while Caterna poured out all the locutions in his marine and theatrical vocabulary.

What was to be done?

"Gentlemen," said Pan-Chao, "I know how things are managed in Pekin and the Celestial Empire. Two hours will not elapse from the time Kinko is arrested to the time he is brought before the judge charged with this sort of crime. He will not only be sent to prison, but the bastinado—"

"The bastinado—like that idiot Zizel in *Si j'etais Roi?*" asked the actor.

"Precisely," replied Pan-Chao.

"We must stop that abomination," said Major Noltitz.

"We can try at the least," said Pan-Chao. "I propose we go before the court when I will try and defend the sweetheart of this charming Roumanian, and may I lose my face if I do not get him off."

That was the best, the only thing to do. We left the station, invaded a vehicle, and arrived in twenty minutes before a shabby-looking shanty, where the court was held.

There was a crowd. The affair had got abroad. It was known that a swindler had come in a box in a Grand Transasiatic van free, gratis, and for nothing from Tiflis to Pekin. Every one wished to see him; every one wanted to recognize the features of this genius—it was not yet known that he was a hero.

There he is, our brave companion, between two rascally looking policemen, yellow as quinces. These fellows are ready to walk him off to prison at the judge's order, and to give him a few dozen strokes on the soles of his feet if he is condemned to that punishment.

Kinko is thoroughly disheartened, which astonishes me on the part of one I know to be so energetic. But as soon as he sees us his face betrays a ray of hope.

At this moment the carter, brought forward by the police, relates the affair to a good sort of fellow in spectacles, who shakes his head in anything but a hopeful way for the prisoner, who, even if he were as innocent as a new-born child, could not defend himself, inasmuch as he did not know Chinese.

Then it is that Pan-Chao presents himself. The judge recognized him and smiled. In fact, our companion was the son of a rich merchant in Pekin, a tea merchant in the Toung-Tien and Soung-Fong-Cao trade. And these nods of the judge's head became more sympathetically significant.

Our young advocate was really pathetic and amusing. He interested the judge, he excited the audience with the story of the journey, he told them all about it, and finally he offered to pay the company what was due to them.

Unfortunately the judge could not consent. There had been material damages, moral damages, etc., etc.

Thereupon Pan-Chao became animated, and although we understood nothing he said, we guessed that he was speaking of the courage of Kinko, of the sacrifice he had made for the safety of the travelers, and finally, as a supreme argument, he pleaded that his client had saved the imperial treasure.

Useless eloquence? Arguments were of no avail with this pitiless magistrate, who had not acquitted ten prisoners in is life. He spared the delinquent the bastinado; but he gave him six months in prison, and condemned him in damages against the Grand Transasiatic Company. And then at a sign from this condemning machine poor Kinko was taken away.

Let not my readers pity Kinko's fate. I may as well say at once that everything was arranged satisfactorily.

Next morning Kinko made a triumphal entry into the house in the Avenue Cha-Coua, where we were assembled, while Madame Caterna was showering her maternal consolations on the unhappy Zinca Klork.

The newspapers had got wind of the affair. The *Chi Bao* of Pekin and the *Chinese Times* of Tien-Tsin had demanded mercy for the young Roumanian. These cries for mercy had reached the feet of the Son of Heaven—the very spot where the imperial ears are placed. Besides, Pan-Chao had sent to his majesty a petition relating the incidents of the journey, and insisting on the point that had it not been for Kinko's devotion, the gold and precious stones would be in the hands of Faruskiar and his bandits. And, by Buddha! that was worth something else than six months in prison.

Yes! It was worth 15,000 taels, that is to say, more than 100,000 francs, and in a fit of generosity the Son of Heaven remitted these to Kinko with the remittal of his sentence.

I decline to depict the joy, the happiness, the intoxication which this news brought by Kinko in person, gave to all his friends, and particularly to the fair Zinca Klork. These things are expressible in no language—not even in Chinese, which lends itself so generously to the metaphorical.

And now my readers must permit me to finish with my traveling companions whose numbers have figured in my notebook.

Nos. 1 and 2, Fulk Ephrinell and Miss Horatia Bluett: not being able to agree regarding the various items stipulated in their matrimonial contract, they were divorced three days after their arrival in Pekin. Things were as though the marriage had never been celebrated on the Grand Transasiatic, and Miss Horatia Bluett remained Miss Horatia Bluett. May she gather cargoes of heads of hair from Chinese polls; and may he furnish with artificial teeth every jaw in the Celestial Empire!

No. 3, Major Noltitz: he is busy at the hospital he has come to establish at Pekin on behalf of the Russian government, and when the hour for separation strikes, I feel that I shall leave a true friend behind me in these distant lands.

Nos. 4 and 5, the Caternas: after a stay of three weeks in the capital of the Celestial Empire, the charming actor and actress set out for Shanghai, where they are now the great attraction at the French Residency.

No. 6, Baron Weissschnitzerdoerfer, whose incommensurable name I write for the last time: well, not only did the globe-trotter miss the steamer at Tien-Tsin, but a month later he missed it at Yokohama; six weeks after that he was shipwrecked on the coast of British Columbia, and then, after being thrown off the line between San Francisco and New York, he managed to complete his round of the world in a hundred and eighty-seven days instead of thirty-nine.

Nos. 9 and 10, Pan-Chao and Dr. Tio-King: what can I say except that Pan-Chao is always the Parisian you know, and that if he comes to France we shall meet at dinner at Durand's or Marguery's. As to the doctor, he has got down to eating only the yolk of an egg a day, like his master, Cornaro, and he hopes to live to a hundred and two as did the noble Venetian.

No. 8, Sir Francis Trevellyan, and No. 12, Seigneur Faruskiar: I have never heard of the one who owes me an apology and a cigar, nor have I heard that the other has been hanged. Doubtless, the illustrious bandit, having sent in his resignation of the general managership of the Grand Transasiatic, continues his lucrative career in the depths of the Mongol provinces.

Now for Kinko, my No. 11: I need hardly say that my No. 11 was married to Zinca Klork with great ceremony. We were all at the wedding, and if the Son of Heaven had richly endowed the young Roumanian, his wife received a magnificent present in the name of the passengers of the train he had saved.

That is the faithful story of this journey. I have done my best to do my duty as special correspondent all down the line, and perhaps my editors may be satisfied, notwithstanding the slip or two you have heard about.

As to me, after spending three weeks in Pekin, I returned to France by sea.

And now I have to make a confession, which is very painful to my self-esteem. The morning after I arrived in the Chinese capital I received a telegram thus worded, in reply to the one I had sent from Lan-Tcheou:

CLAUDIUS BOMBARNAC,
Pekin, China.

Twentieth Century requests its correspondent, Claudius Bombarnac, to present its compliments and respects to the heroic Seigneur Faruskiar.

But I always say that this telegram never reached him, so that he has been spared the unpleasantness of having to reply to it.

THE END

Printed by Libri Plureos GmbH in Hamburg,
Germany